She wanted Jason to take her in his arms and hold her, really hold her, the way a man holds a woman he needs to take to bed. If she allowed herself to think, it would be over, so she chased away the logic clamoring to be heard and closed the distance between them. She slid her arms around his waist and pressed her lips against his shocked mouth. She wanted to soak up his strength, taste forgetfulness on his lips, be herself again, a woman—not a mother, not a wife, not a widow. She didn't want to cry anymore, didn't want to feel like a lost ship on a stormy sea. She wanted an anchor to something real.

She sucked his tongue into her mouth, hearing him groan, feeling his hands drop to her hips. She could feel every inch of his body lined up with hers. He angled his head one way and then the other, giving her only small moments to breathe before he came back for more. She liked the relentless onslaught. She didn't have time to think, only to feel, and she was feeling really, really good, until Jason suddenly jerked away.

He gave her a hard look, searching her face for something—she didn't know what. "Do you really want this, Brianna? Me—you? What the hell are we doing?"

*Turn the page for praise of bestselling author*
*Barbara Freethy's heartwarming romances*

"Freethy has written a suspenseful and captivating story, weaving in human frailty along with true compassion, making every page a delight."

—Reader to Reader Reviews

"Angel's Bay is a place I'll want to visit time and again. . . . Freethy has done a beautiful job of weaving a compelling story while having the patience to fully develop characters who will become our friends, characters with whom we will share joys, sorrows, and all of life's adventures."

—Romance Novel TV

"A well-written, captivating story, with good pacing that will leave you satisfied as it unfolds. There is a little bit of everything—romance, mystery, and inexplicable events—a fascinating story sure to make your summer reading a pleasure."

—Romance Reviews Today

### And for award-winning author Barbara Freethy

"Barbara Freethy delivers strong and compelling prose."

—*Publishers Weekly*

"Fans of Nora Roberts will find a similar tone here, framed in Freethy's own spare, elegant style."

—*Contra Costa Times* (CA)

"Freethy skillfully keeps readers on the hook."

—*Booklist*

"Freethy's star continues to gain luster."

—*Romantic Times*

# BARBARA FREETHY

## In Shelter Cove

POCKET **STAR** BOOKS

New York   London   Toronto   Sydney

Pocket Star Books
A Division of Simon & Schuster, Inc.
1230 Avenue of the Americas
New York, NY 10020

First Pocket Star Books paperback edition May 2010

POCKET STAR BOOKS and colophon are registered trademarks of Simon & Schuster, Inc.

For information about special discounts for bulk purchases, please contact Simon & Schuster Special Sales at 1-866-506-1949 or business@simonandschuster.com.

The Simon & Schuster Speakers Bureau can bring authors to your live event. For more information or to book an event contact the Simon & Schuster Speakers Bureau at 1-866-248-3049 or visit our website at www.simonspeakers.com.

Designed by Jill Putorti

Manufactured in the United States of America

10  9  8  7  6  5  4  3  2  1

ISBN 978-1-4391-7325-1
ISBN 978-1-4391-7326-8 (ebook)

*To Dorothy Freethy,*
*for her always enthusiastic support and for being the*
*best mother-in-law a woman could have!*

# ACKNOWLEDGMENTS

Many thanks to my fabulous editor, Micki Nuding, who has helped me bring the characters of Angel's Bay to life. Much gratitude goes to my writing friends who were always there to offer ideas and share chocolate when my plot and characters were not cooperating—Jami Alden, Bella Andre, Diana Dempsey, Carol Grace, Tracy Grant, Lynn Hanna, Candice Hern, Anne Mallory, Monica McCarty, Barbara McMahon, Kate Moore, Poppy Reiffin, Christie Ridgway, and Veronica Wolff. Thanks also to the local art gallery owners who shared their knowledge of art and gave me a glimpse into their world.

# In Shelter Cove

# PROLOGUE

**150 years ago**

Grief ripped through him as midnight approached.
During the day he could stay busy enough not to
think, but at night the agony always caught up to
him. His fingers tightened around the paintbrush,
his hand shaking from not enough sleep and too
much whisky. His eyes blurred with weary tears; he
could barely see the canvas in front of him.

It was wrong that he was alive to paint and that
his beloved Eve was gone. He could still see the terror in her blue-violet eyes as the waves crashed over
the bow and the ship began to splinter apart. She'd
reached for him, her fingers curling around his, as
she begged him to stay with her. Ruthlessly, he'd had
to break her grip. Not for his sake but for hers. It
was women and children first. He'd forced her to get
into the lifeboat. He'd thought he was saving her life,
but her boat had never made it to shore. For days, he
had walked the beach, searching for her, but she was
lost to him.

Two years later, he was still trying to bring her back.

He dipped his brush into the paint and placed it on the canvas, and her face took shape in front of him: the pure porcelain quality of her fair skin, the soft dip of her dark red hair in the center of her forehead, her delicate shell-like ears, the perfection of her sweetly curved mouth, the soft thrust of her sometimes stubborn jaw, the deep love in her eyes. She'd given up everything to be with him, and he'd never been worthy of such sacrifice.

Tears ran down his cheeks as he gazed into her eyes. She seemed to be trying to tell him something.

*"That's not me. Not really me."* Her voice was sad and a little angry, as if she were frustrated with his inability to paint her portrait. *"Try again. See me, Victor. See me for who I really was. Don't be like the others; see what was real about me. That's who I want you to remember."*

"Not *was,*" he shouted, his voice echoing through the small cottage. He put the painting aside and picked up another canvas. He would get it right— and then she would come back to him.

He painted all night, into the next day and the next after that, until there were three portraits. He called them *The Three Faces of Eve:* the sweet saint, the seductive siren, and the desperate woman.

Exhausted by his efforts, he set down his brush, stumbled to the couch, drank the last bit of whisky, and waited for her to return.

In the dark of his dreams, he saw her arising from the sea, triumph in her eyes. He felt a surge of hope, a certainty that she'd somehow made it to shore, to some sheltered cove, and found her way to where he'd been waiting for so long. But every time she drew close to him, her image began to blur. He fought against the fading colors. He didn't want her to be with the other angels, the lost souls of the *Gabriella*. He wanted her to be with *him*, where she belonged.

When he finally awoke, the sun was high in the sky. He was alone, and the paintings were . . . gone. She'd been taken from him again.

He howled with rage and anguish, raising his fist to the sky. He would do whatever it took to get her back.

# ONE

**Present day, late October**

Brianna Kane shivered as the ocean breeze sliced through her black dress. The hillside cemetery in Angel's Bay overlooked a restless sea, whitecaps crashing against the boulders below, dark clouds blotting out the sun. The ocean was angry, and so was she. This should have been just another Monday morning. Lucas should have been in preschool. She should have been in her own classroom, teaching French to middle-schoolers. And Derek—Derek should not have been dead. Everything about this moment was wrong.

Five years ago, she'd come to Angel's Bay to marry Derek Kane. They'd planned to wed by the edge of the sea. She'd pictured the moment a thousand times. She'd wear an off-the-shoulder white satin dress with a lacy train that went on forever. The wind would blow through her long blond hair, and the sun sparkling off the ocean would light up

Derek's face, his hazel eyes always so beautiful and eager for her.

But she hadn't married Derek on a windswept bluff. She'd said her "I do's" in a cold, sterile room at a prison a hundred miles away, and her husband hadn't been wearing a tuxedo but an orange jumpsuit.

Despite the bad start, she'd believed that one day their lives would get back on track—that Derek's innocence would be proven, his appeal would be granted. He'd be released, and they'd have the life they were supposed to have.

That dream had died five weeks ago, along with Derek, leaving her with nothing but frustration, anger, and a lot of questions.

As the minister prayed for Derek's soul, she glanced around the small group of mourners. They'd waited to have the memorial service until she could pack up her apartment and move to Angel's Bay, where Derek's parents lived. Over the past month, she'd kept herself too busy to think beyond immediate plans. Now she was here and forced to confront what she'd been avoiding—Derek's death and the end of all her dreams.

Her mother-in-law, Nancy, a short, plump brunette, sobbed in her husband's arms. Her father-in-law, Rick, so tall and lean, had lost even more weight in recent weeks and was now almost gaunt as he tried to comfort his wife. Nancy's sister, Margaret, stood across from them, surreptitiously wiping tears from the corners of her eyes with a delicate handkerchief. Wyatt Kane, Derek's grandfather, stood next to her, a grim, forbidding man with fierce brown eyes and shocking white hair that was long and wild. Wyatt, an internationally acclaimed artist, had once been Derek's biggest supporter, but their relationship had been shattered by Derek's conviction. Brianna was surprised he'd come to the funeral. He'd certainly never visited the prison.

Neighbors and friends of the Kanes filled out the group. Most of the mourners were of Derek's parents' generation, with only a few former friends in attendance. The rest had vanished long ago.

"Mommy," Lucas whispered loudly as he tugged on her hand. "How can Daddy fit in that box? Won't he be scared to go into the hole?"

Her stomach turned over at the earnest, worried question. Derek's ashes were enclosed in a small wooden box that would be buried in the family plot. She squatted down, putting her arm around Lucas's shoulders as she tried to think of an answer that wouldn't scare him. How did one explain death to a four-year-old?

"Mommy?" Lucas's curious light eyes were so like his father's it made her heart hurt.

"Daddy's in heaven," she said gently. "He's with the angels now. He's not scared, and you don't have to worry about him."

"Then what's in the box?"

"It's just a symbol, something to remember him by." She hoped the answer would be enough for him.

"Do you think Daddy is looking at us right now?"

"He'll be watching over us wherever we go," she assured him.

Lucas lifted his gaze to the sky, his eyes searching. She'd seen the expression on his face before, and not just since Derek had died. Lucas had always been looking for his father. He'd never understood why Derek didn't live with them like the other daddies did. He couldn't understand why his father stayed in the big ugly house with the bars.

She'd hoped that when Derek got out of prison, he could explain what had happened in a way that Lucas would understand and that after a while the prison years would be forgotten, replaced by happier memories. But Derek had died just before he was due to be released.

When the minister ended his prayer, the mourners filed by, each placing a white rose on the box of ashes. The Kanes took Lucas back to the car to give Brianna a moment of privacy, but Derek's grandfather lingered behind.

"Derek was a damn fool," Wyatt said abruptly. "He could have had everything, but he threw it all away for greed and ambition. He didn't want to work for success. He just wanted to take it."

His harsh words caught her by surprise. "That's not true. Derek was innocent. He didn't steal those paintings from the museum, nor did he assault the security guard. He was set up to take the fall for someone else."

Wyatt gave her a scornful look. "If you still believe that, you're a damn fool. Derek was the best liar I ever met. It might have been his best talent—his only talent. You should forget about Derek, concentrate on your son, and make sure he doesn't turn out like his father did." Wyatt tossed his rose onto the grass and left.

Brianna drew in a shaky breath and slowly let it out, rattled by his harsh words. Her fingers began to sting, and she realized she was gripping the thorny stem of her rose. A drop of blood appeared, bright red against her pale skin, and she stared at it in fascination.

Derek had brought her a lot of pain in recent years, but she still remembered the man she'd fallen in love with, the one who had been outgoing, charming, and handsome, with blond hair and eyes that changed with the colors of the season. Derek had made her feel special and important, as if she were the only one who mattered. He'd swept her off her feet with his big dreams—the places he wanted to go, the life he wanted to lead. And that was the man she mourned now, the one with so much unrealized potential.

Stepping forward, she laid her rose on top of the others. "I guess this is it, Derek," she whispered. "It's hard to believe you're really gone. We should have had more time—a lot more time." She swallowed hard, a knot growing in her throat. "But we have a beautiful son. I'll make sure that Lucas knows who his father was. He'll see where you grew up, and he'll walk in your memories—at least for a while." Tears blurred her eyes. "I'm going to keep fighting for you, too. I won't stop until we get to the truth."

The wind brushed against her face like the caress of a man's hand. She touched her fingers to her suddenly warm cheek and raised her face to the sky. There was a small break in the clouds, a whisper of blue sky . . . then the wind blew, and the dark clouds returned.

As two men began to bury the box of ashes, she stepped back, unable to watch. She turned to move toward Nancy and Rick and caught a glimpse of a man standing just beyond the trees.

Her heart jumped into her throat. He wasn't wearing a police uniform today, but she recognized him all the same—Jason Marlow.

He was the one who'd built the case against Derek and sent him to jail. And he had the nerve to come to his funeral? She was halfway across the grass before she even realized she was moving. She'd kept a tight rein on her emotions for years, but now she couldn't hold them in for one more second.

Jason straightened when he saw her coming. He wore jeans and a black sweater that emphasized his broad shoulders. His hair was sandy brown, his eyes dark and wary. He stood by a dusty Jeep, and judging by his stance, the way he held his keys, he was considering making a run for it. Too late. If he didn't want to talk to her, he shouldn't have come.

"What the hell are you doing here?" she demanded.

"I came to pay my respects."

"To the man you sent to prison? Why?"

She didn't bother to fake politeness. She'd wanted to yell at someone for a long time, and he was the perfect target.

"I grew up with Derek," he said. "You know that."

"Your friendship didn't matter when Derek begged you to help him. Do you really think he'd care that you were here now, after what you did to him?"

Anger flashed in his eyes. "I did my job."

"You sent an innocent man to jail. Now he's dead."

Jason swallowed hard, a battle going on in his eyes. She willed him to try to refute her statement, because she wanted a fight. She needed to release the unbearable tension in her body. Her hands clenched into fists, and it took all of her willpower not to take a swing at him. She'd never hit anyone in her life, but damn if she didn't want to punch him.

Before Jason could speak, Lucas ran over, interrupting them. He threw his little arms around her hips and gave Jason a curious look. "Who are you?"

Jason's face paled; her son was the mirror image of his father.

"He's no one, Lucas," Brianna answered. "Go back to the car."

"Grandma Nancy says to come," Lucas told her. "People are waiting at the house."

"I'll be right there. Go on."

Lucas gave Jason another look and then ran back to his grandparents.

Jason's lips tightened as his gaze met hers. "This must be rough on him."

"Don't pretend to care." She refused to soften at the pain in his eyes. "I can't believe you're here. Did you really think you'd be welcome?"

His gaze burned into hers. "It was probably a mistake. But I couldn't stop thinking about Derek—and about you."

She stiffened. "I'm not interested in what you think about."

"Then why are you still talking to me?"

"I'm not." She turned, then glanced back at him. "I'm not leaving town. I intend to find out what really happened five years ago."

"You know what happened."

"Derek swore he was set up."

"Not by me," Jason said flatly. "You need to let it go, Brianna."

"That would certainly make things easier for you."

"And for you. Be realistic. Your private investigator couldn't come up with any new information because there's none to be found."

She shook her head. "No. You were wrong about Derek, and I'll prove it."

She walked quickly back to the car, feeling Jason's gaze follow her every step.

"What was Jason doing here?" Rick asked, concern etched across the deep lines of his face.

"He said he wanted to pay his respects."

"Maybe after all these years, he's finally sorry for not believing in Derek," Nancy suggested.

Brianna watched Jason drive away. He wasn't sorry at all, but she would find a way to change that.

Brianna's words echoed through Jason's head as he sped through the black iron gates of the cemetery. No way in hell had he sent an innocent man to jail, and there was no possibility that Brianna would be able to prove otherwise. Derek was guilty, and Brianna was blinded by love. He'd thought after all this time she might have come to accept the truth about her husband, but it was clear she was still living in denial—and in pain.

He blew out a breath, thinking about how much she'd changed in the past five years. Her stunning blue eyes were now haunted and weary. Her curves had thinned, and she'd cut at least six inches off what had once been a glorious mane of thick blond hair. She wasn't a girl anymore but a woman, a wife, a mother . . . and a widow.

His gut clenched with anger and sadness, not just for her and her son. Derek had once been his friend, and he missed that happy, carefree, do-anything-once guy who had died at the age of thirty-two, which was a tragedy no matter *what* he'd done. Contrary to what Brianna thought, he'd never wanted to send Derek to jail. He had looked hard for other suspects. There hadn't been any.

In the eyes of Brianna and the Kanes, he was the enemy, the one to blame for the destruction of their family. He'd always believed that putting the guilty behind bars was a noble cause, but even the bad guys had people who loved them.

Too restless to go home, he headed across town to Kara and Colin's house. The Lynches had been his best friends since elementary school. If there were two people he could count on in life, it was them.

As he pulled up in front of their home, he smiled at the pumpkins lining the porch rail and the cobwebs strewn across the hedges. Halloween was one of Kara and Colin's favorite holidays. Last year, he'd helped Colin turn the garage into a haunted house. This year, he suspected things would be a little tamer. Colin was only five weeks into his recovery from a head injury that had left him in a coma for three months. And Kara was busy taking care of her husband and their newborn, Faith, who'd made her arrival just a day before Colin had woken up.

He got out of his car and was halfway to the porch steps when Kara came through the front door carrying a skeleton door decoration. She wore blue jeans and a long-sleeved T-shirt, and her dark red hair was pulled back in a ponytail. She didn't have on a speck of makeup, but she didn't need any. She still had that baby glow.

"Jason, how are you?" she asked, setting down the skeleton to give him a big hug. "I didn't know you were coming by."

"It was a spur-of-the-moment decision."

"Your timing is perfect. Colin just got back from physical therapy, and he's in a bear of a mood. Maybe you can get him out of it." She cast a quick look back at the house to make sure they were still alone. "I don't know what's going on with him. He's extremely irritable, and no matter what I do, I constantly annoy him. I wasn't expecting this, Jason. I thought once he woke up, he'd be ecstatically happy."

Colin's fuse *did* seem shorter, but wasn't that to be expected? "He just needs time to adjust. He's confused, Kara. Three months passed for us while he was frozen in time. He doesn't even remember being shot. Nor does he realize how close he came to dying. He expects to be able to do everything he did before, but he can't, and it's frustrating him."

"You're right. I need to be more patient. It's just not one of my strengths."

"No kidding." He looked past Kara as the door opened and Colin stepped onto the porch, wearing navy sweatpants and a white T-shirt with the Angel's Bay Police Department insignia.

Colin gave Jason a quick nod, then told Kara, "The baby is crying. She's probably hungry, and I can't do anything about that."

"I'll get her. Thanks."

As Colin moved toward the porch bench, Kara gave Jason a pointed look and then disappeared into the house.

Colin let out a sigh as he sat down and stretched his legs out in front of him. He'd regained some color in his face the past few weeks, but his clothes still hung loosely on his big frame.

"How are you feeling?" Jason leaned against the porch railing. "I have to tell you that you look like shit."

"I had a workout this morning. I'm a little tired."

"Maybe you should take it slower."

"Did Kara tell you to say that?" Colin demanded, a fire in his usually calm green eyes.

"I can speak for myself," Jason replied, unintimidated by Colin's bad mood. They'd been friends since the third grade. Neither of them had siblings, and in each other they'd found a brother. They'd grown up together, joined the force, and worked side by side. They'd shared good times and bad. He'd hoped the bad was over, but it looked as if there were still some issues to work through. At least Colin was alive. Everything else could be figured out.

"I don't want to take it slower," Colin continued with a frown. "I need to get in shape, so I can go back to work and support my family."

"You will, but in the meantime you can be home with your daughter and with Kara. What's wrong with that?"

"Nothing is wrong with that." Colin ran a hand through his hair in irritation. "I'm not complaining."

"Aren't you?"

"Look, I know I have a lot to be thankful for. I just want to be the man I was. I need to take care of my wife and my child. It's bad enough that Kara had to go through labor without me." He shook his head, anger etched in every line of his face. "I don't want her to worry about money and working part-time at the quilt store or the real-estate office. I want her to stay home with Faith, the way we planned."

"You're the one who needs to stop worrying about money and work. All Kara needs right now is you at her side."

"She needs more than that," Colin argued.

"No, she doesn't. She's tired, Colin. She sat by your bed every damn day for three long months and prayed for you to wake up. The whole town thought she was chasing a dream, but she wouldn't give in. She wouldn't even go to the hospital when she went into labor; she was so damn determined to be with you when she gave birth to your daughter. She put you first, above herself. You've got a hell of a woman for a wife."

"You think I don't know that?" Colin asked, clearly pissed off. "You think I don't wonder if I'll be enough for her now? I'm *different*. My mind is muddy. I can't find words. I forget things. I don't feel like myself, and who knows if I ever will? I hate feeling weak, out of control. I saw Kara taking out the trash earlier. I *always* took out the trash. It's my job, not hers."

"I'm sure she'll be happy to give you back that job. Stop pushing yourself so hard. You'll be the man you were and more. Kara has been in love with you since you were kids. She's seen you at your worst. She's not going anywhere."

"I don't want her to stay because she feels sorry for me."

"From where I sit, you're the only one feeling sorry for you."

Colin sucked in a sharp breath. "Why don't you tell me what you really think?"

"Fine: I think you should get your head out of your ass."

"If I wasn't so tired, I'd take a swing at you."

Jason grinned. "You'd probably fall over."

"Yeah, probably." The anger faded from Colin's eyes. "You're the only one around here who isn't afraid I'll break. Everyone else treats me like I'm fragile."

"If you didn't break after what you went through, I think you're good to go for another fifty years. I have every confidence that you'll return to normal. So take a breath and enjoy the day—because in spite of everything, you're still alive."

Colin nodded. "I hate to admit that you're right."

"I usually am."

Colin rolled his eyes. "So what's up with you?"

"Just checking in," he said with a shrug.

Colin's gaze sharpened. "Wait a second. Today is Monday. Tell me you didn't go to Derek Kane's funeral."

"I drove by the cemetery," Jason conceded.

"Why the hell would you do that?"

"I couldn't stop myself. It was a remarkably small group for a guy who once had more friends than I could count. It was just his parents, a few relatives, some of the neighbors. Charlotte and her mother were there. Andrew Schilling did the service. I didn't go close enough to hear it." He paused. "Brianna and her son, Lucas, are moving here to be close to the Kanes."

"I heard something about that."

"Did you also hear that Brianna intends to prove that Derek was innocent, that I railroaded him to jail?"

"Who told you that?"

"She did."

"I thought you didn't get close enough to talk to anyone."

"She saw me and came over. She was furious that I was there."

"How did you think she would react?" Colin paused. "Brianna won't be able to prove anything. You double- and triple-checked your facts. The chief rode your ass every step of that investigation, and you didn't do it alone. Everyone in the department was involved. No one wanted to believe Derek was responsible, but the facts were the facts."

"That's what I keep telling myself."

"Then start believing it." Colin's gaze was pointed and direct. "You've always been your own worst critic. Frankly, I've never understood why everyone was surprised by Derek's behavior. He always had his eye on the prize. Even when we were kids, he was hustling at the poker games in the Murrays' garage. Art was his ticket to the top. With his grandfather's connections and his own personal charm, Derek had an entrée into a world of money filled with celebrities and power brokers. There was temptation everywhere he looked."

What Colin said was true, but there was one big question they'd never managed to answer. "I just wish we'd found the paintings."

"Stolen art is rarely recovered; you know that."

"Derek had to hand those paintings off to someone—an accomplice or a buyer, maybe both. I never understood why he'd take the fall. Why didn't he implicate anyone else?"

"He probably never thought he'd actually go to prison. Derek always believed that he was the exception to the rule."

Jason cocked his head, hearing an undertone in Colin's voice that he hadn't noticed before. "Doesn't sound as if you liked him as much as I thought you did."

"He was entertaining. I never thought he had much substance, but you knew him better that I did. I always thought Derek took the easy way out."

"Well, there was nothing easy about serving time. And now he's dead."

"Not because of you," Colin met his gaze. "You need to get a grip. You didn't send an innocent man to jail, and you are *not* responsible for his death. Derek's case is closed. Let it stay that way."

"It won't stay closed if Brianna has anything to say about it." He jerked upright, filled with a restless adrenaline he couldn't seem to shake. "I can't believe she's come back here at all, much less that she's going to go on some crusade to clear Derek's name. It's been five years. The investigator the Kanes hired came up with nothing. I thought by now Brianna would have finally figured out who Derek really was."

"So this isn't about Derek at all—it's about his beautiful widow," Colin said with a speculative gleam in his eyes. "You can't stand that she believed him over you. You're used to being the hero with women, but with Brianna you're the bad guy."

"That's not it," he denied quickly, though there was a grain of truth in Colin's words.

"You don't think you'll change her mind, do you? Because it won't happen. You need to let this go, move on, and stay away from Brianna Kane."

It was good advice. Jason just didn't think he could take it.

# TWO

Brianna gathered up empty glasses and plates and took them into the Kanes' kitchen. A few neighbors and friends remained in the living room, but the postfuneral lunch was just about over, and for that she was grateful. She didn't know anyone well, and their polite, meaningless condolences were beginning to wear her down. She was tired of putting on a face, pretending to feel something when most days she just felt numb.

In five years, she'd gone from being a joyous fiancée on the brink of an exciting life to being the wife of a criminal. Now she was a widow, a single mother, and a dutiful daughter-in-law—but who was she really? She never seemed to have time to find out. She was always playing catch-up, taking on a role she wasn't quite ready for. She needed to take control of her present and her future. She'd let Derek's life shape hers, because once she'd married him, she'd committed herself to supporting him through his prison sentence. She'd believed it was the right thing to do, because she was pregnant and their child needed two parents. But in the end, Lucas had still ended up with one parent.

Now her main concern was making a good life for her son. She'd agreed to move to Angel's Bay because the Kanes were desperate to be near their only grandchild, and she'd wanted Lucas to feel part of a normal family. Her parents had turned their backs on her after she'd married Derek, so the only family she had left was in this house.

She loaded the dishwasher, then looked around the cozy kitchen for any other dishes, but the room was neat and tidy as always. Nancy was a first-class homemaker, as well as an avid collector of pig memorabilia, from salt and pepper shakers to dish towels, coffee mugs, and coasters. Nancy had laughingly told Brianna that she couldn't remember why or when she'd decided to start the collection, but once begun, it took on a life of its own.

Besides the knickknacks, there were memories of Derek all over the house—his carved initials in the round oak kitchen table, the trophies in his bedroom, the walls of photographs marking every year of his life. If there was anyplace on earth where Derek still had a strong presence, it was here in this house. She wondered why she didn't find it more comforting.

"There you are," Nancy said as she entered and set an empty tray on the counter. "I was wondering where you'd gotten to. How are you feeling?" Her concerned gaze swept across Brianna's face.

"I'm okay," Brianna answered. "You've been doing all the work."

"It helps me to stay busy," Nancy said with a sad but determined smile. "Everyone is gone except our old friends Bud and Laurie. We're going to have some tea. Do you want to join us?"

Brianna didn't think she could take one more second of polite conversation. "Actually, I think I'll go to my house and get a start on the unpacking." While Rick and Nancy would have preferred to have her and Lucas live with them, Brianna had drawn the line at sharing a house with her in-laws. She loved them dearly, but there had to be some boundaries, so she'd rented a small house on Drake's Way just a few blocks away.

"Are you sure you want to do that now?" Nancy asked. "I thought you'd wait until tomorrow. Maybe I should come with you. Rick can keep an eye on Lucas. You don't want to tackle those boxes by yourself."

"I appreciate the offer, but please stay here with your friends. I'd like to take a walk around the neighborhood, get my bearings. You can bring Lucas over whenever you're done here. Or I can come back and get him."

Nancy gave her a concerned look. "Are you sure you want to be alone, Brianna? It's been a difficult day."

She couldn't think of anything better than being alone. She needed some time to herself to drop the brave smile and just take a breath. "I'll be fine."

Nancy hesitated, pursing her lips. "Brianna,

you're not thinking about talking to Jason Marlow again, are you?"

A tingle ran down her spine at the unexpected question. Seeing Jason at the cemetery had rattled her. He'd gone from being a dim shadow in her mind to a living, breathing reminder of everything she'd lost. Talking to him again was not high on her list. He unsettled her on a lot of levels. There was something about the way he looked at her . . . the way he'd always looked at her.

"Brianna?"

She realized Nancy was still waiting for an answer. "I don't have any plans to speak to Jason. He'd be the last person who would want to help us find the truth. He thinks he already knows it."

"I appreciate your desire to continue fighting for Derek," Nancy said slowly. "We've all spent a lot of time and money trying to prove his innocence, but every possible lead has always led to crushing disappointment, and I don't know if I can do it anymore." She drew in a deep breath. "Derek is gone, and he's not coming back. My concern now is for you and Lucas to be happy here. If you start asking a lot of questions, I'm afraid the nasty gossip will start up again. It was hard on Rick and me when Derek was convicted, and I don't want to live through it again. I want Lucas to go to school without hearing friends talk about his father and for you to have the opportunity to meet other women your age without Derek's crime hanging over your head. I want us all to live a normal life, to be free of the past."

"I don't think that my asking questions will get people talking; I'm sure they already are," she said, a little surprised by Nancy's attitude. She would have thought that her mother-in-law would want her to continue the fight. "And how can we be free if we don't know the truth?"

Nancy gave a helpless shake of her head. "I doubt we'll ever find it. Can't it be enough to know that we tried?"

It wouldn't be enough for Brianna, because deep down, she knew that it wasn't just about proving Derek's innocence; she had to prove to herself that she'd made the right decision in marrying him and standing by him all these years. But she wasn't going to share that with Nancy, who'd never had a single doubt about her son.

She put her hand on her mother-in-law's arm. "You don't have to try anymore. The past five years, I let you and Rick carry the burden. I was so busy trying to keep my head above water and raise Lucas on my own that I couldn't take anything else on. But I'm here now, back where it all started, and I need to know I did everything I could to find out what happened at the museum that night." She paused. "Rick said that there's a new chief of police now."

"Joe Silveira," Nancy replied with a nod. "He's been here about eight months. We thought about talking to him, but Derek was resigned to letting the clock run out until he was released." Her eyes filled with tears as she bit down on her bottom lip.

"Derek was starting to smile again, the last couple of months. He was looking forward instead of back. We all were."

Nancy's words brought a new wave of pain, and Brianna drew in a shaky breath. No matter how often she tried to escape the past, it kept calling her back. "That's why I have to give this one last try. Maybe a new chief of police will be willing to take another look at the case. We could use a fresh perspective, especially from someone who didn't grow up here and wasn't in the department five years ago."

"I never thought Jason or any of the other boys who grew up with Derek would turn on him the way they did," Nancy said bitterly. "Jason and Derek were as close as brothers. He was part of the family." She squared her shoulders. "Do what you have to do, Brianna, but don't let your guard down with Jason. He won't let you overturn his case without a fight."

"I'm not worried about Jason. But before I do anything else, I need to unpack and put some beds together so Lucas and I have somewhere to sleep tonight."

"You can always stay here another night." The doorbell rang, and an odd expression flitted through Nancy's eyes as they heard Rick's voice, followed by the sound of barking. "Oh, dear," she muttered.

Brianna frowned. "What's wrong?"

Nancy glanced over at the calendar hanging on the wall. "I forgot it was today."

"Forgot what?"

"Derek asked us to do something for him. He wanted to get Lucas a present that would be waiting when he was released."

An uneasy feeling ran through Brianna, maybe because Nancy had never looked as guilty as she did now. "What kind of present?"

Before Nancy could reply, Lucas ran into the kitchen, his face lit with excitement. "Mommy, guess what Grandpa and Grandma got me?"

The sound of barking told Brianna all she needed to know. "You didn't," she said, as Lucas grabbed her hand and pulled her into the living room.

Rick had a squirmy black dog in his arms and a sheepish expression on his face. "I forgot it was today," he told Nancy, who had followed them into the living room.

"So did I," Nancy said.

"Can I hold him?" Lucas asked.

Rick hesitated and then handed the frantically excited puppy to Lucas. Lucas couldn't hang on to the dog, and the two went down together in a mix of barks and giggles.

"We're going to go," Laurie said hastily, giving her husband, Bud, a pointed look. "Let you all sort this out."

Brianna barely registered the neighbors' departure, too caught up in disbelief. Lucas had been asking for a dog for months, and she'd promised him they'd talk about it when his dad came home. Apparently, Derek had made his own plans to surprise his son.

The black Labrador was awfully cute, but the timing wasn't great. She would have preferred to get settled into their house before considering a pet.

"Derek had a black Lab," Nancy told her. "The last time we visited him, two weeks before he died, he said that he wanted to get Lucas a dog. We agreed to set it up for him with some friends of ours who breed dogs."

"After Derek died, I forgot all about it," Rick said.

"I can keep him, can't I, Mommy?" Lucas asked, his arms tightening around the puppy, which was enthusiastically licking his face. "I'll feed him and play with him all the time."

"I guess so," she said. There was no way she could erase the happiest smile Lucas had worn in months.

"We'll help you," Nancy said.

"We've got a head start on supplies," Rick added, motioning to the crate and the bag of dog food. "He didn't come empty-handed."

"What should we name him, Mommy?" Lucas asked.

"I'll let you pick. In the meantime, I'll go to our house and get our beds set up and clear some space for the three of us."

"I'll come with you," Nancy said.

"No, that's okay. I need a few minutes to myself."

"I'm sorry we sprang this on you." Rick offered her a rueful smile.

"It will be fine." And as she watched Lucas playing with his new best friend, she started to believe it would be. This was what she wanted for her son: normal, happy family moments. It was why she'd risked coming to Angel's Bay. There were shadows here, but there was also a lot of love. And she didn't want Lucas to grow up lonely, the way she had.

"I wish Derek could see this," Nancy murmured, her gaze on the child and the puppy. She glanced back at Brianna. "His last gift to his son. I think it was a good one."

"I think it was, too."

Jason headed to the police station after leaving Colin's house. He wasn't on duty, but he wanted to speak to the chief before Brianna did.

Joe Silveira was just getting off the phone when Jason entered his office. In his late thirties, the chief had dark hair, dark eyes, and an unshakably cool manner. He'd spent years working vice in Los Angeles and brought a wealth of experience to this job. Jason had enormous respect for his boss, and they had a good working relationship, but they hadn't moved close to a friendship. Joe was approachable yet distant, the kind of man Jason doubted anyone knew very well.

"What can I do for you, Marlow?" Joe asked, giving him a thoughtful look.

"I wanted to give you a heads-up on a situation that might be developing."

"Let me guess: Derek Kane. I heard you were at the funeral today. Was that a good idea?"

"Probably not."

Joe picked up a thick file from the top of his desk. "I took a look through this earlier. Interesting case. Local boy turns art thief, assaults security guard, lifts three priceless paintings from the museum, and along the way runs into his best friend—you—thereby placing him at the scene of the crime."

"You're up to speed." Jason took a seat across from Joe. He wasn't surprised; the chief made it his business to know what was going on in Angel's Bay.

"The town has been talking about nothing else since the Kanes decided to bury their son in the local cemetery." Joe paused. "So what can you tell me that's not in the file?"

"I can tell you that Derek's widow, Brianna Kane, is convinced that her husband was framed, and she's determined to prove it."

"Are you worried?"

"I don't think I made a mistake. I dealt with the facts I had. I wasn't the only one on the case, and I wasn't Derek's only friend in the department. Everyone knew him. Most people liked him."

Joe stared at him for a long moment. "You were in a difficult position, having to arrest a friend. I'm sure you were torn between wanting to be right and wanting to be wrong."

"I was right," Jason said.

"Then that should make it easier."

"You'd think so," he said with a small sigh. He had no reason to second-guess anything he'd done, but Brianna's stubborn belief in Derek's innocence was playing on his mind.

"From what I read, you conducted a thorough investigation. Unfortunately, you didn't have a lot of hard evidence to go on, and the paintings in question were never recovered." Joe pulled three photographs from the file and spread them across the desk. *"The Three Faces of Eve* by renowned artist Victor Delgado. I don't know much about art, but these look pretty good."

Jason's stomach clenched. It had been many years since he'd studied the photographs of the stolen paintings. The artist was one of the founders of Angel's Bay, having survived a shipwreck off the coast. He'd painted the portraits in memory of his lost love, Eve. In one painting, Eve was a sweet, saintly angel with a halo of heavenly light glowing behind her. There was innocence and wonder in her violet-blue eyes. Behind her was a beautiful landscape with a sandy beach and a light blue sky, the blurred colors creating a dreamlike appearance.

The second portrayed Eve as a sexy, wicked siren beckoning to her lover from where she reposed on a red velvet couch. Her bodice fell off her shoulders, revealing lush breasts, her dark red hair flowing into the background of hot reds, menacing blacks, and fiery oranges.

In the last portrait, Eve appeared frightened and confused as she was swept off the deck of a ship into a stormy sea, her desperate hands reaching out for rescue. There were fine lines in Eve's face, in her hands, as if she were breaking apart in front of the man who loved her.

There was passion and power in the paintings, and desperation bordering on maniacal. Town legend said that Delgado had gone crazy trying to capture the soul of the woman he'd lost. He'd been haunted by her spirit, and she'd mocked him for getting her wrong over and over again.

Jason was only looking at photographs, but he could still feel the pull of the art. It was difficult to look away. He had the bizarre notion that Eve was trying to tell him something. Like maybe where she was . . .

"I wish to hell I could find the paintings," he told Joe. "I spent a lot of time looking for them, but I couldn't catch a lead. Not one of the local artists could point me in the direction of a potential buyer, someone who might have commissioned Derek to steal them. No one ever heard a whisper about their whereabouts. I figured Derek probably stashed them somewhere, letting them cool off until he got out of prison."

"Do you think he was working alone?"

"He never gave up another name. But I always thought he had to have help."

"If he did, they've stayed very quiet."

"They have. And they were certainly willing to let Derek rot in prison. I have to believe that Derek's silence was born of fear. He preferred to serve time rather than implicate someone else, even if that might have meant mitigating his sentence."

"But he did have a private investigator and an attorney working on an appeal."

"He did," Jason agreed. "No one came up with any new information. The P.I. told me frankly that he didn't think Derek was being completely up-front with him. Maybe he was going through the motions so he wouldn't have to admit his guilt to his wife or to his parents."

"If he hadn't assaulted the guard, he might have gotten away with the theft, or at the very least served a lot less time," Joe said.

"It was a bad mistake," Jason said with a nod. "When I was reading through the report, I was struck by the fact that the paintings had only recently been donated to the museum by Derek's grandfather, Wyatt Kane."

"Along with Steve and Gloria Markham," Jason said. "The paintings were lost for a hundred and fifty years; they were believed to have been stolen by Victor Delgado's brother, Ramón, who was also in love with Eve. At least, that was one theory. Another was that Eve's family stole the paintings. She'd run out on the wealthy and highly respected Winstons to jump onboard a ship with a poor Hispanic artist. Her family couldn't get her back, but they could destroy the art that represented her desertion."

"So Derek Kane's grandfather finds the paintings in a small shop in Mexico and brings them back to

Angel's Bay. Ironic that his grandson would wind up stealing them."

"Derek claimed that was exactly why he wouldn't have done it. He knew the paintings meant something to his grandfather, to all the local artists who have been obsessed with Delgado's work for years."

"But you didn't believe him."

"Derek had a lot of issues with Wyatt. I could see revenge being a motive—wanting to take something away from Wyatt that he'd spent years trying to find. There was bad blood between them."

"That makes sense. Art theft always seems to have a personal motive. It's never just about the money." Joe paused. "So what can you tell me about Brianna Kane?"

"She's extremely loyal." Jason stood up. He got angry every time he thought about Brianna marrying Derek after his conviction. Why had she been so willing to tie herself to a criminal? Judging by the age of her son, it was possible she'd been pregnant, but still, surely she'd had other options.

"You need to stay out of this," Joe said, his gaze serious.

"If the case is going to be reopened, I want to be involved."

"It won't be reopened unless there's new information. Right now I just want to hear what Mrs. Kane has to say."

"She'll say I sent an innocent man to jail."

"But you didn't, right? So you have nothing to

prove. Try to remember that. It will make your life a lot easier." Joe cleared his throat. "I also need you to get your head out of the past. With the Harvest Festival starting in a few days, the hotels and inns are at capacity, and we're down a few officers—not a good combination."

"I'll do whatever you need."

"Good. By the way, have you spoken to Colin lately? How's he doing?"

"He's frustrated and impatient to get back to normal."

"Tell him not to rush. He's got a job here whenever he's a hundred percent—if he still wants it. What he went through would make anyone reconsider their career choice."

"He has no qualms about returning to work. He doesn't remember the shooting, so maybe that helps."

"Maybe. Unfortunately, those kinds of memories tend to work their way out at some point," Joe said.

Jason's phone started to vibrate, and his father's number flashed across the screen, sending an uneasy feeling down his spine. His father had been dodging his calls the past few weeks, which usually meant only one thing—another woman was about to enter their lives. "My dad," he said to Joe. "I should get this."

"Take it."

"You'll keep me posted on the Kane case?"

"You'll be at the top of my list," Joe promised.

As he left the office, Jason answered his phone. "Dad?"

"I need your help," Hal Marlow said, his voice laced with excitement. "I'm heading to Vegas in a couple of hours."

Jason's stomach turned over. The last time his father had gone to Vegas, he'd come home with his third wife. "I'm on my way."

"You don't have to come over here, I just want to—"

"I'll be there in ten minutes," he interrupted. He usually didn't get a lot of warning before impending nuptials. Maybe this time he could talk his father out of making yet another mistake.


After divorcing his third wife, Jason's father had moved into a one-bedroom apartment over Dina's Café. Hal Marlow opened the door with a big, broad smile and an eagerness in his brown eyes that made him look a lot younger than his sixty-one years. He'd lost some weight in recent weeks, and he'd exchanged his usual faded work jeans for khaki slacks. Even his hair looked a little less gray—all signs of a new woman.

"You didn't have to come running over here," his father said as he headed into the bedroom, where he was in the middle of packing.

"Of course I did. You only met Patty three weeks ago. You barely know her."

"I know exactly who Patty is, and if you gave her a chance, you might like her," Hal said as he placed a sweater in his suitcase.

"Do you know how many times you've said that to me since Mom died?'

"Patty is different."

"And how many times have you said *that?* Lois was special, Rita was exotic, Tammy was interesting, and Jeanette was unlike anyone you'd ever met. Should I go on?"

"Please don't," his father said, an irritated gleam flashing through his eyes.

"Dad, come on. You want to date Patty, fine, but why marry her? You've got enough ex-wives. Do you really need one more?"

Hal shook his head, disappointment shading his eyes. "Patty is different," he repeated. "She's real. She's herself. And I'm crazy about her." He zipped his suitcase and set it on the floor. "But I'm not going to marry her in Vegas. We're just closing up her apartment there and arranging to have the rest of her things moved here."

"You say that now, but once Patty gets you near a wedding chapel and drunk on champagne, who knows what you'll do?"

His father's brown eyes sparkled with amusement. "I think I'm a little too old to be warned about the dangers of drinking in combination with Las Vegas wedding chapels. I'm the father. You're the son."

That might be theoretically true, but Jason had watched out for his dad almost his entire life. His mom had died when he was seven, leaving his devastated father heartbroken and lonely. For years, he'd barely made it out of bed; then he'd tried to fill the void in his life with women. Some had made him happy for a while, but no one had lasted. Jason wanted to see his father happy again; he just didn't think Patty Pease was the answer.

"You could do better, Dad." The words slipped out before he could stop them.

His father's smile disappeared, and he shook a warning finger at him. "Don't ever say that again. Patty is a fine woman."

"She's a *stripper*. Granted, she's got a lot to offer, and I mean *a lot*, but you don't need to go to Las Vegas with her."

"Watch your mouth, Jason. Patty is no longer an exotic dancer."

"She's playing you."

"No, she's not." Hal paused. "What are you so worried about? I know it's not your nonexistent inheritance." His gaze narrowed. "In fact, I don't even think it's me or Patty that's got you so on edge."

His father rarely paid any attention to his life, which made his current scrutiny surprising. "I'm fine. I'm just not in the mood for any more surprises."

"Any more? What's happened? Wait, I know. Derek's funeral was today." He gave Jason a compassionate smile. "Dina said you went to the cemetery."

Apparently, everyone in town knew about his impulsive trip. "I had to see it for myself. I can't quite believe Derek is dead."

"That's understandable. You were good friends for most of your childhood. When you weren't with

Colin, you were with Derek, and the Kanes were practically your second family."

They'd been his only family for some of the years his father had been wandering through life in a drunken stupor.

"I can't imagine what they're going through, losing their son like that," Hal continued. "I couldn't stand it if something happened to you." He cleared his throat, a guilty expression tightening his mouth. "I know I wasn't always the best father, especially in those early years. You lost out big when your mother died. She knew how to make a family. I wasn't very good at it."

"You did your best."

"And you're being generous," Hal said with a smile. "At any rate, the reason I called you was that I need your help. I want you to watch Patty's pets while we're gone. She's been staying at her mom's house since Shirley went into the convalescent home, and she doesn't want to drag her animals on the plane. She's got an itty-bitty dog, a couple of cats, and a bird. All you have to do is sleep there, feed the pets, let them out, and maybe spray some water on the flower garden."

"I don't think I can. The Harvest Festival starts in two days. I'm going to be pulling some double shifts with all the tourists in town. I won't be around much."

"You can fit it into your schedule," his father said, ignoring his excuse. "And it's not like you'd be leaving a wife or a girlfriend at home alone. You've had quite the dry spell the last few months."

"I've been busy, and it hasn't been that dry," Jason said with a frown.

"Hasn't it?" his father asked with a knowing gleam in his eyes. "I know you were watching over Kara while Colin was in the hospital, but now that he's home, you should get back out there. You can't spend your life playing third wheel to those two."

"I'm out there." He just hadn't had anyone catch his interest in a while. Brianna's image flashed though his head, but that wasn't going to happen. Derek had always been between them, and he always would be.

"Come on, Jason, I'd really appreciate your help. Patty is important to me. I want to make this work." His father's expression grew serious. "I know I don't have the best track record with women, but she's—"

"Different," Jason finished, meeting his father's gaze.

"Yeah, she is," he said sheepishly. "I haven't felt this way in a long time, like a young man on the verge of something exciting. It's a great feeling— exhilarating, almost like jumping off a cliff."

"Jumping off a cliff might be cheaper."

His father slapped him on the back. "You're such a cynic. I hope my divorces haven't ruined you for love. It *is* out there, Jason. I had it with your mother, and I'm going to have it again."

"Well, you're certainly due."

Hal smiled more broadly. "That I am. The keys to Patty's house are on the table. Whatever you do, don't lose one of her pets. She's crazy about those furballs. They're her children."

"And whatever *you* do, don't marry her until you get a prenup."

"Prenups are not romantic," his father said with a breezy wave of his hand.

"No, but they will keep you out of bankruptcy."

"Where's your sense of adventure? Marrying someone is always a risk, but it does have some advantages. You get a lot of sex."

Jason quickly put up his hand. "I don't want to discuss your sex life."

"Wasn't going to tell you. Wouldn't want to make you jealous," Hal said with a twinkle in his eye. "Thanks again. I'll bring you something from Vegas." He grabbed his suitcase and headed toward the door.

"Just make sure it's not a new stepmother," Jason called.

# THREE

It was almost midnight before Brianna settled into bed. As she stared at the ceiling, watching the shadows dance in the moonlight, she felt tense and jumpy. She wasn't used to the way her new house breathed yet. And it was so quiet in Angel's Bay. She'd become accustomed to falling asleep to the sounds of traffic on the highway by her apartment building, sirens as the nearby fire department answered calls, and loud thumps coming from her upstairs neighbors. Those noises had comforted her, made her feel less alone. While Derek might have died a few weeks ago, he'd been gone for five years. They'd never lived together before their marriage or afterwards. But even though she'd been on her own for a long time, it felt different now, more final.

As if sensing her need for noise, the puppy began to bark and whine, long, pitiful, high-pitched cries. Despite Lucas's plea to let the dog sleep with him, she'd insisted on putting the puppy in a crate in the kitchen. She didn't want to set a precedent that she wouldn't be able to change. Unfortunately, the dog was testing her willpower.

Pulling the pillow over her head, she told herself that Lucas had learned to sleep through the night on his own, and so would the dog—the yet-to-be-named dog. Lucas was debating among Oscar, Snickers, and Digger. After seeing what damage the puppy had already done to the backyard in the short amount of time he'd been in it, she was voting for Digger.

Ten more minutes of pathetic dog cries finally drove her out of bed. She pulled a sweatshirt over her camisole and cotton pajama bottoms and walked into the hall. She stopped at Lucas's bedroom to pull the door shut, then went into the kitchen. The puppy bounded to his feet when he saw her, barking and yelping even louder. She closed the kitchen door, hoping the noise wouldn't wake Lucas.

Kneeling next to the crate, she gave the dog a firm look. "It's bedtime. You're supposed to go to sleep."

He barked in delight, as if she'd just told him it was time for a walk. She stuck her fingers through the mesh, and he licked them with enthusiasm, bringing a reluctant smile to her lips.

"Okay, I get it. You don't want to sleep. But you can't keep barking." Maybe if she let him out, he'd run around and get tired. She took him out of his crate, and he squirmed in her arms, licking her face and hands and anything he could get his puppy tongue on. Then he jumped to the ground and ran around the kitchen, sliding into the table legs and the walls.

She opened the back door, and the dog flew around the dark yard, exploring the shadows under the bushes and trees. There was a great deal of overgrown foliage; she'd need to do some gardening. It was nice to have such a big backyard; Lucas would probably enjoy it as much as the dog did.

Glancing toward the house next door, she saw lights on at the back of the house. Someone was up late. The Realtor had told her that an elderly woman owned that house. On her other side was a family with three older children—she hoped she'd find a babysitter among them.

With the dog digging in the dirt, she returned to the kitchen and put on some water for tea. Maybe it would help her relax enough to sleep. Like the puppy, she was finding it difficult to settle down in her new surroundings. While she waited for the water to boil, she unpacked one of the half-dozen boxes on the kitchen floor—one fewer task to do tomorrow. When the water boiled, she poured it into her mug and stepped out onto the deck.

The puppy was nowhere to be seen, and her uneasiness grew. Just as she saw the hole the puppy had dug under the neighbor's fence, she heard barking, a decidedly unfamiliar yap, and then a crash followed by male swearing—all coming from next door.

"Damn," she muttered as the barks and swearing grew louder.

She ran alongside her house and found a gate that led into the neighbor's property. There a tiny white puff of fur ran around her feet, chased by her puppy and a very pissed-off man, who was also wrestling with an irate, spitting cat.

"Digger, puppy!" she yelled, but he was too busy chasing the other dog to pay attention to her. Then the small furball squeezed under the bottom of the deck, in a space so small that her puppy could do little but bark furiously at his escaped prey.

The man let out another curse as the cat sprang from his arms. He put a hand to his cheek, and as he stepped into the light, she saw a long red scratch on a face that was very familiar.

Her heart jumped into her throat. "No way!"

Jason looked as shocked as she felt.

"You can't possibly live here," she said. "I was told this house belongs to an elderly lady."

"It does. Shirley Pease. She had a stroke a few months ago and went into a care facility. Her daughter, Patty, is living here now."

"You don't look like her daughter." Her gaze slid down his body. His jeans were slung low on his hips, and his button-down shirt was unbuttoned, revealing a tantalizing glimpse of a broad, muscular chest. His bare feet and tousled hair made him look as if he'd just rolled out of bed. She swallowed hard at the thought, a wave of heat running through her. She'd forgotten how sexy he was. Forgotten how his gaze had always made a little tingle run down her spine. But Jason was the cop who'd ruined her husband's life, and she could never forget that.

"I'm house-sitting for Patty, my father's girl-friend," Jason said. "You need to get your damn dog under control. He's digging a hole under the deck."

Jason was right. Dirt was flying through the air with her puppy's exuberant efforts to get under the deck. She grabbed the dog, thankful he was still small enough to hang on to.

Jason got down on his knees and peered under the deck. "Come on, Princess," he called. "It's safe to come out now."

"Princess?" she echoed.

Jason flung her a scowl. "She's not my dog. I didn't name her."

"She seems to like you," Brianna said as the tiny princess threw herself into Jason's waiting arms, whimpering with relief. "Unlike the cat. That's a nasty scratch she gave you."

"She lured me in, rolled over on her back like she wanted me to pet her, then took a swipe at me," he said with disgust. "Do you see her anywhere?"

Brianna scanned the yard. "No, It looks like she took off."

"Great. First night, and I've already lost one of them."

"How long are you going to be house-sitting?" She couldn't handle the idea of Jason being right next door; it was way too close.

"A few days, maybe a week." His gaze dropped to

the puppy in her arms. "He looks like Buster, Derek's old dog."

"I'm sure that was the intention. The Kanes got him for Lucas at Derek's request. I'd better get back. Lucas is asleep in the house."

"Hang on." He opened the door to the house and thrust Princess inside. "I'll go with you. The cat might be in your yard."

Brianna walked down the path between their houses, keeping an eye out for the cat, but a large shadow by the front windows of her house gave her pause. She stopped so abruptly Jason bumped into her.

"What's wrong?" he asked.

She took another step forward, knocking into the trash can, and the shadow moved through the trees. "I think someone is in my yard," she said in shock.

"Stay here." Jason moved past her quietly, quickly.

She hesitated for a moment, but the idea of Lucas being alone in the house propelled her forward. Jason met her on the lawn. "I don't see anyone. It was probably just the wind moving the trees."

She cast a quick look around. Maybe he was right. There were tall trees on both sides of the property, and it was pretty dark, the nearest streetlight three houses away. "I need to check on Lucas."

"Did you come out the back door?"

"Yes."

"I'll walk around with you."

Her back door was open the way she'd left it. She

hurried inside to check on Lucas. He was still asleep. As she came out of the room, she saw Jason checking her bedroom.

"What are you doing?"

"Just looking around. Everything seems to be fine."

"It was probably just my imagination."

"More than likely. It looks like you have a lot of unpacking to do."

"Tell me about it." She walked into the kitchen and put the puppy in his crate. He immediately started barking. "He really doesn't like that thing."

"I can't say that I blame him." Jason slid onto a bar stool, making himself a little too comfortable. Then again, it was nice not to be alone in the house. She didn't know why she was so jumpy. It had to be the new house, the new town. She just needed to get her bearings.

She refilled the teakettle and turned on the burner. "Tell me again, who lives next door?"

"Shirley Pease owns the house, but she had a stroke a few weeks ago, and her daughter, Patty, is moving in—if she doesn't rope my father into marriage before that," he grumbled.

"Is that a possibility?" She really shouldn't have been encouraging conversation, but she couldn't seem to stop herself.

"Absolutely. Patty is an ex-stripper, which doesn't bother my father at all. She has certain noticeable attributes, if you know what I mean."

"Got it."

"My father is a trusting romantic who always thinks he's about to embark on the greatest love of all time—up until the moment he ends up in divorce court. He's been married three times already."

"What number was your mother?"

A dark shadow passed through his eyes. "She wasn't a divorce. She died when I was seven."

"Oh—I'm sorry." It felt strange to say those words to Jason, even stranger to feel anything but hate for the man. She didn't want to see any other side to him than the one he'd shown the day he testified against Derek.

Unfortunately, Jason didn't look like that cold, ruthless cop now, with his wavy, mussed-up hair and bare feet. He looked like the guy she'd first met in the bar five years ago, the one who'd shamelessly flirted with her until he'd realized she was taken.

She needed to tell him to go. Why wouldn't the words come?

"Feel like making me a cup of tea?" he asked as the kettle began to sing.

She hesitated, then grabbed another mug.

He met her gaze as she slid it across the counter. A sharp gleam entered his eyes. "You must be spooked to let me stay. Is there a reason?"

She shrugged, not wanting to get into a discussion about her motives. "So you said your father remarried a couple of times?"

"You're not going to answer my question, are you?"

"Are you going to answer mine?" she countered.

"All right. The first couple of years after my mom died, my father was destroyed. He couldn't get out of bed in the morning, and when he did get up, he drank too much. He lost his construction business and the house he'd bought with my mother. We would have ended up on the streets if my uncle hadn't shown up and dragged us here to Angel's Bay. My dad got better eventually, recovered his desire to be married, and has since tied the knot a couple of times. Even though he's devastated with each failure, he keeps going back for more pain. I suspect he's headed for his fourth trip down the aisle as we speak."

"Maybe this one will work."

"That's what he said. He's always optimistic. I'll give him that."

"He doesn't sound at all like you." She lifted her mug to her lips as she leaned against the counter.

"We're very different," Jason agreed. "It was just the two of us for a while, and someone had to be practical. It wasn't going to be him, so if I wanted to eat, I had to look out for both of us."

"You don't have any other siblings?"

"Nope. Only child. You, too, right?"

"Yes," she said without elaborating.

For a moment there was nothing but quiet in the room. Even the puppy had fallen into an exhausted sleep.

"So what have you been doing the last five years?" Jason asked.

"Surviving," she said shortly.

"Are you sure coming back here was a good idea? Angel's Bay can't hold many happy memories for you."

"It's where the Kanes are."

"What about your parents?"

She cleared her throat. "They're not part of my life anymore." He stared back at her, a myriad of questions running through his eyes, none of which she wanted to answer. "But I didn't just come to Angel's Bay for the Kanes—I came for the truth. I won't find it anywhere else." She paused. "And I think it's time for you to leave."

He met her gaze head-on. "Is it really that simple to blame me for everything?"

His words hung in the air for a long moment. "It was simpler when you weren't standing in front of me," she admitted.

He drew in a quick breath at her words. "That's a start."

She immediately shook her head. "No. I might be willing to concede that you were part of a larger investigation, but you led the charge, Jason. You took the stand and testified against Derek. You were the last one to speak before the verdict came in. Besides all that, you were his friend. Your betrayal hurt him and the Kanes beyond measure. The relationship you had with them should have mattered. You should have tried to help Derek fight the charges. Instead, you went after him."

He paled at her harsh words. "I had to do my job, Brianna. If I could have taken myself off the case, I would have. But this is a small town with a small police department, and I saw Derek on the museum grounds. I talked to him minutes after the guard was assaulted. I was subpoenaed to testify. I had no choice but to tell the truth."

"You shaped the truth to fit the case. You were a young cop, and you needed to prove yourself. You used Derek to do that."

"Is that what he told you?"

"He didn't have to tell me. I was there."

"You heard only one side."

"And you saw only one side, the side that sent Derek to jail. What was a job to you was the end of my dreams."

"Derek is the one who destroyed your dreams—why don't you blame him?" he challenged.

"Because . . . because he's *dead.*"

All the emotions of the past few years assaulted her at once. She'd been trying to hold it together for Lucas and the Kanes, but she couldn't do it anymore. The room began to spin, and the mug slipped from her hand, hot liquid splashing her fingers. She was almost glad for the physical pain; at least it would pass. It was something she could make better.

Jason grabbed her arms and pulled her up against his solid chest. His body was warm, his embrace secure, comforting. She hadn't had anyone to lean on in a very long time. She'd been holding herself up for so long, and she was so tired. But she had to fight the temptation to linger. Jason was the wrong man to rely on.

She pushed him away and staggered to the kitchen table, sitting down quickly. Drawing in several deep breaths, she forced herself not to look at him, even though she was acutely aware of his gaze.

"Please go," she said, staring at the tabletop.

"Are you all right?"

She had no idea how to answer that question. Finally, she lifted her gaze to his. "I will be."

Clearly concerned, he said, "I'm sorry, Brianna. I know it's been a rough day. I didn't mean to make it worse."

"It's been a rough five years."

"I wish you could see that I'm not your enemy."

"I wish you could see that it doesn't matter to me *what* you are."

His lips tightened. "Okay. Make sure you lock the door behind me."

After he left, she let out a breath, completely drained by the encounter. She got up and slid home the dead bolt on the back door. The puppy barked, drawing her attention back to him. He'd woken up and looked ready to play again.

She knelt down on the floor next to the crate. "This was your fault. Jason never would have been here if it hadn't been for you charging into the yard next door." He barked in reply, his adorable face too sweet to bear. "Okay, not completely your fault, but we need to stay away from him." She didn't want

Jason to try to convince her that Derek was guilty. She didn't want him to confuse her. She *had* to believe she was right about Derek, and tomorrow she would start figuring out a way to prove it.

"Without any new evidence, I have no reason to re-open the case," Joe Silveira told Brianna late Tuesday morning. He'd listened patiently to her impassioned declaration that her husband had been set up for a crime he hadn't committed, but she hadn't told him anything he didn't already know.

"The stolen paintings were not found in Derek's possession," she persisted. "The police searched his apartment and mine, the Kanes' house, and the gallery where Derek worked in L.A. He didn't have them."

"He could have handed them off," Joe suggested. "But this case wasn't just about stolen art. A security guard was assaulted and injured. You know that."

"I also know that Derek swore he was innocent. Not once in five years did he waver from that position." She paused for a moment. "My husband was killed in a prison fight three weeks before he was supposed to be released. Everyone says it was an accident, but I'm not completely convinced."

Joe had found the timing interesting as well. "Why would you have doubts?"

"Because Derek was a model prisoner. He didn't fight. He got along with the other prisoners. And he was looking forward to his release date."

"It's my understanding he didn't instigate the

fight but was provoked. In the process, he slipped and hit his head on the concrete, suffering a fatal blow." Brianna flinched, and he wished he'd chosen his words better. "It was ruled an accident."

"I know, but I wonder if someone didn't *want* him to get out."

"Why?"

"Maybe Derek had something on someone else, information he could use when he was released. I just want someone to take an objective look at the case. It's been five years. A new perspective might bring a new conclusion."

He appreciated her determination. He even found himself wanting to help her—not because he was under the impression that her husband had been wrongly convicted but because she was willing to fight so hard for the man she'd married. He hadn't seen that kind of loyalty in a long time. Unfortunately, he couldn't give her the answer she wanted.

"I've read through the file, and I also noted that we shared our reports with an independent investigator hired by your in-laws. I'm sorry, Mrs. Kane. I don't see any suggestion that the case was handled improperly."

Her blue eyes filled with frustration, but there were no tears, thank God. She was hard enough to resist, with her fragile, haunted beauty. But he couldn't allocate department resources to reinvestigating a case that had already been prosecuted to a satisfactory conclusion.

"What about the fact that Jason Marlow was Derek's friend? Wasn't that a conflict of interest?"

"Several officers worked the case. But as I said before, if you bring me any new information, I'll be happy to take a look at it."

"Then I'll be back," she said, lifting her chin as she got to her feet. "Because I don't believe that we know everything about what happened that night."

After Brianna left, Joe gathered the loose papers together in the file, his eye falling once again on the photographs of the paintings. There was something about the mysterious Eve that intrigued him. Or maybe it was the artist's torment that got to him— Delgado's inability to see the woman he loved for who she really was.

And suddenly, Joe wasn't seeing Eve's face anymore but his wife, Rachel's. Rachel, with the long black hair, the white skin, the enormous dark eyes, the full lips, and the soft body that had once welcomed him home.

Rachel had had more than three faces; she'd had half a dozen, and lately he hadn't seen any of the happy ones. The woman he'd loved at fifteen, married at twenty-five, and lived with for fourteen years was more a mystery to him now than she had ever been. He didn't know how to make her happy. He didn't know if he even wanted to try anymore.

He'd thought the move to Angel's Bay would be a fresh start for them, but it hadn't turned out that way. Rachel was tied to L.A., to her real-estate business, her friends, and a life that she couldn't seem to give up for him.

He'd fallen in love with a life here that he couldn't seem to give up for her.

Was it time to cut their losses and move on?

Or was it time for him to give up Angel's Bay, go back to L.A., and be the husband she wanted him to be?

Shaking his head, he refocused his gaze on Eve. There was something about her eyes that seemed angry and disgusted, as if she couldn't believe the artist was getting it so wrong.

"Maybe you should have just told him who you were, Eve," he muttered. "Save him from having to guess and getting it wrong. But that would have taken all the fun out of it, wouldn't it?"

His door opened, and his assistant walked in. Betty Jones was a no-nonsense fifty-five-year-old mother of three, who kept the department running like a well-oiled machine. She was one of the few people who didn't find him intimidating.

"Who are you talking to?" she asked.

"No one. What do you need, Betty?"

"Charlotte Adams is here. She wants to know how many spots we're taking at the chili cook-off on Friday. The fire boys are putting up three entries. We've got Hamilton and Laughton signed up, but Lynch is out this year, and no one else around here can cook worth a damn. Are you up to the challenge?"

He'd heard something about the long-standing

rivalry between the police department and the fire department at the chili cook-off, but he had no idea exactly how it worked. "Why don't you send Dr. Adams in?"

Betty rolled her eyes. "She's just going to tell you what I did."

"Then I'll hear it from her."

He got to his feet, ignoring Betty's knowing smile as he tried to calm the sudden jump in his pulse rate that always seemed to occur when Charlotte was nearby.

Charlotte had on a black suit, and her expression was all business. He was disappointed. He liked seeing her in her jeans or, better yet, her running shorts, her thick blond hair blowing in the wind, her cheeks pink, her blue eyes bright. Actually, he just liked seeing her—but she'd been avoiding him for a few weeks, ever since Rachel had left town. At least, he thought she was avoiding him. Maybe she just didn't find him as fascinating as he found her.

"I didn't want to bother you," Charlotte said as Betty closed the door behind her.

"It's fine." He waved her into the chair in front of his desk and sat down again. "Is your medical practice so slow that you have time to run the chili cook-off?"

"I'm on my lunch break. The cook-off is my mother's baby, but she's been down with a cold, and she's now frantic that we don't have enough chili makers. So I was told to find more entrants or don't bother to come home."

Joe grinned. Monica Adams was a force of nature; he doubted anyone could say no to her. He could see why she and Charlotte butted heads so often. But one thing they had in common was a desire to help people.

"So what's it going to be, Chief? Are you going to let the fire department send three entries while you only send two?" Charlotte challenged.

"I have no idea how to make chili."

"There are lots of recipes on the Internet. I'm sure a smart, capable, and community-spirited man like yourself could find a way to whip something up."

"Nice job on the flattery. You really are desperate, aren't you?"

"I am," she admitted with a guilty smile. "Some of the regulars dropped out this year, and if the hall isn't filled with chili pots, my mother will lose face, and many other bad things will happen—mostly in her head. But I'll have to hear about them. And it will be completely my fault."

"I'll tell you what. Find me a recipe, I'll put it together."

"It's a deal." She got to her feet with a happy smile.

He came around the desk and extended his hand.

She hesitated and then put her hand in his. Her warm touch made his fingers tighten around hers. One swift pull, and he could have her in his arms. He could almost taste her sweet mouth under his.

She yanked her hand from his and cleared her throat, her eyes a little too bright. "I'll drop off a recipe with Betty tomorrow. I'd better run. I'm meeting Annie at the church. Andrew thinks he might have found a couple to adopt her baby, " she added, quickly changing the subject.

"I didn't realize Annie was interested in giving her child up."

It probably wasn't the worst idea. A pregnant eighteen-year-old, Annie Dupont had no family support and would have been on the streets or in a shelter if not for Charlotte and her mother.

"She's considering her options. It might not be easy to find a couple willing to adopt her baby without a release from the biological father, whom Annie is unwilling to name."

"I don't understand why she's protecting him. Unless she doesn't know who the father is."

"Oh, I think she knows. But so far she's been very good at keeping the secret."

"She's lucky to have you looking out for her."

"It's actually nice having her in the house. She's a good buffer between my mother and me." She paused, her gaze thoughtful. "You never talk about your family. Do you get along with your parents?"

"Yes, very well. I'm one of six kids, though, so no one got too much attention."

"It sounds fun and chaotic."

"Add in my mother's Irish temper and my father's Spanish passion, and you get even more drama."

"So where do you get your calm demeanor?"

"I put it on with my suit and tie when I come to work," he said with a small smile.

"Really? So I'm not looking at the real Joe Silveira right now?"

"You're looking at the chief of police."

She nodded, her gaze meeting his, a charge of electricity flowing between them. "It's too bad both of you are married."

She was out the door before he could tell her that he might not be married for very much longer.

# FOUR

Charlotte thought she'd grown out of being impulsive, but telling Joe she wished he wasn't married hadn't been one of her smartest moves. They'd been casually flirting with each other for months, but both had been careful never to step over the line. She'd even kept her distance since Rachel left town. She hadn't wanted to put herself in the middle of their troubled marriage, but deep down she had to admit she missed him, missed that little tingle that ran through her body when he turned those dark, sexy eyes in her direction. He was always unfailingly polite, but once in a while she caught a glimpse of a far more passionate nature.

As she drove away from the police station, she couldn't help wondering what Joe's wife was thinking. Why was Rachel so determined to conduct her marriage long-distance? And why was Joe allowing it to happen? She didn't get it. If they loved each other, why wasn't one of them willing to sacrifice? Not that she wanted Joe to leave, but obviously someone had to budge.

As she turned into the church parking lot, she saw Andrew Schilling on the steps, talking to the gardener who'd worked at the church for as long as she could remember. She shut off the engine and sat for a moment. It still felt odd to see Andrew as the minister, a position her father had held for more than thirty years. In high school Andrew had been a smooth-talking, party-loving jock.

She had no idea what he'd been up to since then—not because he wasn't interested in telling her but because she kept putting him off. She wasn't sure how to handle his renewed interest in her. Their breakup had been messy and ugly and filled with adolescent angst. While they'd both grown up, she was reluctant to rekindle their old flame.

High school had been a painful time for her, a period of rebellion, indecision, restlessness. The role of minister's daughter didn't suit her well, not like her older sister, Doreen, or her younger brother, Jamie. Her mother had been continually disappointed in her behavior, and her father, while much more kind and compassionate, had been frustrated by her inability to accept that certain behaviors were required of a minister's family.

Eventually, she'd left Angel's Bay and gone to college and medical school, along the way coming into her own. She knew who she was now. As for what she wanted . . . well, that was still to be determined. She wasn't very good at long-term relationships. She'd never figured out how to let someone all the way in. It was too damn scary to be that vulnerable; it was much easier to keep things light and fun.

She got out of her car and crossed the lot. Andrew gave her a wave as he finished his conversation. His black slacks and black shirt were set off by his neatly combed blond hair; despite his conservative dress, he was a handsome man. At sixteen, he'd made her heart jump into her throat, and she wasn't immune to his charm now, especially when he flashed her his golden-boy smile. He'd probably gotten the closest to her of anyone—but look where that had ended.

"Thanks for coming," he said as she joined him on the steps. "I'm glad you could get away from work."

"No problem. Is Annie here yet?"

"No, but the Lowells have arrived. I had Jeannie take them into my office." He glanced down at his watch. "I hope Annie didn't forget."

"She mentioned it this morning." Charlotte hoped that Annie hadn't backed out. "But she is nervous. She isn't sure that she wants to give the baby up. I don't want you to push her, Andrew."

"Do you think that's what I'm doing?" he asked in surprise. "I just want her to explore all of her options."

"I know, but you're also very persuasive. Annie wants to do the right thing, and she doesn't want to disappoint you." She remembered a time when she hadn't wanted to disappoint him either, but she shook that errant thought out of her head.

"Adoption is a good solution for her situation, Charlotte. You and your mother have been generous to take Annie in, but do you really want to take on a baby, too? And if you don't, where will Annie go?"

She understood his argument all too well. "It still has to be her decision. Did you explain to the Lowells that Annie is unwilling to name the biological father?"

"Yes. They're hoping that Annie will change her mind, but they've been waiting for a baby for a long time, and they're willing to take the chance."

"It's a risk. If the father suddenly appears and wants the baby . . ."

"I agree. But let's take it one step at a time."

"I wish they were Angel's Bay people, so we'd know more about them," Charlotte said.

"It might be good that they live in Montgomery. It could be difficult for Annie to live in the same town as her child and not be able to mother her. But I also have some Angel's Bay couples who are interested in adopting." He paused, giving her a considering look. "I would think that as an ob/gyn, you'd be cheering on the idea of adoption. You must run into a lot of infertile couples desperate to have a child."

"I do, and I'm in favor of adoption. But Annie has become like a little sister to me, and I know how connected she is to this child. She's always stroking her belly and talking to the baby. She reads parenting books and eats all the right things. This baby gives her a family again, and she really wants that. At the same time, she wants to give her child more than she had. She's torn."

"Sometimes the right thing to do is the most difficult."

"Now you sound like a minister."

He raised an eyebrow. "Is that a bad thing?"

She offered him an apologetic smile. "I didn't mean it that way. Actually, I wanted to tell you that I thought you did a great job at Derek's memorial service yesterday. You really personalized it. I'm sure it meant a lot to the Kanes to have you perform the service."

"I hope so." His gaze turned reflective. "Sometimes I don't know how your father presided over so many funerals for people he knew and cared about. Last week at Mrs. Johnson's service, I could hardly keep it together. She used to make me cookies and drive me to baseball practice, and only a month ago she was attending Sunday service. Her husband couldn't stop crying after she died. He came to me looking for wisdom, hope, peace, and I didn't know what to say. I felt like a fraud."

She saw the uncertainty in his eyes and realized that Andrew was still finding his way. "I'm sure you gave him exactly what he wanted. You have a gift for being able to see what people need. I've watched you the last few months, and people respond to you. You say things in a way that means something to them. That's a gift."

"It means a lot to me to hear you say that." A

smile curved his mouth. "But if I have that gift, why can't I see what *you* need? Why can't I give you what you want, Charlotte?"

She drew in a surprised breath. "Because I—I don't know myself."

"We could be good together. We *were* good together."

She shook her head. "We were terrible together, Andrew. We fought, we lied, we drove each other crazy."

"And I cheated on you," he finished. "But I've grown up since then. Give me another chance."

She let out a sigh. "You do tempt me, but—"

"No buts," he said, cutting her off. "Let's leave it with the fact that I tempt you. That way, I still have a chance. And Annie's here."

Charlotte turned around to see Annie waddling across the lot. In her last month of pregnancy, she was all baby. With her jeans and T-shirt and her long blond hair in a braid down her back, she looked far too young to be having a child.

"I'm sorry I'm late," Annie said breathlessly as she joined them on the steps. "Did they leave?"

Charlotte thought she detected a hopeful note in her tone. "They're inside," she said. "Are you all right?"

"I'm nervous," Annie confessed.

"All you have to do is say hello and get to know them a little," Andrew said.

"They'll think I'm bad for being unmarried and pregnant."

"No one is judging you. Just try to relax and be yourself. There's no pressure. You don't have to make any decisions today."

"Okay," Annie said. "But I need to use the restroom first."

"We'll meet you inside."

"You really are good at getting people to do what you want them to do," Charlotte murmured as Annie entered the church.

"Prove it. Have dinner with me tomorrow night."

"Andrew, you need to stop asking me out," she said in exasperation.

"Not until you say yes. Come on, Charlie, it's just dinner. Are you afraid you'll fall in love with me again over lobster at the Blue Pelican?"

"Yes, lobster always makes me a little giddy," she said lightly.

"Then you can order something else. I just want to talk to you for more than five minutes in passing. What do you say—one dinner for old times' sake?"

"You only want me because I'm saying no. You always liked a challenge."

"Then say yes, and maybe I'll lose interest," he said.

"Fine. One dinner. And I'll meet you there. I don't want my mother to get any ideas about us."

"Your mother likes me."

"Exactly—another strike against you." She marched past him into the church. "Let's go meet the Lowells. I have to get back to work soon."

*   *   *

After her frustrating trip to the police station, Brianna spent several hours unpacking and setting up the house. By three o'clock, she was more than ready for a break, so when Nancy stopped by to ask if she and Lucas would like to take a walk into town, she readily agreed. They dropped the puppy off with Rick and then headed down the hill.

"I thought we'd stop in at the new bakery that just opened," Nancy said. "It's called Sugar and Spice, and it's run by a local girl, Lauren Jamison. Lauren was a year younger than Derek, but she spent time with him and some of his friends. I've heard that the bakery is really good."

"Sounds great. Lucas, wait for us to cross the street," she added as her son skipped ahead to the corner.

Nancy smiled at her. "Lucas has so much energy, just like Derek did. We used to take this same walk when Derek was a little boy. We'd say hello to Rick at the hardware store, then we'd pop in at the quilt shop so I could pick up new threads, and our last stop would always be Martha's Bakery, where we'd get a tart filled with whatever fresh fruit was in season. Those were good days."

Brianna saw the tears gathering in Nancy's eyes and slipped her hand into hers, giving her fingers a reassuring squeeze. "Now you can share the tradition with Lucas."

"I'm so happy you agreed to move here, Brianna. It helps to have you and Lucas nearby. It makes me feel closer to Derek." She cleared her throat. "But we're not going to be sad today. There have been enough tears."

"I agree." Seeing the prison walls every night outside her window had made her feel as trapped as Derek. The view from the hills of Angel's Bay was quite different, and she loved the infinite beauty of the landscape. "It's a gorgeous day." The clouds from yesterday had blown by, and there was nothing but blue skies and bright sunshine.

"I hope the weather holds for the Harvest Festival this weekend. You're going to love all the festivities. And then next week we head right into Halloween. Does Lucas know what he wants to be?"

"He's changed his mind half a dozen times already, and I don't think he's done yet."

"I'm sure the preschool will have a lot of activities. Lucas is set to start next Monday, right?"

"Yes," Brianna replied. "Which means I need to find a job. The local schools don't have any openings for teachers, but they put me on the sub list. The high school principal is fairly confident they can use me in the spring, but in the meantime, I have to find something else."

"There's an opening at the quilt shop." Nancy said. "It's only about fifteen hours a week, but it would be a little cash, and it's a great place to meet people. I can watch Lucas for you."

Brianna gave her mother-in-law a suspicious look. "Don't you work part-time at the quilt store?"

Nancy grinned unrepentantly. "Well, I did, but I'd much rather spend time with Lucas. I talked to

Fiona Murray, the owner, and explained how wonderful it would be if you could take my place for a
while. She was quite agreeable. She'll be there this
afternoon if we want to stop in."

"So this wasn't just a casual walk," Brianna said.

"We don't have to go today; it's up to you. If it's
too soon, Fiona will understand. She comes across as
a tough old broad, but she's a sweetheart inside."

Brianna thought about the offer as they crossed
the street. It *was* soon, but why not start working
right away? She could always use the money, and
perhaps people would be more inclined to talk to her
about Derek and the theft if she wasn't such an out-
sider. "I'd like to do it, if they'll take me on," she said
finally. "I've never worked in retail."

"You'll pick it right up. You already know how to
sew and I've shown you the basics of quilting."

"That's true," Brianna murmured.

You'll meet people, too. Quilting is very popular
around here. Our community quilting nights draw
quite a crowd," Nancy added.

"What's that over there?" Lucas asked, interrupting their conservation. He pointed to the hillside
above the beach, where a dozen kites were flying.

"They're practicing for the kite-flying competition this weekend," Nancy answered. "Your father
won it three years in a row when he was a kid."

"He did?" Lucas asked, clearly impressed. "Can I
do it, Mommy?"

"Sure, I guess so." She knew nothing about flying
a kite, but how hard could it be?

"They have kite-building kits at the quilt shop," Nancy told her. "We can pick one up when we're there."

As they neared the waterfront, the streets grew more crowded. It was long past lunch, but the smells of garlic and fish still lingered in the air. People were lined up at Carl's Crab Shack to buy clam chowder in bread bowls. Coffee was brewing at the Java Hut and warm, salty pretzels were being sold on the corner by a street vendor. It was like a picture postcard: the boats rocking in their slips, people riding their bikes or strolling along the bay. A beautiful, idyllic seaside town.

But as they turned a corner, Brianna's sense of peace fled. Amid the clothing boutiques and cafés was the Markham Gallery, anchoring the far corner with its impressive brick-walled presence. There Derek had gotten his first exposure to the world of art dealing and had made his initial contacts. The gallery was one of the first places he'd taken her to when he'd brought her to Angel's Bay. Everyone had been so happy to see him, greeting him like a long-lost friend. How quickly that had changed after the robbery.

"There's the bakery," Nancy said. "Why don't we get our treat before we go to the quilt shop? I'm a little hungry."

"Can we, Mommy?" Lucas asked eagerly.

Brianna hesitated. "Why don't you two go ahead? I'll window-shop for a few minutes and meet you back here."

Nancy took Lucas's hand and crossed the street. Once they had entered the bakery, Brianna headed toward the gallery, which was housed in a three-story brick building with floor-to-ceiling windows. She stepped inside the airy space, feeling as if she were stepping back in time. A wall of beautiful mirrors greeted her, their cut glass sparkling under the light. Tall white columns divided up the space, and paintings hung prominently on the walls. A black granite counter fronted a small reception area, where a young woman sat behind a computer. She appeared to be in her late twenties, with dark brown hair pulled back in an elegant updo. She spoke on the phone in low tones, lending an air of hushed importance to the room. When she saw Brianna, she ended the call and rose to her feet with a welcoming smile.

"Can I help you?" she asked.

Brianna hesitated, not sure where to start. The Markhams had been interviewed by the private investigator and the police. What on earth could she hope to find out?

"I know you," the woman said suddenly, her gaze narrowing. "You're Derek Kane's wife, aren't you?

"Yes, I am," Brianna replied, surprised. "Have we met?"

"No, but I saw you at the trial. I'm Katherine Markham. My aunt and uncle, Gloria and Steve Markham, own this gallery. I was really sorry to hear about Derek's death. He was a good guy."

There was no judgment on Katherine's face, which was surprising. The local art community had turned on Derek. He'd stolen paintings of great importance to the community, and the breach in security had led to the abrupt end of the art festival, which had never been reinstated. Brianna cleared her throat. "Did you know my husband well?"

"A long time ago. Derek and I both worked here in high school, and we occasionally painted together in Wyatt's studio. Derek was a fantastic artist. I was disappointed when he stopped painting and went into the business end. I thought it was a terrible waste of his talent. Then again, Derek wasn't big on living the life of the starving artist, so I guess it made sense."

Brianna frowned at the mention of Derek's artistic talent, which he'd always been unwilling to share with her. When she'd asked to see some of his work, he'd cut her off, telling her flatly that there was no work to be seen. He'd destroyed it all after his last conversation with his grandfather, who had apparently deemed his art a failure.

"So you know Wyatt, too," Brianna said.

"Oh, sure, everyone in the art community knows Wyatt. He's a crazy-good artist but also demanding, ruthless, and a little cruel. He and Derek had their battles." Katherine paused, giving her a curious look. "So you're living here now?"

"Yes, we just moved in this week. I have a son, Lucas."

"I heard. I can't imagine Derek with a son. He never quite seemed like a grown-up to me, even after he grew up."

That was true. Derek's boyish charm had been one of his most appealing traits. "Were you here during the art festival five years ago? Derek introduced me to a lot of people, but I don't remember meeting you."

"I was out of town on a buying trip. By the time I got back, Derek's trial was already under way. I was stunned when he was found guilty." Katherine paused as the phone rang. "I'd better get that. Feel free to look around."

As Katherine took the phone call, the front door opened, and Wyatt and the Markhams entered the gallery. Brianna's heart skipped a beat, and her throat felt suddenly dry. Derek's grandfather was dressed all in black, which seemed to be his usual attire, the dark clothes contrasting with his wild white hair.

Steve Markham was a sophisticated, well-dressed man in his mid-forties, with short brown hair that matched the color of his eyes. Gloria appeared a few years younger, with black hair and olive skin that gave her an exotic beauty. She wore a sophisticated turquoise sheath dress adorned with colorful beaded jewelry. The three had been engaged in a lively debate, but when they saw Brianna, their conversation ended abruptly.

"Brianna, what are you doing here?" Wyatt asked sharply.

"Just looking around." She turned her attention

to the other couple. "Mr. and Mrs. Markham—I don't know if you remember me."

"Of course we do," Steve said smoothly. "We're sorry for your loss, Mrs. Kane."

There wasn't a hint of honesty in his polite words. Apparently, the Markhams held the same animosity toward Derek that Wyatt did. She doubted they would be interested in helping her prove Derek's innocence.

"Brianna?" Wyatt repeated. "What's going on? I hope you're not still under the delusion that you'll be able to prove someone else stole the paintings."

"Wouldn't it be wonderful if I could? Wouldn't you want me to clear your grandson's name?" she challenged.

"That won't happen. We all know that Derek stole art that was the heart of Angel's Bay, and he did it to get back at me. He deserved what he got."

"He deserved to die?" she asked, anger overtaking her amazement. "How can you not care that your grandson is dead, that he left a child behind? What kind of man are you?"

"Of course I care that Derek is dead." His jaw tightened, his eyes narrowing to hard, black beads of anger. "I gave that boy every opportunity to be the best, to succeed. I opened doors that would have slammed in his face if it weren't for me. He threw it all away. You shouldn't be asking what kind of man *I* am. You should be asking yourself what kind of man would steal something so important to the people who loved him. What kind of man would marry a woman while he was serving a prison term? What kind of man would—"

"Stop!" She put up a hand in protest, his words making her stomach turn over. "I know who Derek was. I was his wife."

"And I was his grandfather. I watched him grow up. I taught him how to paint. I listened to his dreams. You had a six-month fairy-tale romance, followed by a five-year relationship conducted over a prison telephone. You can't *begin* to compete with what I know about Derek and what you don't. And if you keep asking questions, you might be surprised to find that the answers are even worse than you imagine. If you want to save some scrap of Derek's reputation for your son, then leave the past alone."

Wyatt stalked toward the back of the gallery, motioning to the Markhams to follow him.

Brianna let out a breath, shaken by his harsh and cruel words. He seemed so certain of Derek's guilt. Did he know something she didn't?

She saw Katherine's speculative gaze on her and was grateful that the gallery was otherwise empty.

"Wyatt loved Derek," Katherine said quietly.

"Did he?"

"The people you love are the only ones who can hurt you that badly."

Maybe that was true, or maybe Wyatt was just an egotistical ass who couldn't see past his own importance. With a muttered good-bye, Briana left, relieved to be out in the open air.

Perhaps she needed to take a step back and think

about her approach. There was so much anger toward Derek that she doubted anyone in the art community would be willing to help her, especially with Wyatt standing so firmly on the other side. And the police had no interest in reopening an investigation that might only make one or more of their officers look bad. She would have to find another way into the past.

Heading down the street to the bakery, she saw Nancy and Lucas sitting at an outside table. Her son's eyes sparkled with delight when he saw her, and his smile was all she needed to put the world right again. Whatever mistakes she and Derek might have made, Lucas wasn't one of them. And she would do whatever it took to keep that smile on his face.

# FIVE

"We had tarts," Lucas told her with a delighted grin. "My favorite is raspberry. Daddy's was, too."

Brianna suspected Nancy had made the comparison for him. She was a little worried by how often the Kanes compared Lucas to Derek. She wanted Lucas to be loved for himself, not as a replacement for the son they'd lost.

"Would you like one?" Nancy asked, nodding to the pink bakery box on the table. "I got some for us to take home."

"Maybe later." Her stomach was still churning from her recent conversation with Wyatt.

"I guess we're ready to go to the quilt shop, then," Nancy said as she got to her feet. She gave Brianna a curious look as they started walking. "Are you all right? You look a little pale."

"I ran into Wyatt at the Markham Gallery," she said.

Nancy's eyes filled with worry. "Oh, dear. Was he horrible?"

"Yes. I knew he thought Derek was guilty, but I didn't realize how deep his anger went."

"He's been angry his whole life. Rick tried to please his father in so many ways but never could, and Rick's mother fell short, too. Wyatt divorced her when Rick was about ten years old. He's had half a dozen women since then, but no one stuck around very long."

"So Derek was just the last in a string of family disappointments in Wyatt's mind?" Brianna kept an eye on Lucas, who was walking a few steps ahead, delightedly jumping over the sidewalk cracks.

"Once Wyatt makes up his mind, it's impossible to change it." Nancy paused, her gaze still concerned. "Brianna, why did you go to the gallery? The Markhams were never on Derek's side. If you think they'll help us clear Derek's name, you're mistaken."

"I know. It was just an impulsive decision. I keep thinking those paintings have to be somewhere, and if I can find them, the truth will follow."

"A lot of people have tried. Sometimes I think those paintings are cursed. They were lost for more than a hundred years; maybe they were never supposed to be found." Nancy stopped in front of the door to the quilt shop. "How about we change the subject?"

"I think that's an excellent idea."

"Good, because as much as I want to clear

Derek's name, I'm most interested now in making sure you and Lucas are happy here. I want you to settle in, make friends, have a life."

"I want that, too," Brianna said.

"Then let me show you one of my favorite places in town and maybe we'll get you a job at the same time."

Nancy's optimism lifted her spirits. "Lead on," she said.

As they stepped into the store, Brianna felt a rush of warm energy. The store was alive with colors and conversation, a delightful buzz of activity. Women were chatting by the cash register, another group was working at sewing machines in the back of the store, and others were picking out materials and threads. Upstairs, an appliqué class was in progress. The sense of creative anticipation in the building was intoxicating. No wonder the store was one of Nancy's favorite places. Brianna felt immediately comfortable, welcomed by the cheerful smiles that greeted them at every turn.

"There's Fiona," Nancy said, leading her toward the cash register, where an older woman with bright red hair and fiery blue eyes was completing a transaction. "Don't let her scare you. She's more bark than bite. She's eighty-two years old but you won't meet anyone with more energy."

Brianna drew in a deep breath. She didn't know why she suddenly felt nervous. But as Fiona's sharp eyes landed on her, she felt as if she were being stripped bare. It had been a long while since anyone had looked so closely at her.

"This is Brianna and my grandson, Lucas," Nancy said, introducing them.

Fiona nodded. "I'm sorry I missed the funeral. My deepest condolences."

"Thank you," Brianna said.

"So you need a job, do you?" Fiona asked. "Nancy says you're a teacher. Why do you want to work here?"

"I've been teaching French at a middle school the last couple of years. I'm hoping to get a teaching job here in town, but there aren't any openings at the moment. So I'm looking for something part-time."

"Then I guess you're hired."

"Just like that?" Brianna asked in surprise.

"Yes," Fiona said, her gaze contemplative. "I think you might need this shop as much as we need you."

Brianna had no idea what that meant, but she didn't have a chance to ask.

"You can take over Nancy's shift starting tomorrow," Fiona continued. "I assume babysitting won't be a problem."

"I'm always available," Nancy cut in quickly.

"I guess I'm covered," Brianna said. "I appreciate the opportunity. I won't let you down."

"I know you won't," Fiona said with a confident smile. "Now, Nancy, why don't you bring this cute boy of yours upstairs. I know some ladies who are just dying to meet him."

"Do you mind?" Nancy asked Brianna, an eager light in her eyes.

"Go right ahead. I'll look around."

Lucas was happy to accompany his grandmother. A curious child, he was always eager to see what was upstairs or around the corner or in the next room.

Brianna wandered the aisles, making mental notes of where things were. Judging by how quickly the interview had gone, training would be done on the fly as well. She was grateful to Nancy for the job and the babysitting. Her mother-in-law was doing everything she could to make the transition go smoothly. She and Rick wanted her to love Angel's Bay, and there was a lot to like.

She'd always wanted to live in a small town, something she'd never dared tell her academic, globe-trotting parents. While she'd been exposed to incredible opportunities, she'd missed having roots, having friendships that went from kindergarten to college.

She'd missed having parents, too. They'd hired a series of nannies and tutors to make sure her basic needs were met, but there hadn't been much love or even attention. That had changed when she'd met Derek. They'd adored him and thought he was the perfect man for her—until he'd been arrested. Then they told her that if she went ahead and married him, she'd lose them forever. But when had she really had them? At any rate, that was all in the past. Today was about starting fresh.

"Brianna?"

She looked up to see a woman with dark red hair, brown eyes, and a smattering of freckles across her nose, who bore a distinct resemblance to Fiona. She also looked quite familiar.

"I'm Kara Lynch. I don't know if you remember me."

"Yes," Brianna said slowly. "Derek introduced us at Murray's Bar. You and your husband, Colin, went to school with him."

"We were all good friends back in the day. Fiona is my grandmother. She told me that she just hired you. I occasionally work here as well, so I'm sure we'll be seeing a lot of each other." Kara's eyes sparkled with friendliness. "I met your little boy upstairs. He's the spitting image of his father at that age."

"So everyone says. Do you have children?"

"A little girl, five weeks old."

"You're kidding! You look great."

"Thanks. I'm tired, but it's a happy exhaustion. So, are you a quilter?"

"I know the basics. Nancy showed me the Kane square that goes in the Angel's Bay quilt." She glanced toward the quilt, enclosed in a glass case on a nearby wall. "That's the original over there, isn't it?"

"That's right. The squares honor the shipwreck survivors who founded the town. The Kane square was sewn by Francine Kane, who lost her husband, Marcus, but she remained in Angel's Bay with her two children, and her in-laws."

Brianna felt a little shiver run down her spine at how the story echoed her own life. She wondered how Francine had felt, living in a family that wasn't truly her own.

"Francine used material from the dress she'd been wearing when the ship went down," Kara continued. "And the quilting design details the overland journey they took from Missouri to San Francisco for the Gold Rush and then their final treacherous sail down the coast as they attempted to go home." She looked back at Brianna. "I'm sure Nancy will want you to continue the quilting tradition so that you can pass it on to your son's future wife."

"That's a long way off," Brianna said. "He's only four and a half."

Kara smiled. "True, but the women around here can be relentless about passing on our quilting traditions, especially to descendants of the original twenty-four. Well, I'd better go find my baby. My mother took her upstairs, and I haven't seen her since."

"So they're not really learning appliqué techniques up there; they're just admiring our children," Brianna said.

Kara laughed. "A lot that goes on in this shop has nothing to do with quilting. It's basically a female hangout, although occasionally someone's husband is sent in to pick up some fabric. They usually leave as quickly as possible, especially when the conversation turns to childbirth or PMS."

Brianna smiled. "I can imagine."

Kara hesitated, something obviously on her mind. "Brianna, I'd like to be friends, but in the interest of full disclosure, I have to tell you that Jason is one of my closest friends. In fact, he just helped me get through a really rough time in my life. He's a good guy, but I know that he and Derek ended up on opposite sides."

"No question about that," Brianna replied. "I know that most people believe Derek was guilty. I hope to prove that he wasn't."

"I can respect that. I just spent three months fighting for my husband to wake up from a coma. If you love someone, you have to go to bat for them. I just hope we can still be friends."

Brianna liked Kara's directness. This was a woman who didn't play games, who stood up for the people she cared about. Too bad Jason was one of them.

Jason walked into Murray's Bar on Tuesday afternoon. He'd had a busy shift, with no time for lunch, and he wanted to grab a burger and a beer before he checked in on Patty's pets. The bar was usually empty in between lunch and happy hour, so he was surprised to find Colin sitting on a stool, nursing a beer, and watching a basketball game. He hadn't seen Colin out on his own since his miracle recovery.

Colin gave him a scowl as he sat down. "I thought you were working."

"Just got off. What's up with you?"

"I'm having a drink," Colin said, in a terse tone that didn't bode well for a cheerful conversation.

"Okay." Jason called to Michael Murray, the bartender. "Can you get me one of Casey's burgers with that beer you're pouring?"

Michael slid the mug in front of him and said, "Double meat, no cheese, extra sauce?"

"Yep." He glanced at Colin. "You hungry?"

"Kara would kill me if I came home full before dinner."

"How's she going to feel if you come home drunk?" He'd shared enough liquor with Colin to know when his friend had a buzz on.

"Why don't you sit somewhere else?" Colin suggested.

"And miss all the fun here? Who are you pissed off at, besides me?"

"No one. I'm great. I'm alive. What more could a man ask for?"

Jason took a sip of beer and let the question slide.

"Kara went to the doctor today," Colin said a moment later. "Charlotte said she's good to go—in the bedroom."

"Oh." Jason cleared his throat. "Well, that's great news, right?"

Colin drained his beer and beckoned to Michael for another one.

"Maybe you should slow down, or *you* might not be good to go," Jason warned.

Colin shot him a dark look that told him far more than he wanted to know.

"Oh. Have you talked to your doctor?"

"I shouldn't have any problems, according to him, but I'm not feeling it." Colin let out a breath. "I've always felt it with her, since I was thirteen years old. Every damn second, I wanted to be with her. I love her. I'm crazy about her. She's the only one for me. I should have thrown her down right there on the couch, the way I used to. Instead I told her that I had to check in with my physical therapist, and I came here."

"It's going to be fine."

"You don't know that."

"I do actually," Jason replied confidently. "And so do you. You just panicked, the way you did the first time you kissed her. Remember how you flipped out? You were sure she didn't like it. You avoided her for days. I told you *I* was going to kiss her if you didn't try it again."

"Don't even think of suggesting that now," Colin said, a touch of humor back in his voice.

"Then give me that beer." Jason grabbed the glass that Michael had just set down in front of Colin. "Go home to your wife. And stop pushing so hard to get everything back the way it was."

Colin sighed. "I want to feel normal again."

"Just feel what you're feeling now, and tell Kara. You know how women are—once you share your feelings, they get all hot for you."

A reluctant smile curved his lips. "It's that easy, huh?"

Jason shrugged. "Where you and Kara are concerned, I don't think it's going to take much to light the fire. But even if it does, what's the rush? You're recovering from a head injury. Kara just had a baby.

There's a lot of stress in your life. It sucks, but you'll get over it. Go home."

Colin took his beer back. "Kara is at the quilt store. Tell me what's up with you. Any more contact with Brianna Kane?"

"Actually—"

"Oh, man, I knew it. You can't stay away from her."

"It's not like that. I agreed to house-sit for my father's girlfriend, and she lives next door to Brianna."

"No shit? So you saw her again?"

"Last night. Her dog got out." He took another swig of beer, thinking of how coldly she'd dismissed him. For a moment, he'd thought she was softening her stance against him. She'd actually let him hold her—until she'd remembered he was the enemy. He felt Colin's gaze on him. "What?"

"I know this face," Colin said, a troubled look in his eyes. "Are you out of your mind?"

"I don't know what you're talking about."

"You like Brianna."

"I wouldn't go that far."

"Good, because that would be a suicidal idea."

"I know that. She holds me personally responsible for Derek's death. She told me that flat-out."

"Then leave her alone."

That was exactly what he should do, but he couldn't let it go. "I need to make her see that Derek was guilty. I need to find those paintings and connect the dots back to him. That's the only way Brianna will believe that I didn't send an innocent man to jail."

"And where does that get you?" Colin challenged. "Jason, she hates you. I know you like a challenge, but dude, find another woman."

"I didn't say I was going after her. But what the hell kind of marriage could she have had, with her husband in prison?"

"Whatever she had, you have to respect it."

Jason shook his head. "I don't know why she tied herself to Derek. It had to be because of her son. It was loyalty more than love."

"You don't know that. And staying together for the sake of a child isn't a bad reason." Colin frowned. "How long have you been thinking about her? Because it sounds like a lot longer than the few days she's been back in town."

"I've thought about her and Derek over the years," he admitted. "How could I not? Derek and I were friends. It killed me to arrest him."

"I know how wrecked you were, but you always believed you were right. I thought that would help you get through it."

"I still believe I was right. And I have to make Brianna see the truth."

"Why? So you can have her?"

Jason ducked Colin's inquisitive gaze. "I didn't say that."

"But you're thinking that. Here's the way I see it: if you can prove to Brianna that Derek was guilty, you'll destroy her life all over again. You'll be right, but you'll never get her, because you'll always be the guy who ruined everything. It might be illogical, but that's how she'll think of you." Colin let that sink in before continuing. "And if the unthinkable happens, and she proves that Derek was innocent and you sent him to jail, then *she'll* be right, and you'll still be the man who destroyed her life. There's no way to win, Jason. Cut your losses and move on."

"I can't stand that she thinks I screwed Derek over," Jason muttered, unwilling to believe there wasn't a way he could win.

"It sucks. Get over it. Isn't that what you just told me?"

"You didn't make it right. It's not working," Lucas complained as he ran across the backyard, trying to launch his new kite into the air.

Brianna frowned. What the heck was wrong with the thing? She'd followed the directions, but the kite didn't look anything like the picture. It sagged in the middle, looking limp and pathetic. Still, she was pretty sure their main problem was a lack of wind and space to run. "We'll take it down to the beach tomorrow and test it out there."

"But I want to fly it *now*," Lucas protested.

She knew he was frustrated and tired; he'd been going nonstop all day. She needed to be patient.

"We don't have enough room here to run, and it's too dark to go out front. Tomorrow we'll find a big, wide-open space, and the kite will take off—you'll see." The phone rang inside the house. "Why don't you bring the kite in and we'll make some dinner?"

She jogged through the back door, grabbing her cell phone off the counter. "Hello?"

"Mrs. Kane? This is Will Isaacs."

She was surprised to hear the voice of one of Derek's former attorneys. Mr. Isaacs had left the case last year after being diagnosed with cancer. "What can I do for you?"

"First of all, I'm sorry for your loss. It was tragic, what happened to Derek."

"Thank you."

"I'm sorry I wasn't able to come to the funeral."

"I know you've been ill. I hope you're feeling better."

"I just got back from Germany yesterday. I underwent some experimental treatment, and so far, so good, but that's not why I'm calling. Last year Derek gave me an envelope and instructed me to give it to you in the event that anything happened to him before his release. I apologize for neglecting to make sure that happened immediately after his passing."

"You have a letter for me from Derek?" she echoed in shock.

"Yes. I don't want to entrust it to the mail, and it's been delayed too long already. I'd like to drive it down there tomorrow, if that would be convenient."

"Do you know what it says?"

"It was sealed when Derek gave it to me."

She leaned against the counter, her heart racing, her palms sweaty. "I don't understand why he'd leave me a letter. If he had something to say, why wouldn't he have just said it? He couldn't have been anticipating his death. It was an accident. It was unexpected."

"I'm sorry that you have to wait until tomorrow to find out. But I can be there around five o'clock."

"That's fine." She licked her lips. "Mr. Isaacs, you worked with Derek for a long time, and you reviewed all the private investigation notes, correct?"

"Up until about six months ago, yes," he agreed.

She hesitated. "Do you believe that Derek was innocent?"

She heard him take a quick breath. "Well, that's not the question I was expecting."

"Do you?"

His answer was slow to come. Finally, he said, "I don't honestly know. Derek insisted that he didn't take the paintings, but I always felt he was holding out on us in some way. The investigators we hired concurred. I told Derek that he if wanted us to help him, he had to help us. He said he'd done all he could do."

"Perhaps he just had no idea who stole the paintings, and it wasn't about being uncooperative."

"Possibly. At some point, Derek became resigned to serving out his sentence and moving on. If you want to talk more, we can do so tomorrow."

"Of course. Thank you." She hung up, still shocked about the letter. It didn't make sense.

She suddenly became aware of the silence in the

house and in the yard. It was quiet—too quiet. And where a four-year-old was concerned, that was a sure sign of trouble. "Lucas!" she called, turning toward the back door.

There was no reply, no happy bark.

Nothing.

# SIX

Jason was about to turn onto Drake's Way when he saw a small figure chasing a black dog and dragging what looked like a kite behind him. It was Lucas Kane, with no Brianna in sight.

He pulled his car over to the curb and got out as Lucas went flying by. His little four-year-old legs were no match for the puppy, who appeared to have a cat in his sights.

Jason ran after them, catching up with Lucas. "Stay here," he told him. "I'll get your dog." He kept running, but he could hear Lucas's little feet pounding after him. Where the hell was Brianna? She didn't strike him as a mother who would let her small child play outside on his own, especially with night coming.

The dog dashed to the bottom of the tree and began to bark as his prey escaped to a higher branch. Jason swooped down and wrestled the puppy into his arms as Lucas came to a breathless halt beside him. The little boy's eyes sparkled with excitement.

"You caught him!" Lucas said, amazement in his voice. "You run really fast."

"Thanks. Where's your mom?"

Lucas shot a quick look over his shoulder, his expression going from happy to worried. "I better go home."

"That sounds like a good idea. I'll go with you. What are you doing out here by yourself?"

"Trying to fly my kite, but it wouldn't work." His little mouth turned down in a pout. "It's broken." He gave the kite a disgusted kick.

Jason took a quick look at the kite, which didn't appear to be put together correctly. "I think we can fix it."

"Really?" Lucas asked hopefully. "I want to fly it in the contest. My daddy won three times. I'm going to win, too."

"I bet you will." Lucas sounded so much like Derek, not just in his voice but also in his determination to succeed.

Lucas let the kite trail along the sidewalk as they headed around the corner. "I wish my daddy was here," he said a moment later, heaving a big sigh. "He could show me how to make the kite fly. But he's in heaven. He's an angel now."

Jason nodded, feeling a wave of sadness for Lucas. He knew what it felt like to lose a parent when you were just a little kid. He'd also never been reassured by the idea that his mother was in heaven. All it had meant to him was that she was somewhere far away. She might be watching over him, but he couldn't feel her presence.

His father, on the other hand, seemed to have had more than one encounter with the angel form of his wife. Jason had dismissed most of those events as a result of his father's alcohol intake or his desperate need to hang on to the woman he'd loved.

"Do angels make the wind?" Lucas asked. "Grandma Nancy said that the winds come from heaven. Maybe Daddy will make the wind blow really hard so my kite will fly."

"That sounds right."

"Do you know how to fly a kite?" Lucas asked curiously.

"I do."

"Could you show me?"

"I could." He doubted Brianna would appreciate his answer, but he wasn't going to lie to Lucas.

"Did your daddy teach you how to fly a kite?"

"He did," Jason said.

"Did he live with you all the time?"

"Yes." An uneasy feeling ran through him as he sensed where Lucas was headed with his questions.

"My daddy never lived with Mommy and me," Lucas announced. "He did something wrong, and they wouldn't let him come home, even if he said he was sorry." He paused, tilting his head to the side to give Jason another speculative look. "Did you ever do anything wrong?"

Before he could reply, Brianna came flying down the sidewalk, shouting Lucas's name.

"Uh-oh," Lucas said worriedly. "I'm not supposed to talk to strangers." He took off, running toward his mother.

"What are you doing out here?" Brianna demanded.

Jason could see her arms shake as she grabbed Lucas and squeezed him tight.

"You *know* you're not supposed to leave the backyard." Brianna held Lucas away from her so she could make sure he wasn't hurt, but she still had a tight grip on his arms. "How did you open the gate?"

"I climbed on the bricks and reached over the top," Lucas said, proud of his accomplishment.

"Why did you do that?"

"There are too many trees in the back. I wanted to see if the kite would fly in the front," he replied. "I wasn't going to leave the yard, but Digger saw a cat and started running, and I had to go get him so he wouldn't get lost."

"*You* could have gotten lost," Brianna said. "You are never, *ever* to leave the backyard again without me. Do you understand?"

"I'm sorry, Mommy. Will they send me away for being bad like they did to Daddy?"

"Oh, God, of course not." She hugged him again.

Jason's heart broke a little at Lucas's question and Brianna's desperate assurance. The kid was barely four and already messed up by his father's crimes. No wonder she was so determined to clear Derek's name.

"You and I will be together always," Brianna said,

looking Lucas straight in the eye. "But you have to listen to what I say. I'm trying to protect you and keep you safe. That's why we have rules. Okay?"

Lucas nodded. "Okay."

Brianna slowly stood up, turning her gaze on Jason. "Where did you find them?"

"Around the corner."

"I can't believe he went that far on his own. I just went inside the house for a few seconds to take a phone call. I never imagined that Lucas would leave the yard. He's never done that before." She cleared her throat. "I can take the dog."

"I've got him." Selfishly, foolishly, he wanted to spend a little more time with her, and as long as he had the dog, he had a hostage.

"He said he knows how to fly a kite," Lucas said, pointing his finger at Jason. "He said he could help us fix it, Mommy."

"We don't need his help," Brianna said quickly.

"But you don't know how to do it," Lucas complained. "And I want to win the contest."

"I think I can figure it out, and it's not about winning. Flying a kite is about having fun."

"Daddy would want to win," Lucas proclaimed.

Jason wondered how much time Lucas had spent with his father. How well could he have gotten to know Derek during short prison visits?

"Your father would want you to enjoy the experience," Brianna corrected as she led the way into her backyard. "We don't need your help," she told Jason.

"You might. I don't think you put the kite together right." Once Brianna had shut the gate, he let Digger down. The dog celebrated his freedom with a sprint around the yard.

Lucas held up the kite for Brianna's inspection. "It's all messed up, Mommy."

"Why don't I take a look at it?" Jason suggested. "It's a little dark out here, though. Can I come inside?"

"No," she said flatly.

"Mommy," Lucas wailed in protest. "I want him to fix my kite."

"Lucas, please go in the house."

"No," he said, stomping his foot. Then he burst into tears.

Brianna swung him up in her arms and carried him into the house, and he screamed even louder.

Jason picked up the dropped kite and followed them inside. He could hear Brianna talking to Lucas in his bedroom while the boy continued to cry, and he felt a little guilty. He could have refused to help and drawn Lucas's anger, instead of pitting Lucas against his mother. But he was tired of being the bad guy where the Kanes were concerned. Besides, it wouldn't take much to fix the kite, so wouldn't that be best for everyone?

He set the kite on the kitchen table and took a look at its construction. He doubted it would win any contests, even at the preschool level. The contestants took their kites seriously—or at least their parents did—and to compete, Lucas would need a kite with a much more aerodynamic design.

While he waited for Brianna to return, Jason

glanced around the kitchen. Fresh flowers sat on the kitchen table, and colorful vases and bowls adorned the open kitchen shelves. The front of the refrigerator was covered with photographs of Lucas and childish hand-drawn pictures. He liked the vibe of the room, pretty and warm.

"You're still here. Why am I not surprised?" Brianna said when she returned to the room. "Every time I turn around, there you are."

"Well, I suppose I could have kept on going and let Lucas find his own way home."

She frowned. "I already said thank you."

"Actually, you didn't," he pointed out. He could see the battle going on in her eyes. She didn't want to be grateful to him for anything, but her innate politeness eventually won out.

"Thank you," she said tightly.

"You're welcome. How's Lucas?"

"He fell asleep mid-cry. He was exhausted. I shouldn't have started this kite project today, but he was so eager." She ran a hand through her hair, her blue eyes weary.

It couldn't be easy starting over in a new place, especially a place that held some bad memories. Not that she'd want his sympathy.

"Just when I think I know what Lucas is capable of, he surprises me." She gave a bewildered shake of her head. "I never imagined he'd be able to open the gate and leave the yard." Her gaze moved toward the kite. "It does look pathetic. I don't get it. I followed the directions."

"I can help you fix it, but if you want to have a fast, high-flying kite, this one won't cut it."

She frowned at him. "Lucas is four and a half years old and less than three feet tall; I don't think the kite has to fly that high."

"I'm just saying that this isn't a competitive kite. It doesn't have the right aerodynamic shape to really take off. If you want to stick with it, at least let me make a few adjustments."

"Why do you care whether or not this kite will fly?" she challenged, suspicion in her eyes. "What's in it for you?"

"Nothing is in it for me. But your kid seemed excited about the idea of a high-flying kite. And I've been there—it's an amazing feeling to watch your kite take off into the sky."

"It's really that big of a deal?"

"I guess your parents never took you kite flying."

"It never would have crossed their minds." She moved past him and grabbed a glass out of the cupboard, taking a moment to fill it with ice and water. "Do you want some?"

"Thanks."

She handed him the glass, then filled another for herself.

"So what are your parents like?" He knew she came from money and that her parents sported some impressive educational credentials, but beyond that he had no idea.

"They are academic, studious, globally adventur-

ous, community-oriented, and ecologically responsible," she said.

He put up a hand. "Whoa. I've never heard
anyone describe their parents that way before. You
sound like a magazine article. Do you want to give it
another shot—in English this time?"

"My parents are professors. They've taught at
several Ivy League schools. My mother specializes
in immunological medicine, and my father has a
doctorate in world history. They spend every holiday, summer vacation, and sabbatical traveling the
world. They always have a purpose, like working in
an AIDS clinic in a remote African village, or taking medical supplies down the Amazon, or bringing
music to some ancient Indian tribe in South America. They're incredible people, and the words I used
to describe them are the way they were written about
in an issue of *Time* magazine several years ago."

"Very impressive."

"Very," she agreed, but there was a cool note in
her voice.

"So where are they? They weren't at Derek's trial.
They weren't at the funeral. They don't seem to have
a presence in your life."

She pulled out a chair and sat down. "I don't
know where they are. They didn't like my decision
to stand by Derek. They thought I was a fool." Her
gaze met his. "I'm sure you agree with that."

He wasn't about to touch that comment. "But
you have a child, their grandson. Don't they want to
see Lucas?"

"Not so far," she replied, taking a sip of water.

He took a seat across from her. "I no longer find them impressive."

"Few people would agree with you."

"It must have been rough, not having their support these past few years."

"I've never had their support. They weren't interested in being parents; I was an accident. My parents always felt that they were destined to do more important things with their lives than raising a child, so they left that to nannies and tutors. They prefer to spend their time solving big problems like world peace and poverty."

"How are they doing on that?" he asked dryly.

A hint of a smile played around her lips. "Not even making a dent."

"It doesn't sound like you had much of a childhood." No wonder Brianna had been drawn to the Kanes, who had showered her with love from the moment they met her.

"It wasn't bad. I lived all over the world, had plenty of money, clothes, and educational opportunities. It was hard to keep changing schools, tough to hang on to friends, but I always had my books. I was a huge reader. And my favorite place in the world was the library—the smell of all those books, the promise of all those adventures. I couldn't get enough. I still—" She stopped abruptly.

"Still what?" he asked, curious.

"Nothing. Anyway, I'm going to give Lucas a different kind of life and all the time with me he wants.

I want to be there for him—especially now that it's just me."

"Hasn't it always been just you?"

Her lips tightened. "Yes, it has. Thanks for the reminder."

"Why did you marry Derek, Brianna? Was it because you were pregnant?"

She stared at him for a long moment, a glint of steel in her eyes. "I married Derek because I loved him. That's not what you want to hear, is it?"

"If that's the truth, then that's the truth." But he didn't quite buy it.

A moment of tense silence passed between them. "I did love him," she reiterated, "but I was also young, pregnant, and scared."

"You had other options."

"Did I?" She shrugged. "To be honest, those days are all a blur now. Everything happened so fast. One minute I was planning a wedding, and the next I was talking to cops and lawyers, listening to accusations of robbery and assault." She shook her head. "For the longest time, I thought I was having a nightmare. I believed I'd wake up and it would be over."

"Derek was lucky to have you stand by him."

"He told me that he was innocent, that he'd win his appeal, he'd get out, and we'd go on with our lives. But—" Her gaze narrowed. "Why am I talking to you?"

"Because I'm a good listener?" he suggested lightly.

She shrugged. "Or maybe I've just been a little short on adult conversation."

"Do you remember the first time we met?" Jason asked.

"At Murray's Bar. I actually thought we were going to be friends."

"Really? I thought we were going to be more," he said.

She stared at him in surprise. "Why?"

"Because in the hour we spent talking and laughing, you never once said you were engaged. I didn't find that out until Derek came in and kissed you and invited me to the wedding." He took a breath, knowing he was heading into dangerous territory, but he couldn't stop himself. "I think for a few minutes you forgot you were with him."

"Don't be ridiculous," she said, but there wasn't much force behind her words.

He pressed on. "For a few minutes there, you wished you were still single."

"Why? So I could have you?" Anger flashed in her eyes. "Your ego is unbelievable. Just because I didn't announce my engagement to you doesn't mean I was interested in you. We had a casual conversation in a bar. That's it."

He held up his hands. "Okay, my mistake." If he pushed any further, he'd be out on his ass, and now that he had her talking, he didn't want to stop.

"You really thought I was into you?" she asked.

"Maybe I just wanted you to be."

"Is *that* why you went after Derek? Was it about me?" She jumped to her feet and ran a hand through her hair. "My God—I never even considered that possibility."

He stood up. "No, I went after him because I ran into him on the museum grounds right after the guard was attacked and because Derek was acting nervous and changing his story every other second. I didn't have a personal agenda. I didn't want him to be guilty. He was my friend."

"He was your rival. Derek told me the two of you competed for everything. In fact, that's probably why you wanted me. I was just another trophy to play for, wasn't I?"

"I didn't know you belonged to Derek when we first met," he pointed out. "And when I found out, I backed off. I don't take women away from other men."

"You need to leave."

He'd known that statement was coming ever since he'd stepped through the door. "Look, we got off track."

"We've never been on track."

"Let me fix the kite for Lucas. It's not a big deal, and I'd really like to do it for him."

"Why?"

"I lost a parent when I just a little older than Lucas. I feel sorry for the kid."

She gazed at him in confusion. "I don't know what you want from me, Jason."

He wasn't entirely sure, either; he just knew he

didn't want her to spend the rest of her life thinking he was the enemy. "Right now I just want to fix the kite."

"Derek wouldn't want you to help Lucas. He wouldn't want you to be here in this kitchen with me."

"Derek's not here. So why don't you tell me what *you* want, Brianna?"

She hesitated one last second, but in the end, her love for Lucas was stronger than her hate for him.

"Fine," she said. "But only because Lucas has had more disappointments than any little boy should have."

"I agree."

"But you're not fixing it here," she said firmly. "You can take it with you and bring it back when you're done."

"I thought Lucas might want to help me."

"Don't push it, Jason. And after all your bragging, that kite better be good."

"It will be." He grabbed the kite and headed toward the back door.

"And just to be clear," she added, "this does not in any way mean that I like you."

He gave her a smile. "Maybe not yet."

When the doorbell rang twenty minutes later, Brianna tensed. She wasn't up to another round with Jason tonight. His earlier comments had shaken her up. She hadn't thought about that night in the bar in years;

she'd pushed that sexy, flirtatious guy to the back of her mind. It hadn't been difficult. After Derek's arrest, Jason had turned into a cold, ruthless cop.

When she opened the door, it wasn't Jason on her porch but Katherine Markham, dressed now in jeans and a jacket.

"Hello," Katherine said with a smile. "I stopped by the Kanes' house, and they gave me your address. I hope you don't mind, but I felt really bad after you left the gallery earlier, and I wanted to talk to you for a minute."

"Come in," Brianna said, waving her inside, more than a little curious to hear what she had to say.

"Who's here, Mommy?" Lucas walked into the room, wiping the sleep out of his eyes, his cheeks a rosy pink.

"This is Katherine," Brianna said, putting her hand on Lucas's shoulder. "She was a friend of your dad. This is Lucas."

"Hi there," Katherine said tentatively. She glanced back at Brianna. "He's a mini-Derek. I had no idea."

"Can I have a snack?" Lucas asked.

"Yes, you can have a banana. We're going to eat dinner soon." She turned to Katherine as Lucas ran into the kitchen. "Can I get you a drink?"

"No, please don't bother."

Brianna gestured toward the couch. "Have a seat."

"Thanks. I just couldn't get your face out of my mind. Wyatt was hard on you."

"Harder on Derek," she said, sitting down in the chair across from Katherine. "I can't understand why he would choose to believe the worst about his grandson."

"Wyatt thought that Derek threw away everything he gave him. He felt betrayed. I'm not saying he was right—just that that's how he saw it." Katherine's gaze moved across the room, to where a large, ornate mirror was propped against the wall. "That was Derek's," she murmured, an odd note in her voice. "He bought it at an estate sale even though there was a crack in the glass. He never fixed it, I guess."

"I guess not," Brianna replied. "I just started unpacking the boxes that came from Derek's townhouse. Nancy had put all of his things in storage when he went to jail, because I was moving into a tiny apartment and barely had space for my own things. I'm not even sure what all he had." She paused for a moment, noting the pallor in Katherine's face. "Is something wrong?"

Katherine started. "No. I'm sorry. It just hit me again that Derek is really gone."

Brianna nodded. "I completely understand. I think I have it all together, and then something triggers a memory, and the pain sends me reeling."

"So I wanted to come by and let you know that if I can help you find out what happened to the paintings, I'd be more than happy to do so. I didn't have a chance to help Derek before. I'd love to do that now. To that end, I spoke to my aunt after you left. I asked her if she'd heard any rumblings about those paintings. I thought Derek's death might have caused someone to break their silence."

Brianna had wondered the same thing. "What did Gloria say?"

Katherine frowned. "Unfortunately, nothing helpful. Both she and my uncle believe that Derek had a private buyer lined up, who either received the paintings and has them hidden away in a vault or was waiting for Derek's release in order to complete the transaction."

"That's one thing I don't understand," Brianna said. "Why would someone go to the trouble of stealing paintings that they couldn't display?"

"It happens all the time. Collectors can be very eccentric. Some have private rooms filled with art of questionable provenance. And highly publicized stolen art can stay hidden for decades."

Brianna leaned back in her chair, her momentary optimism vanishing. "So I should give up?"

"I didn't say that. I just want you to be realistic. It may take some time. And you won't get a lot of help around here."

"Aren't you concerned about helping me?" Brianna asked curiously. "I'm sure the Markhams wouldn't want you to get involved in this."

"They don't own me," Katherine said lightly. "And while everyone seems to think of Derek only as a thief and a criminal, I remember a different guy. Derek was charming and funny, and he was a really talented artist. He always found the most interesting and unique perspective from which to paint. I was in awe of his talent. But I'm sure you know how good he was."

Brianna didn't comment. She'd never known Derek as an artist, only as a savvy businessman with a passion for art. When he'd left Angel's Bay to go to Los Angeles, he'd left that part of his life behind.

"Does your son like to paint?" Katherine asked.

"He scribbles a little. I haven't seen any sign of genius, but he's only four."

"I have a sketch pad with some of Derek's earliest work on it. I found it the other day when I was cleaning up. Maybe I'll bring it by, and you can give it to Lucas."

"That would be great. Not even the Kanes have much of his work. I guess he did most of his painting at Wyatt's studio, and apparently, Wyatt destroyed whatever Derek left behind."

Katherine nodded. "Wyatt was angry with Derek long before *The Three Faces of Eve* went missing. But losing those paintings made him crazy. Wyatt was obsessed with Victor Delgado's work. He spent most of his adult life looking for Eve." She paused. "I never understood why Wyatt agreed to donate the paintings to the museum. My aunt and uncle must have talked him into it. The three of them discovered the paintings when they were together in Mexico. They purchased them as a group."

Brianna stared at Katherine, reading between the lines. "Are you suggesting that Wyatt might have wanted the paintings for himself but somehow got talked into giving them up? He doesn't seem like a pushover."

Katherine shrugged. "I don't know. I could be completely off base, but I have wondered if Wyatt's hostility is a cover for some other emotion—like guilt."

"Well, that's something I've never considered," Brianna said in bemusement.

"I would be surprised if Derek didn't consider it," Katherine said, giving Brianna a curious look. "Didn't you two talk about who might have taken the paintings, since Derek didn't do it? He had to have had some idea."

"He never mentioned his grandfather as a likely candidate," Brianna replied. "To be honest, our visiting time was so short that Derek didn't want to waste it talking about art. He saved those conversations for his attorney and the private investigator we hired. Now I wish I'd pressed him more. I keep wracking my brain trying to remember something he said that might have been a clue, but so far I've just gotten a headache."

"Maybe you should just let the past go. Those paintings can't free Derek now."

"No, but if they can clear his name, I have to try to find them. I have a son to consider."

Katherine stood up. "I understand. Be careful if you speak to Wyatt. Where art is concerned, he has no boundaries and no patience for people who get in his way."

Which made Wyatt sound more and more

like the real thief, Brianna thought, as she ushered Katherine out of the house. She couldn't remember anyone ever mentioning Wyatt's name in conjunction with the theft, but then, why would they? He'd been the one to donate the paintings to the museum. Maybe Katherine was right—maybe he'd been forced to make the donation, forced to find another way to get those paintings for himself.

But would Wyatt have let his grandson rot in a prison cell for five years over some paintings? She had to find out.

# SEVEN

Brianna woke up Wednesday morning with a headache. She'd spent a long night thinking about Wyatt and Derek and the paintings. She doubted confronting Wyatt would get her anywhere. He'd simply sneer at her in his condescending way and tell her she was on a fool's errand to prove her husband's innocence. And while Katherine's suggestion that Wyatt might not have wanted to donate the paintings resonated with her, did she really have any new information to take to Joe Silveira? She didn't think so. She needed more. But more would have to wait. She had a job to get to.

After dropping Lucas off with his grandparents, she started her shift at the quilt shop. At the end of three hours, she knew how to work the cash register and cut fabric, and she had a pretty good handle on where everything was. She'd also gotten to know two of her coworkers. Stella was a big-hearted, loud-talking forty-something divorcee who'd recently discovered Internet dating, and during slow periods at the store, she'd shown some of her favorite male profiles to Brianna, lamenting the fact that none of the men lived in Angel's Bay. How far did she want to go to get a little something, she'd asked with a laugh. It was a question Brianna couldn't begin to answer, since she hadn't had a "little something" herself in a long time.

He other coworker, Erin McCarthy, was a quiet woman in her mid-thirties. Upon prodding from Stella, Erin had confided that she and her husband were trying to adopt a baby, and that there was a local teenager who might be giving her child up, but apparently there was quite a bit of competition. After that, she'd shut up, worried that she might be jinxing herself by talking about it.

The shop had done a steady business all morning, and by noon Brianna had lost track of all the people she'd met. She could see why Nancy enjoyed working at the store; there was a sense of camaraderie and community. People came in eager to create something new, and their hopefulness and joyous anticipation were infectious. Brianna had already started plotting out possible quilt designs in her head, and she had a feeling it wouldn't be difficult to become an obsessed quilter herself.

She'd also learned that quilting in Angel's Bay wasn't just about the craft; it was also about business. Besides providing materials and classes for individuals, a core group of employees constructed a line of Angel's Bay quilts that were sold all over the world.

Two women whose sole purpose was to handle the Internet orders worked in the back office. She'd never imagined that the store was supporting so many families.

Speaking of family . . . she smiled as Nancy and Lucas entered the shop. Lucas immediately ran into her arms, giving her a big hug and a kiss. She introduced him to Erin, who was just finishing up with a customer.

"He's beautiful," Erin said, with maternal yearning in her eyes. "I can see you in him. He has your nose, I think."

Erin was the first person who hadn't seen only Derek in her son, and it was refreshing. "Thanks."

"Grandma and Grandpa took me to the pumpkin patch," Lucas announced.

"And the bakery?" she asked, wiping away the smear of red jam by the corner of his mouth.

"I only had a little tart. Grandma said I have to wait until after lunch."

Brianna was relieved to hear her mother-in-law was capable of imposing some rules; Rick and Nancy tended to spoil Lucas like crazy.

"Any word on babies, Erin?" Nancy asked.

"We're still praying."

"Well, don't give up hope," Nancy said.

"I won't," Erin promised. She turned to Brianna. "If you'd like, I can show Lucas the kids' room while you check out with Fiona."

"That would be great," Brianna said, setting

Lucas back on his feet. "Fiona needs me to sign something before I go," she added to Nancy.

Lucas went off with Erin with a happy smile, always happy to explore.

"So how did it go here?" Nancy asked.

"Great. It was busy, and I made some mistakes, but Stella and Erin and Fiona were great. They were very welcoming."

Nancy beamed. "I'm so glad. I know it's not a teaching job, but that will come soon. Do you want to find Fiona, and then we'll go to lunch?"

"Let me just take this customer. I think she's about ready."

Nancy turned to make room for the older woman approaching the counter. As the two saw each other, they both stiffened. Nancy's usually happy expression vanished. The other woman's lips drew into a tight line, and the air between them crackled with tension.

The woman finally looked away from Nancy and set her fabric on the counter. When she turned to Brianna, her dark eyes widened in disbelief. "You!"

Brianna wasn't sure how to respond. The woman looked vaguely familiar, but she couldn't remember why. She had a rather nondescript appearance—brown hair streaked with gray, a thin face, no makeup except for a streak of pink on her lips.

"So it's true. You're here now," the woman said, "Donald told me that, but I didn't believe it. You have a lot of nerve."

Brianna looked to Nancy for some help, but her mother-in-law seemed frozen.

Then Stella came around the counter, gently pushing Brianna to the side. "Fiona is looking for you, Brianna. I can take care of you, Mrs. Hanlon."

*Hanlon.* Lorene Hanlon, the wife of the security guard Derek had allegedly assaulted. Brianna swallowed hard.

"My husband still has headaches and dizzy spells," Lorene Hanlon said, her eyes burning with anger. "He hasn't been the same since Derek attacked him. And now you're back trying to convince everyone he didn't do it? Who the hell do you think you are?"

"Here's your change, Mrs. Hanlon," Stella interrupted. "And your fabric. You're all set."

Lorene took the money and the bag from Stella, then left, giving the door a furious slam on her way out.

"You okay, hon?" Stella asked with concern.

"I'm fine," Brianna said as she took a deep breath to slow her racing heart.

"I forgot to warn you that Lorene comes in here sometimes," Nancy said, finally finding her voice again. "We usually just avoid each other."

"I'll have to do the same."

"I'll get Lucas," Nancy said, moving away.

Brianna turned to Stella. "Thanks for stepping in."

"No problem. Listen, whatever Derek did or didn't do, you're not him. Most people around here understand that. And those that don't, well, that's their problem."

Unfortunately, it was her problem, too, and one reason she'd worried about bringing Lucas to Angel's Bay. She could deal with Lorene Hanlon, but she wasn't about to let anyone make Lucas feel bad for something that Derek probably hadn't even done. *Probably?* She shook the doubt out of her mind. She couldn't stop believing in her husband now.

After her shift at the quilt shop, Brianna went to lunch with Nancy and Lucas at the Crab Shack, then they picked up some groceries and stopped by the Kanes' house to get Digger. When she finally returned home with Lucas and the puppy, Brianna found a note taped to her front door. It was short and to the point: "Kite flying, three o'clock."

Jason hadn't signed it, but she knew it was from him. It was also almost three.

"Who's it from, Mommy?" Lucas asked.

For a moment, she was tempted to lie to him. In fact, she was tempted to track down Jason and tell him not to come, but it was a little late for that. She'd already told Lucas that Jason was fixing the kite.

"Jason is going to bring your kite by in a few minutes," she said as she unlocked the door.

Lucas squealed with delight. She hoped he was more excited about the kite than about seeing Jason, but she suspected it was a little of both. Lucas craved

adult male attention, and while his grandfather provided some of that, Jason was younger and more like
a father figure. She just had to make sure that Lucas
didn't start seeing him that way.

A few minutes later, the doorbell rang. Lucas was
on her heels as she answered it. He greeted Jason
with an exuberant hug that seemed to take the man
by surprise, but he quickly recovered.

"Hey, buddy. Look what I've got." Jason held up
a red and purple kite that looked nothing like the
one they'd made the day before.

Lucas stared at it in amazement. "It's so big."

"And not at all familiar," Brianna added. "Did
you buy a new kite?"

Jason shrugged. "I made this one. I used some
parts of yours."

If he had, she couldn't recognize any of them.

"Ready to give it a test run?" Jason asked.

"I guess we can go out front," she said somewhat
reluctantly. She'd rather not be seen running around
the neighborhood with Jason Marlow.

"We need more room," Jason said. "I know a
good spot. You'll need jackets; lucky for us, the wind
is picking up."

"I don't know," she said, hesitating. "I can't leave
Digger here alone yet. He'll tear up the house. And I
just brought him back from the Kanes'."

"Your puppy will love where we're going. There's
a lot to explore, and he can't get into any trouble."

She was more concerned about the trouble *she*
might be getting into going out with Jason. But if

they were going to do this together, she'd rather do it away from her house. "All right. Let's go."

Jason's Jeep was parked in Patty's driveway. As he opened the back to stash the kite, she caught a glimpse of a wetsuit and a couple of beach towels.

"Do you dive?" she asked.

"Some, but mostly I surf. We get some good waves along the coast, especially when the storm pattern is right."

"Sounds dangerous and cold."

"It's challenging and fun," he returned, a sparkle in his eyes. "Man against nature. It's the ultimate contest. You should try it."

"I don't think so."

"Sometimes it's more fun to actually have an adventure, instead of just reading about it in the library," he said with a smile.

She was already regretting sharing that with him. Ignoring his comment, she settled Lucas into the backseat with Digger, then got into the front and fastened her seat belt.

"So where are we going?" she asked as Jason pulled out of the driveway. "Somewhere out of town, I hope?"

He shot her a quick look. "It's been a long time since a girl wanted to hide me from her parents."

"I don't want to hurt Rick and Nancy. They mean a lot to me."

"I don't want to hurt them, either. There's a good spot just south of here, where the wind blows like a freight train and there's a lot of room to run. Derek and I used to fly our kites there. It took a while to get there on our bikes, but it's not far by car."

Turning her gaze out the window, she watched the streets go by, picturing two young boys pedaling to the beach with their kites. What an innocent time that had been. Neither of them would ever have imagined their lives would turn out the way they had.

As they left the downtown area, the scenery turned more rural. Although there were several large houses going up along the coastline, eventually those were fewer and far between. She saw a sign for Angel's Bay Art Colony, and in the distance she could see a circular building with lots of windows. Next to it was a string of small cottages. "What's over there?"

"A community art center. Wyatt and some of the other artists had it built about fifteen years ago. The studio is in the main building; the smaller cottages overlook the sea and provide artistic inspiration for visiting artists. The local art scene has grown tremendously in the past decade."

"Is that where Derek painted?"

"Sometimes, but he usually worked at Wyatt's house. He lives about a mile down the road. You can't see his place from the highway."

A few minutes later, Jason pulled off to the side of the road and parked at the edge of a wide, flat field. Good. She didn't want to worry about Lucas and the puppy running along a narrow cliff.

Lucas had his seat belt unbuckled the second Jason turned off the engine. He was reaching for the door when Brianna reminded him to wait. She wanted to get hold of Digger's leash before he took off without them. The puppy was just as excited as Lucas to explore new territory. When she got the dog out of the car, he hit the ground running, taking her along with him. Fortunately, he ran only a few yards before stopping to sniff the wildflowers and paw at the ground.

While Digger was digging, Jason squatted down next to Lucas, showing him how to hold the kite. Brianna didn't think they'd have any trouble getting it up in the air; it was windier than heck. She'd pulled her hair back in a ponytail, but several strands had already blown loose and were whipping about her face. Her skin tingled from the sun and the salty breeze. Even though she was a little cold, she also felt invigorated for the first time in a long time.

"Okay, Lucas, give it a shot," Jason said, stepping back.

"Aren't you going to show him how to do it first?" she asked, surprised by his willingness to turn the kite over to Lucas.

"It's his kite. He should be the first one to fly it." Jason gave Lucas an encouraging nod. "Just hang on tight, Lucas."

Lucas took off running, and in seconds the kite blew up behind him. Brianna felt a sudden rush of worry. What if the kite went too high and dragged Lucas toward the edge of the bluff? But Jason was already running next to Lucas, keeping pace with her little boy.

They were shouting and laughing as the kite blew toward the heavens, the red and purple colors lighting up the grayish sky. Unexpected tears gathered in her eyes. She'd never seen Lucas so happy, so free from the somber quiet that had surrounded them for so many years. This was exactly what she had wanted for him.

She stumbled as the leash suddenly jerked in her hand. Digger had decided the guys were having too much fun without him, and soon she was running just as fast as they were. She didn't know how many trips they made back and forth across the bluff, but finally Lucas and the dog got tired, both collapsing to the ground in a mix of delighted barks and giggles.

Jason pulled the kite back to earth. His hair was tousled from the wind, his eyes lit with pleasure. He looked young, happy, and carefree.

"Your turn," Jason said, holding the kite out to her with a smile.

"I'm fine."

"You can't come out here and not fly the kite."

"I just ran two miles chasing you, Lucas, and the dog."

"Give me the leash." She saw nothing but encouragement in her eyes. "You should do it, Brianna. It's exhilarating to let the wind carry you away. I want you to feel it."

His words held a promise that was too tantalizing to resist.

Lucas offered words of advice as she started to

jog down the bluff. She didn't intend to go far, but once the kite took flight, she felt as if she was soaring right along with it. It *was* an incredibly freeing feeling. Her feet had been planted on the ground for years, her head down, plowing through her daily life without any real joy. She couldn't remember the last time she'd looked up, the last time she'd dreamed about anything.

The wind wrapped around her like a blanket of love. She heard voices whispering in the air and had the absurd thought that the angels were singing. And somewhere in that chorus was Derek's voice—lighter now, not filled with sadness and guilt but buoyed by love and hope. *It's time for your dreams now, Brianna. Make them big, make them bold, make them real.*

She didn't realize she was crying until she stopped running, and Jason and Lucas looked at her with concern.

She wiped her cheeks with her hand and smiled. "Just the wind," she lied. "That was incredible. Thank you."

Jason nodded, his knowing gaze seeing past her excuses. "You're welcome. You deserved that."

"Do you think I'll win the contest, Mommy?" Lucas asked.

"I don't think it matters, honey, as long as you have as much fun as you did today."

"The fun isn't over yet," Jason said unexpectedly. "Do you feel up to a little more exploring?"

"I do! I do!" Lucas said, the dog barking in agreement.

Jason laughed. "I've got two takers. What about you?"

He held out his hand to Brianna, and she took it without thinking. His fingers curled around hers, jolting her with delicious heat. She hadn't felt so warm or so connected to a man in a long time. It was terrifyingly good. She pulled her hand from his grip and took Lucas's hand instead. This was the guy she needed to hang on to.

Jason led them down a long, winding path to the beach below. Surrounded by the tall bluffs, the beach was very protected, the wind surprisingly nonexistent.

"It's called Shelter Cove," he told her.

"I can see why. It's so calm."

"It provided shelter for three survivors of the *Gabriella*," he said. "They were clinging to boards from the ship when the storm tossed them here."

"It's beautiful." The shallow water was a pretty blue-green, the current gentle. Only hundreds of yards away on the other side of the point were wild, crashing waves, but a natural land barrier protected this strip of the beach.

"Digger wants to go in the water," Lucas announced.

She glanced down at Digger, who was straining on the leash held by Jason. "Should we let him go?"

Jason nodded. "I don't think he can get into too much trouble here." He let the dog off the leash, and Digger dashed toward the sea.

Lucas immediately followed.

"Don't get too close to the water," she warned him. Lucas had taken swimming lessons since he was two and loved the water, but he'd never been in the ocean. Fortunately, he was distracted by the shells lying along the beach and squatted down to explore them.

She drew in a breath and let it out, feeling even more at peace in this quiet cove where the wind had dulled to a dim roar. "I do like the sea. There's something about standing on the edge of the continent that makes me feel both big and small at the same time."

"Any desire to see what's on the other side of the horizon?"

"I've already been there."

"That's right; you're a world traveler. I forgot." He picked up a rock and tossed it into the ocean. "The farthest trip I've made is to Hawaii."

"To surf?" she asked.

He smiled. "There are some monster waves over there."

"I can imagine." She sat cross-legged on the sand, letting her fingers trail through the grains.

Jason sat down next to her, stretching out his long legs, and they watched Lucas and the dog playing on the beach. She hadn't felt so content in a long time.

"You're quiet," Jason commented.

"It's peaceful here."

Another minute ticked by, and despite the beauty of the scene, she could feel tension building between them. "Why don't you just ask me whatever it is you want to ask?" she said finally.

Jason shot her a quick look. "What are you talking about?"

"I can feel your curiosity." She crossed her arms in front of her chest, feeling as if she needed to be careful, needed to protect herself.

"Why Derek?" he asked finally.

She drew in a quick breath. It was an easy question, wasn't it? She'd met Derek at his art gallery. She'd been invited to an exhibit by one of her parents' friends. She'd been running late, having gotten caught in an unusual Southern California rainstorm. She'd dashed into the gallery and paused by the front mirror to check her appearance. As she'd run her fingers through her hair, a man came up behind her, his gaze meeting hers in the mirror. She'd been startled by his beautiful hazel eyes, which seemed to change colors as he stared at her. She hadn't been able to look away, and neither had he.

"So many people looked past me," she murmured. "I was practically invisible to my parents, but Derek saw me. He made me feel like I was the most important person in the room. When we met, he told me that if he were still painting, he would have wanted to paint me, because he'd never seen eyes as blue as mine." She cleared her throat, feeling a little awkward. "I suppose you think that was quite a line."

"You do have beautiful eyes," Jason commented.

"Derek had great eyes, too. He swept me off my feet. We had a six-month whirlwind relationship of dinner and dates. Everything was fast and intense. I was twenty-five years old, and I'd never had as much fun with anyone as I had with him. I didn't want it to end, so when he asked me to marry him, I said yes. And when he brought me here to Angel's Bay and Nancy pulled me into her arms and squeezed me as tight as she could, I felt like I'd come home. She told me I was going to be the daughter she never had. And Rick was just as warmhearted and generous. The Kanes were everything I'd imagined a family to be."

"And you never had a doubt, never thought to yourself, This is a little too fast? Do I really know this guy?" he asked

She moistened her lips. "Maybe I did. But I was young, and when Derek was around, it was easy to push those doubts aside. He had a big presence. When he was in the room, everyone knew it."

"That's true." Jason's gaze clung to hers. "But what about after the trial, Brianna? You sat in that courtroom and heard the testimony. You didn't believe any of it? You didn't see the holes in Derek's story?"

"I saw the holes in your case," she retorted.

"And during the last five years, no doubts? None whatsoever?"

"Let's talk about something else," she said abruptly.

"Am I getting too close?"

"Tell me more about this cove and the survivors who washed ashore here. Or else let's just go."

Jason hesitated, "Fine, we'll change the subject for now. There were three men who landed here.

They had no idea that most of the survivors had made it to land a few miles north. They lived on the beach, in the caves when the weather was bad." He pointed to the outcropping of rocks at the far end of the beach. "When the tide is low, you can go inside. The caves extend deep into the bluff. There are still some etchings on the walls from when the men hid out there."

"Can we see?" she asked, feeling a tingle of excitement at the prospect.

"The tide is coming in now, so it would be too dangerous. While the water doesn't reach the back of the cave, you could easily get stuck in there for a few hours. We can come back when it's low—it's something to see. Derek and I discovered the caves together. We went in expecting to find a skeleton or gold from the wreck, but all we found were some marks on a wall. That didn't stop other kids from exploring. Colin got sucked out to sea by a riptide one day and almost drowned. He claims an angel saved him, but I think he just got lucky. After that, the caves were roped off for a while, and most people just forgot about them. They're off the beaten track."

"Who were the shipwreck survivors who landed on this beach?"

"Caleb Hughes, Peter Danforth, and Ramón Delgado."

She tensed at the mention of one of the Delgado brothers. "I thought Ramón and his brother, Victor, were together when they came ashore."

"No, they didn't reunite for several months, when

the men finally made their way up the coast. When Ramón discovered that Eve was dead, he blamed his brother."

"Which is why some people think that Ramón stole *The Three Faces of Eve* from Victor," she finished with a sigh. "We always come back to those paintings, don't we?" She paused. "I spoke to Katherine Markham yesterday. Do you know her?"

"Sure. She's a local girl."

"She suggested that Wyatt might not have wanted to donate the paintings to the museum but was forced into it by her aunt and uncle."

Jason's gaze didn't waver. "Are you accusing Wyatt of stealing the paintings?"

"Did you ever consider that a possibility?"

"He owned the paintings. Why donate them if he wanted to keep them? And as for the idea that Wyatt could be forced into something by the Markhams . . ." He shook his head. "No possible chance. Wyatt is a force of nature. What he wants he gets."

"Exactly."

"Brianna, I know you want to find someone else to blame, but I think you're going down the wrong road."

"I'm keeping an open mind—something you choose not to do."

"I know Wyatt. You don't. It makes it easier for me to see which roads are dead ends." He took a breath. "And I knew Derek, too, maybe better than you did. His dreams might have changed over the years, but they didn't diminish in size. The day before the robbery, he came to my house while you were shopping for your wedding dress. He talked about all the connections he'd made in L.A., the celebrities he was working with, and the money people were willing to spend on art. He said his life was shaping up just the way he planned."

"He worked hard, and he had ambition, but a lot of men do. You put everything Derek said or did that week in the context of him being the thief."

"I worked with the facts that I had. You have to let this go, Brianna. It will eat you up inside, and for what purpose? You gave up five years of your life to fight for Derek. How many more will it take? If you don't let go of the past, you'll never have a future. That's not fair to Lucas. He needs a mother who's living in the present, not in the past." He put up a hand, apology in his eyes. "I'm sorry. That didn't come out the way I intended, but I won't lie to you, Brianna. That's a promise."

"Just because you're honest doesn't mean you're right." Glancing down at her watch, she realized Derek's attorney would be at her house in a few minutes. She got to her feet. "I have to get back. I have a meeting at five."

She grabbed the kite off the ground and called for Lucas. He ran back to them with a dripping-wet puppy at his heels. Digger's black coat was soaked, and he was covered with a thick layer of sand that he was vigorously shaking onto the rest of them.

"He's kind of dirty," Lucas said.

"Not a problem," Jason replied. "I've got towels in the car." He took the leash from Lucas's hand and led the way toward the car.

Jason gave Digger a quick towel dry before putting him in the back next to Lucas and shutting the door. Brianna slid into the front seat.

"Thanks for today," she said as he started the engine. "It meant a lot to Lucas."

"I had fun. And I think for a while you did, too," he said pointedly.

She looked away. More than she'd ever imagined.


When they arrived at her house, there was a black BMW parked in front. Mr. Isaacs was waiting on the porch. He was in his early sixties, but his illness made him look older. His hair had grayed, and his black suit looked a size too big.

Jason gave her a speculative look. "Isn't that Derek's attorney?"

"Yes, he has something for me." As she saw the large manila envelope in the lawyer's hand, she felt a wave of panic. She wasn't sure she was ready to read whatever Derek hadn't been able to tell her in person.

"Who's that man, Mommy?" Lucas asked, always inquisitive.

"He's just a friend." She glanced at Jason. "I know I shouldn't ask, but is there any way you could take Lucas into the house for me and keep him busy for a few minutes? This shouldn't take long."

"I've got a better idea. Why doesn't Lucas come meet some of Patty's pets? She's got a talking bird."

"Can I, Mommy?" Lucas asked. "Can Digger come, too?"

"Sure," Brianna said with relief. "Thank you, Jason."

"No problem."

She stepped out of the car and walked up to greet Mr. Isaacs while Jason took Lucas and the puppy next door.

"I'm sorry I'm late," she said. "I hope you haven't been waiting long."

"Just a few moments," he said.

She swallowed hard at the sight of Derek's familiar scrawl across the front of the envelope, which she took with a shaky hand. It was thicker than she'd expected. There was more inside than just a simple letter. "Do you want to come in?" she asked.

"No, thank you. It's a long drive, and I'll be heading back."

"I appreciate the personal service. Are you sure I can't get you a drink before you go?"

He gave her a sympathetic smile. "Not anxious to open that, are you?"

"Can you give me a hint what's inside?"

"I honestly don't know. Derek gave it to me almost a year ago, said to give it to you if something happened to him. I never thought I'd have to deliver it. I'll leave you to it." He nodded his head and walked to his car.

After he drove away, she sat on the love seat on

the porch and stared at her name. What a coward she was. There was nothing to be afraid of. Derek had probably written her a love letter, words to cherish for the rest of her life.

Unfortunately, that thought didn't make her feel any better. While she'd just told Jason how Derek had dazzled her during their courtship, it had been a long time since she'd really felt his love—even longer since she'd felt her own love. Sometime in the past few years, she'd gone numb. She'd lost touch with her senses, her emotions, her heart. Derek had become a ghost in her life long before he died, a phantom presence holding her captive. She'd battled daily with the desire to stay and the need to run. No one who hadn't been in her position could ever understand what it meant to love someone who was in jail.

Still, whatever he had to say to her, she wanted to hear it. Sliding her finger under the flap, she opened the envelope.

# EIGHT

Brianna didn't know what she'd been expecting, but it certainly hadn't been a stack of pencil sketches. She flipped through them, her confusion growing with each page. The sketches were incredibly detailed and seemed to depict important people and places in Derek's life. There was even one of her standing in front of the mirror at the gallery where they'd first met, the shadow of a man behind her. Was this how Derek had passed the endless days of his sentence? Why hadn't he ever told her he was drawing?

Setting the sketches aside, she picked up a smaller white envelope and pulled out a letter. Her heart sped up as she began to read.

> *Dear Brianna,*
>
> *When you come to visit me, there are so many things I want to say but I can't seem to find the words. Our time is always so short and I don't*

*want to waste it. I want you to know that I feel
incredibly touched by your loyalty and your love,
but also guilty for tying you to this terrible life.
I never should have let you marry me, but I've
always been a selfish man. I thought about what
was good for me and not what was best for you.
In the beginning I believed it would only be days
until I got out. I never imagined that I would still
be here now. I've told myself that I'll make it up to
you when I get out, but it would be impossible for
me to ever return the years I took from you.*

The words blurred, and she blinked away the
tears.

*I haven't always told you the truth. Honesty
doesn't come easy for me. My secrets run deep. I created the life I wanted to live a long time ago, and
I began to believe in my own lies. I thought I could
take what was fake and make it real. I thought I
could fool the world, but the glass always reflects
the truth, and I should have known better.*

*I didn't steal The Three Faces of Eve, but
I'm not completely innocent, either. I'm not the
man you think I am. If I get the courage to tell you
all this to your face, you'll never see this letter or
the sketches I've done, but just in case . . . I'll sleep
better knowing that one day you'll know the whole
story, even if I'm not here to tell it.*

*I hope we'll have a long life together, but
things happen in prison. Every day someone seems*

*to fall sick or die. If something should happen to
me, take care of yourself and our son. Know that
whatever lies I told, there was always one truth:
I loved you, and I loved Lucas, more than I ever
thought I could love anyone. You both made me
want to be a better man. I hope someday I'll have
a chance to exceed your expectations, to replace
these years with ones we'll both want to remember.*
                                        *Love, Derek*

Derek's voice was so clear in her head, his eyes beseeching her to understand. Tears streamed from her eyes like the rush of water from a broken dam. She cried for the man who had died too young and the little boy who would grow up without his father. She cried for the death of all their dreams and because she had to let out the pain. She'd been holding it together for weeks, putting on a brave face for her son, but this moment was just for her.

Finally, she was spent. She wiped her eyes with her sleeve and put the letter and sketches back into the envelope. Then she went inside to run cold water over her puffy eyes. After giving her face a brisk rub with a towel, she stared at herself in the bathroom mirror. Her hair was a mess of tangles from the windy beach, her eyes were still red and a little too bright, but the evidence of her weeping was fading. She'd gotten good at pretending to be all right, and this day wouldn't be any different.

Derek said he'd been pretending, too. His words ran around in her head. *"I'm not who you think I am."*

Who was he, then? And what had he meant, telling her that he hadn't stolen the paintings but he wasn't completely innocent, either? If he'd wanted her to know the truth, why be so cryptic? Why continue to keep secrets when he was already serving time in prison? None of it made any sense. With a sigh, she turned away. She needed to get Lucas.

She went next door and rang the bell. Jason answered it a second later.

"Where's Lucas?" she asked, stepping into the living room.

"He's in the kitchen, trying to teach the parrot to talk."

"I'll get him." She started to move past him, but he grabbed her arm.

"He's fine. You, on the other hand, don't look so good." He followed her gaze down the hall. "Don't worry, Lucas can't hear us. The kitchen door is closed. The other pets don't care for your puppy, so I had to isolate him. What happened? What did Derek's lawyer want? Why have you been crying?"

She tried to pull away from him, but he had a tight grip on her arm. "Nothing's happened."

"I don't believe you."

"Let me go," she said desperately. Her emotions were too highly charged; she couldn't tangle with Jason now.

He stared at her for a long moment, indecision in his eyes. "I know I *should* let you go."

She caught her breath at the look in his eyes. It had been a long time since a man had gazed at her with such desire—and since she'd felt the same pull. An electrical charge lit up the tense air between them; anticipation licked up her spine. She wanted what she shouldn't want, needed what she shouldn't need. If only he would look away—if only she could.

She thought he would kiss her, but he released her arm and stepped back, digging his hands into his pockets as if he were afraid he might reach for her again.

She was afraid, too. Because beyond all reason, she wanted his touch. She wanted him to take her in his strong arms and hold her, really hold her, the way a man holds a woman he needs to take to bed.

Her brain said, *Think.* Her body cried, *Act.*

She closed the distance between them, sliding her arms around his waist and pressing her lips against his shocked mouth. She wanted to soak up his strength, to taste forgetfulness on his lips, to be herself again, a woman—not a mother, not a wife, not a widow. She didn't want to cry anymore, didn't want to feel like a lost ship on a stormy sea. She wanted an anchor to something real. She wanted to feel something better than pain.

She sucked his tongue into her mouth, hearing him groan, feeling his hands drop to her hips. He pulled her into his hard groin. She rubbed her breasts against his chest and thrust her hands under the hem of his shirt, running them restlessly over his hard abs. Jason was all muscle and heat, passion and tenderness. His intensity was overwhelming, intoxicating. A delicious fever overtook her.

Jason backed her against the wall, angling his mouth over hers to deepen the kiss. She could feel every inch of his body. She liked the relentless on-slaught of his mouth on hers. She didn't have time to think, only to feel, and she was feeling really, really good—until Jason suddenly jerked away.

He stared at her, his breathing rough and hard. "What the hell are we doing?"

She didn't have an answer. As the seconds ticked by, she could hear the parrot squawking, reminding her that Lucas was in the next room. What if he'd come out and seen them? She never should have given in to such a reckless impulse.

"Brianna?" Jason's dark gaze searched her face.

"I don't know. I'm sorry."

"I don't want an apology," he said tersely. "I want an explanation. One minute, you hate me; the next minute, you're trying to rip my shirt off."

"You kissed me back," she reminded him.

"Of course I kissed you back. I've wanted to since the second I saw you in Murray's Bar five years ago."

"That's not true," she said, shocked by his statement.

"It's absolutely true. When I saw you sitting on that bar stool, drinking white wine, your long hair down to your waist, your eyes a beautiful sky blue, your lips . . ." His gaze dropped to her mouth. "So soft and perfect. I thought to myself, This is her, this is the one I've been waiting for."

His words took her breath away. "You did not think that."

"I felt like I was falling off a cliff. I never thought about women in terms of longer than a night or a week, maybe a month. But you . . . I don't know what came over me. You spouted off all these intellectual facts about wine making, and I was a goner."

"I sometimes babble when I'm nervous."

"So *you* felt something, too. That's why you didn't tell me you were engaged."

She had enjoyed talking to Jason that night. He was funny and sexy and interesting, and a lot better listener than Derek, who tended to dominate most of their conversations. She didn't know if she'd consciously left out the fact that she was engaged or if it just hadn't come up. But nothing had happened between them, and nothing *would* have happened, even if Derek hadn't walked into that bar.

"Look, we had a couple of drinks together a long time ago," she said. "Maybe you felt something for me, but I was in love with Derek. I'm sorry if that hurts, but it's the truth. And you're the one who wants nothing but the truth between us."

He gave her a long look. "Okay, so you were being friendly then." He took a step closer to her, and she instinctively backed up. "Is that what you were being tonight? Friendly?"

His breath fluttered against her cheek, and the challenge in his eyes only made him that much more attractive. But she couldn't go there again. "Would you please move?"

"Why did you kiss me, Brianna?"

"I was upset. You were here. It just happened."

"Why were you upset?"

She hesitated, reluctant to get into the letter, but she needed something to distract him, distract both of them. "Mr. Isaacs gave me a letter that Derek had written. It was something he wanted me to have in case he died."

Jason's eyes turned speculative. "What did it say?"

"It's personal. But the gist was that he loved me, and he didn't steal the paintings, two things I'm sure you don't want to hear."

"So why were you so upset?"

"Wouldn't it bother you to get a letter from someone you loved after they died?"

"I might find it comforting, unless they said something that surprised me. Is that what Derek did?"

She wasn't about to give Jason any more ammunition. "Lucas is probably wondering where I am. I should get him."

"You're going to just walk away, pretend nothing happened between us?"

"I think it's best if we both do that. Whatever you felt for me five years ago, whatever you feel now, it doesn't matter."

"What about what *you* feel?"

"You want to know how I feel?" she asked, searching for words. "I'm numb, frozen. Maybe I kissed you because I wanted to feel something. But it didn't mean anything. Nothing can ever happen between us."

"It's already happening, Brianna."

"Then we need to stop it, because Derek will always be between us."

"Only if you keep him there."

"I have to. I'm raising his son, and I'm indebted to his parents."

"So that's it? You'll never have another relationship?"

"I don't know about never, but not now, not with you."

"This isn't over," he said sharply. "But for now . . . I'll get Lucas."

Brianna let out a breath as he walked down the hall. She lifted her left hand and gazed at the diamond solitaire that Derek had placed on her finger so many years ago. The ring had grown loose in recent months, and as she played with the band, it slipped easily over her knuckle. She'd considered taking it off many times since Derek's death, but if she let go of Derek, what would she have left?

She knew how to be Derek's wife, even his widow—but she had long ago forgotten who she was.

Brianna tossed and turned most of the night, her mind jumping between Derek's disturbing letter and Jason's unexpectedly disturbing kiss. She didn't understand either one of them—or herself, for that matter. She'd certainly never expected to feel so torn between them.

Jason had reminded her of that girl she used to be, the one in the bar who'd babbled about wine and flirted with a sexy stranger and had so many possibilities in front of her. Was it possible to get her back? Or was it too late?

She'd been fighting for Derek. Maybe it was time to fight for herself.

She got up in the morning with new resolve, and for the first time in a long time, she felt hopeful.

After getting Lucas fed and dressed, she reached for her car keys. She needed to drop Lucas and Digger off with Nancy, then head to the quilt store to work her morning shift. Lucas was a little sleepy-eyed and moving slowly. Digger, on the other hand, was straining at the leash.

As they finally made their way out of the house, she saw Jason taking his surfboard off the back of his Jeep. His hair was wet, his cheeks red from the water or the wind, a shadow of beard on his jaw. He wore sweatpants and a T-shirt that clung damply to his skin.

"Hi, Jason," Lucas called out, following up his greeting with a running hug.

Jason hugged him back. "Where are you off to?" he asked, smiling at the boy warmly.

"Grandma and I are going to make cookies while Mommy works."

"That sounds like fun."

"Do you want to come?" Lucas asked with the innocence of youth.

"I can't. I've got to go to work."

"Lucas, take Digger and get in the car," Brianna said, handing him the leash.

"Can we fly kites later?" Lucas asked Jason. "I need to practice before the contest."

"We'll see," Jason said, his gaze moving to her.

She knew she should get into her car, but she found herself lingering. "Did you just come back from surfing?"

"Yeah, there were some good waves out there this morning. You should come with me one day."

"I'm not a very strong swimmer."

"I wouldn't let anything happen to you," he said.

An undercurrent flowed between them that she knew Jason was just as aware of as she was. She was also aware that Lucas was waiting, as were her mother-in-law and the quilt shop. So why wasn't she moving? "About last night," she began.

He cut her off. "Don't go there."

"I shouldn't have kissed you," she said, lowering her voice to just above a whisper. "I was feeling, I don't know, a little emotional, a little reckless."

"Next time I won't stop," Jason warned.

"There won't be a next time."

"Sure there will."

"I'm leaving now."

"Okay," he said with a small smile. "I'm just going to watch you walk away."

"Why?"

"You really don't want to know." His smile broadened into a grin.

She flushed under his flirtatious gaze and was about to beat a quick retreat when another car pulled up alongside them. The driver's-side door opened, and Kara stepped out.

"Hey there," she said, her gaze curious as it moved between them. "Is this where you're house-sitting, Jason?"

"Yes, it is," Jason said. "Are you on your way to your parents' house?"

"Yes, Faith needs some grandparent time."

"You've got the baby in there?" he said, moving toward her car. "Let me see her."

As Jason opened the back door, Kara turned to Brianna. "I'll see you at the shop later. Some of us are meeting at noon to work on a baby quilt for Annie Dupont. Maybe you can join us for a while after your shift. Charlotte is going to stop by; I think you've met her. It will be fun."

"I'll see if Nancy can watch Lucas for an extra half hour," Brianna said, not wanting to get in a long conversation. "I'd better go now. I don't want to be late." She got into her car and backed out while Jason was busy with Kara and the baby. She probably should have turned down Kara's invitation. Once Kara got her alone, she was probably going to have some questions. Well, she had three hours to think of some good answers.

"You two looked pretty chummy," Kara told Jason as Brianna pulled out of her driveway.

"Just being neighborly," he replied.

"Is that what they call it these days? Come on, Jason, what's going on with you two? I thought Brianna disliked you, but she didn't look like she was hating you a second ago."

"We've gotten to know each other a little better."

"That's all you're going to give me? Your oldest and dearest friend?"

"There's nothing to give."

"I guess this house-sitting job came in handy. You'll have to thank your father." Kara paused, her smile dimming a bit. "I am worried about you, though."

"No reason to be."

"You don't let very many people in. As soon as a woman gets too close, you usually head for the door. And Brianna isn't just any woman. She's tied to Derek, and you were wrecked after Derek's trial. I don't want Brianna to take you back to that dark place."

He was touched by her concern. "There's nothing to worry about."

"So you don't have a thing for her, like Colin said?" she persisted.

"Colin talks too much."

"Is it the challenge? You need to convince her that you were the good guy and Derek was the bad guy?"

He sighed; Kara was like a dog with a bone when she was on to something. "I'd like the truth to come out," he admitted. "But it's not that simple."

He'd realized just how complicated it was after

she'd let down her guard last night and kissed him, inviting him in. And what had he done? He'd put up his own walls and shoved her out. As Kara said, when it got intense, he tended to bolt.

Kara's gaze was steady on his face. "Wow. You *do* have it bad. I've been waiting a long time to see you really fall for someone, but I wish it wasn't her. I'm not sure this can end well. Some things can't be overcome. You're tied up in all of her pain, Jason— and then there are the Kanes. Can you imagine what they would think of you even sharing a driveway like this?" Kara shook her head. "She can't be the one."

"I don't think I said she was."

"Be careful, Jason. Brianna isn't just a woman; she's a mother, and she wants to clear Derek's name for her son. You're in her way. Don't forget that."

# NINE

"Mother," Charlotte called, as she let herself into the house just before noon. "Are you ready to go?" She set her purse down on the hall table, hearing an unfamiliar man's voice in the kitchen. An odd tingle ran through her. It felt strange to even have a man in the house. Since she'd helped her mother move out of the home she'd shared with her father for forty years, it had been just her mother, Annie, and herself, women of three different generations trying to survive under one roof. The other two were getting along great; she, on the other hand, was still trying to find some way to connect with the woman with whom she shared blood but little else.

She opened the kitchen door to find her mother smiling and laughing with a gray-haired man in a business suit.

"Charlotte," her mother said quickly as she got to her feet.

Was her mother actually blushing?

"This is your daughter?" the man asked.

"Yes, this is Charlotte. Charlotte, this is Peter Lawson. He's an old friend."

An old friend she'd never met before? "It's nice to meet you," she said, shaking his hand.

"And you. Monica has told me a lot about you," he said.

She was surprised, since she'd heard absolutely nothing about him. "Are we still going to the quilt shop to work on Annie's quilt?" she asked her mother.

"Oh, dear, I forgot to call you," her mother said. "Peter and I are going to look at a house he's interested in acquiring."

"I'm afraid I only have this hour available before I have to get back to San Francisco," he added, giving an apologetic smile.

"So you live in San Francisco?"

"Temporarily," he said. "I'm planning to change that. I hope you don't mind me stealing a bit of your mother's time. She's always had such an eye for interior design."

"How do you know that?" she couldn't help asking.

"Charlotte," her mother said, looking a bit appalled by her blunt question.

Peter smiled. "I saw what she did with my sister's house."

"Beverly Thomas is his sister," Monica added. "You remember Beverly, don't you?"

"I do. I just didn't realize you'd helped her decorate her house."

"Well, you were gone for a long time," her mother said somewhat sharply. "Please tell the ladies I'm sorry that I can't help with the quilt today." She grabbed her purse off the counter, then paused at the door. "Oh, Charlotte, I meant to tell you that Annie is meeting with Erin McCarthy and her husband today. I guess they're interested in adopting now."

Charlotte wasn't surprised. Erin's last miscarriage had taken a lot out of her.

"And Rabbi Ziegler called and said the Goldmans would like to set up a meeting. I'm not sure Annie would want her baby raised out of her faith, but Adam Goldman is a highly respected lawyer. I heard he's thinking of running for a state office next year."

"I'm not convinced Annie really wants to give up her baby," Charlotte said. "I've been wondering if we should talk about how we could help her if she wants to keep it."

"I don't quite know how much I can help," Monica said with a vague wave of her hand. "I'm not sure what kind of time I'll have, but we'll discuss it later." She paused her gaze narrowing. "You should really do something about your hair before you go. I can't believe you wear it that way to work."

And with that, she was off. Charlotte dismissed the hair critique, more curious about whether her mother's newfound concern about her time had anything to do with Peter Lawson. It was mindboggling to think of her mother with another man. There had only ever been one man, and that was

Charotte's father. They'd been together since they were twenty years old. They'd been so in love with each other they'd been able to finish each other's thoughts—at least, her mother had always seemed to know what her father was thinking. She suspected it hadn't worked quite so well the other way around, because her mother was a bit of a mystery. Monica Adams had a face she put on for the world, a face that very few people ever got past. But that face had been missing in the kitchen today. The woman heading out the door with the giddy smile of a teenager was no one Charlotte recognized. She'd thought her mother was done surprising her—but apparently not.

"My mother is on a date," Charlotte told Kara as they met up in the upstairs sewing room at the quilt shop. One of the instructors was finishing up a private lesson, and they had a few minutes before the rest of the group arrived. "Can you believe that?"

"Not really," Kara admitted, raising one eyebrow. "Are you sure?"

"I just ran into the two of them together." She couldn't get the image of them out of her mind. Her mother had been smiling and flirting.

"Do you want some tea?" Kara asked, moving toward the coffee and hot water urns at the back of the room.

"I'm so shocked, Kara," Charlotte said as Kara made the tea. "I come home to take care of my lonely, ailing mother, who doesn't think she'll be able to survive a day after my father dies, and now, less than a year later, she's off on a date. What's going on?"

"Life is going on—the way it's supposed to. So who's the guy?"

"Some silver fox named Peter Lawson. I didn't recognize him, but he's Beverly Thomas's brother. He's thinking of buying a house here in Angel's Bay, and he wants my mother's help, because she's apparently a great interior decorator." Another fact that had escaped her notice. "I knew she was a good homemaker, but I had no idea she had some incredible design talent."

"She did a beautiful job on Phyllis Fletcher's house. It was highlighted on the kitchen tour last Christmas." Kara handed her a cup of tea.

She absentmindedly took a sip. "I didn't know that, but then, how could I? She doesn't talk to me except to criticize."

Kara tilted her head, giving her a thoughtful look. "You're really upset about this. Why? It's not like your mother is cheating."

"It's just out of character. She's been so rigid about dating and love and sex—oh, God, you don't think they're having sex, do you?" The idea disturbed her on so many levels.

Kara laughed. "I doubt they're having sex right now. Your mother doesn't seem like the afternoon delight type."

Charlotte sighed. "She doesn't seem like any type.

She was never affectionate. I rarely saw my parents kiss. Whatever they did, they did in the bedroom, in the dark, and very quietly." She paused as a group of her mother's friends entered the room. "I wonder if they know what she's up to," she murmured.

"Your mother is helping an old friend find a house. You need to chill," Kara told her. "Look on the positive side. If your mother finds someone, that gets you off the hook. You can move out, get your own place, have a life, maybe even some sex of your own," she added with a wicked smile. "Speaking of which, how's Andrew doing?"

"I have no idea. Yesterday he was begging me to go to dinner with him tonight, but this morning I got a cryptic message that he couldn't make it. No explanation. I finally said yes, and now he says no."

Kara frowned. "That *is* puzzling. He's been trying to get you to go out with him for weeks. It has to be something important."

"Maybe it's fate, telling me not to go down that road again."

"You don't believe in fate," Kara reminded her.

"Maybe I should start." She paused as one of her patients, Victoria Baker stopped by the table to get some coffee. "Hey, how are you?" she asked. Victoria was a tired-looking brunette with deep shadows under her eyes that made Charlotte worry. "Is everything okay?"

"I couldn't sleep last night. I wasn't sure I should come to this," Victoria admitted.

"Why not?" Kara asked. "You're one of our regulars."

Victoria drew in a shaky breath. "David and I talked to Reverend Schilling about possibly adopting Annie's baby."

Charlotte's heart skipped a beat. She knew how hard Victoria and her husband had been trying to have a baby and how much money they'd already spent on in-vitro.

"I don't know if I should be working on the quilt," Victoria added. "It might make it even harder if we don't get the baby." She paused. "You don't know what Annie's going to do, do you, Charlotte?"

"I can't say, I'm sorry."

"I shouldn't have even asked. Erin McCarthy and her husband are hoping to get the baby, too. Erin and I have been commiserating over our fertility problems for some time. It's strange to think we're now in some sort of competition."

"Annie may keep the baby," Charlotte said with a compassionate smile. "She hasn't decided yet."

Victoria nodded. "Well, that's certainly her right. I couldn't imagine giving up my own child."

"Hey, I saw your brother yesterday," Kara interrupted. "He was having an argument with some goth-looking teenager in front of Dina's. Has he moved back to town?"

"For the time being, and that goth-looking teenager is Nick's daughter, Megan," Victoria said. "She just arrived, and she's not at all happy to be here. I'm hoping to get her involved in the theater next week when we start preproduction on the Winter Workshop. Speaking of which, we're going to have some parts for locals, and I would love to have you audition, Kara."

"Me?" Kara stuttered in surprise. "Why?"

"You were great back in high school."

"My drama days are behind me."

Victoria smiled. "You might say that now, but I'm going to keep asking," she said as she moved away to greet another friend.

"You *were* good in high school," Charlotte told Kara. "You should do it."

"Oh, please. I was not good, nor do I have time to be in a play. I'm a mother."

"Colin loved watching you act. I bet he'd support the idea, and doesn't the Winter Workshop just run until Christmas?"

"Let's talk about something else," Kara said quickly. "There's Brianna."

"Brianna Kane?" Charlotte echoed in surprise.

"She's working here now, and I invited her to come."

"Really?" Kara and Jason were best friends, and as far as Charlotte knew, Jason was still enemy number one when it came to the Kanes.

"Brianna," Kara called, motioning her over. "I'm so glad you came. You've met Charlotte, right?"

Brianna nodded, giving Charlotte a tentative smile. "A few times. I really appreciate your coming to Derek's funeral."

"I'm sorry I couldn't make it to the house afterwards. A patient went into labor."

"That's fine." Brianna cleared her throat, her gaze sweeping the room. "I don't know if I should stay, Kara. I don't think I belong here. I'm an employee, not one of the quilters."

"Of course you belong here," Fiona said, interrupting their conversation. "You're one of us now, Brianna, and you'll be a quilter before you know it."

Charlotte straightened as Fiona turned her sharp gaze on her. "Where's your mother, Charlotte? Shall we wait for her?"

"She can't make it. She has an engagement, but I'm here to represent the family."

"Yes, you are," Fiona said, clearly unimpressed. "Kara, keep an eye on her. Charlotte doesn't always care that much about what she's doing."

"I care," Charlotte said defensively, although quilting wasn't really her thing. "She should see the way I stitch up my patients," she added to Kara when Fiona moved along to talk to someone else. "I'm damn good."

"She should have told you to watch me," Brianna put in. "I haven't sewn in a long time."

"We'll help you. And while we're sewing," Kara said, "you can tell me how you and Jason are getting along."

A guilty look flitted across Brianna's eyes. "What's going on with you and Jason?" Charlotte asked curiously. "Jeez, am I behind the curve on everything around here?"

"He's just house-sitting next door to me," Brianna said quickly. "It's hard to avoid him, but eventually he'll be gone. And that will be that. End of story."

"Somehow I don't believe that," Kara murmured to Charlotte as Fiona called Brianna over to meet some other women.

"I didn't even know there *was* a story," Charlotte said. "How come you didn't tell me?"

"I don't like to gossip," Kara said with smile.

Charlotte grinned back at her. "Since when?"

Kara's smile dimmed. "Since I started worrying that one of my best friends might get his heart broken."

"I thought Jason and Brianna hated each other."

"I don't think what's between them has anything to do with hate—at least, not anymore."


Jason stopped by Patty's house after lunch to check on the animals. Brianna's car was still gone, and he assumed she was at the quilt shop. As he got out of his car, he was surprised to see someone coming down Brianna's side yard—and even more shocked when he realized it was Steve Markham. What the hell was he doing there?

"Officer Marlow," Steve said, stopping abruptly when he saw him. His gaze flickered past him. Jason didn't know if he was looking for a quick escape or if someone was with him.

Jason looked over his shoulder, noting the gray sedan parked at the end of the street. Markham certainly hadn't wanted to advertise his visit. "Mr.

Markham," he said, turning his gaze back to the gallery owner. "Are you looking for Brianna?"

"Yes, I was. She didn't answer the door, so I went around the back. I thought she might be in the yard, but she wasn't."

"Do you want me to tell her you came by?"

"Why would you be talking to her?" Steve asked, his gaze sharpening.

"I'm house-sitting next door," he replied.

"That must be . . . uncomfortable."

"What are you doing here?" Jason asked, tired of the polite charade they were playing.

"Brianna stopped in at the gallery the other day. I didn't have a chance to express my condolences."

"And that's what you wanted to do today? I don't buy it, and I doubt Brianna will, either. You made your position against Derek quite clear."

"As did you," Steve said smoothly.

"Yes, I believed Derek was guilty of everything he was charged with. Nothing's happened to change my mind." He tilted his head. "So why don't you tell me why you're really here?"

Steve hesitated for another second, then said, "I want the paintings. I went to the prison last year to speak to Derek, to tell him how much we wanted to get the art back—those pieces are important to the history of this town. But Derek wouldn't see me. I hoped that when he was released, we might able to come to some terms. Either he could sell us the paintings for some exorbitant price, or perhaps he'd own up to who had them, and we could make a deal with them."

"And now?"

"Now I'm hoping that Derek's widow can help us find the paintings."

"If Brianna had the art, she would have handed it over a long time ago."

"Not necessarily. Not if doing so would confirm Derek's guilt."

"If she believed Derek was guilty, she wouldn't have spoken to Joe Silveira about reopening the case," Jason pointed out.

Markham looked surprised at that piece of information. "I didn't realize she'd done that. Well, putting all that aside, I understand that Derek's belongings were placed in storage and recently shipped here. Perhaps she has some clue that she doesn't realize she has."

"I would think with your connections, you would be in a far better position to find those paintings than Brianna. She's not tied to the art world."

"She's tied to Derek, and he was the last one to have them." Steve paused. "I always knew Derek was ambitious, that he could look the other way if big money was involved, but I never thought he'd steal from us. Gloria and I introduced him to so many people. We gave him his start. We were practically family."

"Speaking of family," Jason said, "was it Wyatt's idea to donate the paintings to the museum or yours?"

"We agreed as a group. We could have sold them for a great deal of money, but it wasn't about the cash. It was about the art."

"I'll let Brianna know you were here," Jason said as Markham moved past him. "Next time, you might want to just park in front of the house, save yourself the walk."

Markham didn't answer, heading down the street at a brisk pace.

Jason walked down the side of Brianna's house and into the backyard. He checked the back door. It was locked. It didn't appear that Markham had gone inside, but it bothered him that he'd been in the backyard at all. And if Markham thought Brianna had a clue to the missing paintings, Jason couldn't help wondering who else might think the same thing—and how far they'd go to find out.


"What are you making, Mommy?" Lucas asked, joining Brianna at the dining-room table. He climbed onto the chair next to hers, gazing down at the fabric and threads she'd picked up at the quilt shop.

"I'm not sure," she said with a smile. "Maybe a quilt for your bed." Nancy had given her an old sewing machine, and after selling quilting materials all day, she'd gotten the itch to make one of her own.

"I like this." Lucas said, picking up some bright green fabric.

She'd figured he would. Green was one of his favorite colors.

"What's this?" he asked, grabbing for the other bag she'd set on the table.

"That is the Halloween costume you wanted," she said as he pulled out the pirate costume.

"Did you get a sword, too?" Lucas asked with excitement.

"You don't need one."

"But all pirates have swords," he said, dismay written all over his face.

"Well, *this* pirate carries a big plastic pumpkin to collect candy in," she said, pulling out the pumpkin.

"That *is* big," he agreed, happier now. "I can get a lot of candy in there."

"Yes, you can," she said. "So do you want to try on the costume?"

He had his shirt off before she finished the question. A few minutes later, he was decked out in his pirate gear, complete with eye patch. He ran into the living room to look in Derek's big mirror that was still propped against the wall and immediately started striking poses.

She loved watching him caught up in his imagination. In Lucas's world, anything was possible.

The sound of a car pulling into the adjacent driveway caught his attention, and he headed for the front door.

"I want to show Jason," he said.

"Wait." But he was out the door before she could stop him. When she stepped onto the porch, he was showing off his costume to Jason, who was expressing warm enthusiasm.

Jason was good with kids. He was patient, and he looked right at Lucas, listened to him, shared in his joy.

Moisture gathered in her eyes as a wave of bittersweet emotion ran through her. This moment belonged to a father and a son. Derek should have been the one coming home from work, the one her son couldn't wait to see. But Lucas had never had a moment like this with his father. The only time he'd spent with Derek had been in the visiting room at the prison. She'd read him letters from his dad, told him stories about Derek, and put up photographs of his father all over the house, but she'd never been able to produce the actual man.

She blinked away the tears. It shouldn't be Jason sharing this moment, but it was. And Lucas didn't mind at all. Jason was quickly becoming a superhero in her little boy's eyes.

Lucas turned and ran back to her. "Mommy, Jason got pizza, and he said we can have some."

Jason took a large pizza box and a six-pack of beer out of the car, then kicked the door shut and ambled across the lawn.

"I've got plenty to share," he said.

"It's a little early. It's not even five."

"I skipped lunch."

"I'm hungry, Mommy," Lucas declared.

"You're always hungry," she said with a laugh, rumpling his hair with her hands. "It does smell good."

"Then invite me in," Jason said with a coaxing smile.

If she said no, she'd probably send her son into a

screaming fit, and for what? It was just pizza. They'd eat, and Jason would go home. Nothing else was going to happen. "All right, come in."

"Really?" Jason asked with surprise.

"Lucas, why don't you take off your costume and wash your hands before we eat?" she added as they entered the house.

As Lucas headed to his bedroom, Jason followed her into the kitchen and set the pizza on the counter. "Before Lucas comes back," he said, "I wanted to let you know that I caught Steve Markham coming out of your yard earlier today."

"Steve Markham?" she echoed in surprise. "What was he doing here?"

"He said he went around back to see if you were there, but I noticed that he parked down the street as if he didn't want anyone to know he was at your house. I thought that was odd."

"So do I. What did he want?"

"He wanted to know if you have any idea where the paintings are."

"If I did, I would have produced them already."

"He thinks you might have a clue you don't know you have. He seemed to be aware of the fact that you'd had Derek's things shipped here. With Derek gone, you're the closest link to those pictures."

Uneasiness ran through her. "Do you think Lucas and I are in some sort of danger?"

"I hope not."

She didn't like his answer. "That's not exactly reassuring."

"I don't believe Markham is a danger to you, but I am concerned that someone else might see you as their best lead."

"But I'm not! I don't have the paintings. I don't know where they are. I wish I did."

"Have you gone through all the boxes that came from Derek's place?"

"Not yet. Some of them are still in the garage, but we both know that the paintings were never in his apartment. It was thoroughly searched before Nancy boxed anything up."

"True. But since you stuck by Derek all these years, it might be assumed that Derek told you where the paintings are."

"And again, if he had, I would have returned them to the museum. But Derek didn't tell me, because he didn't know, because he didn't do it. And if Mr. Markham wanted to speak to me, he could have done it when I was at the gallery the other day. Unless . . . he didn't want to say what he had to say in front of Wyatt." She broke off as Lucas came back. "We'll talk about this later." She grabbed some plates out of the cupboard.

"Do you want a beer?" Jason asked. "Or are you only a wine drinker?"

"Beer is fine." Although she probably could have used something a little stiffer. Having Steve Markham wandering around her property made her uneasy. The Markhams and Wyatt were the closest to Derek, the closest to the paintings, yet they had all made themselves quite unavailable during the investigation, the trial, and the past five years.

"How was the quilt shop today?" Jason asked as they settled around the table.

"Busy. I sat in on a group quilting project during lunch."

"With Kara, right?"

"Yes, and Charlotte Adams was there, too. They're a lot of fun." She paused. "Kara is very protective of you."

"She's protective of all her friends."

"I think you're in a special category."

Jason nodded. "We've known each other since the third grade."

"Did you ever like her as more than a friend?"

"Aren't *you* curious all of a sudden."

"And aren't *you* evasive all of a sudden," she replied.

He tipped his head with a conceding smile. "I might have had a little crush on her back in the day, but she only had eyes for Colin. He was her first, last, and always, and she was the same for him. The two of them would die for each other. And I'd die for them."

She believed him but she couldn't help wondering why he hadn't felt such loyalty to Derek. "I don't have any friendships that go that deep or that far back. It must be nice."

"Those kinds of friendships are fairly common in Angel's Bay. People grow up here and stay, or they leave for a while and come back to raise their own kids."

"You never wanted to be a cop anywhere else?"

"I like it here. That's probably hard for someone who's lived all over the world to understand."

"It wasn't my choice to move as often as we did or to travel far and wide."

"You don't think you would have lived that same jet-setting life with Derek?" he questioned.

She cast a quick look at Lucas, who was stuffing pizza into his mouth and kicking a ball to Digger under the table. He wasn't paying any attention to them, but still . . . "Maybe," she said. "But I can see the charm of a small community. The women at the quilt shop have been very nice to me. The only bad run-in I had was yesterday, when Mrs. Hanlon came in."

He frowned. "What did she say to you?"

"The same old accusations. In her mind, Derek and I are the same person."

"I'd avoid her and her husband whenever possible, and her son, too. He's a loose cannon."

"I forgot they had a son," she said. "He's our age, right?"

"A couple of years older," Jason replied.

"Jason, look," Lucas interrupted, a long strand of cheese hanging from his mouth to his plate.

"Lucas," Brianna scolded. "Food is not to play with."

"Your mom's right," Jason said, adding his support.

Lucas quickly shoved the cheese into his mouth.

He might have argued with her but not with Jason.

As they ate, conversation turned to the upcoming Harvest Festival, Jason giving her a rundown on all the events. The atmosphere was easy, relaxed, almost surreal, Brianna thought. After their encounter the night before, she'd dreaded seeing him again, but here they were, seated around the table like a family. She'd never imagined that one day she'd be sharing a meal with Jason and not be unhappy about it.

"So I was thinking," Jason began, as Lucas took his empty plate to the counter and then headed out of the kitchen. "You should take me up on my offer to teach you how to surf."

"I don't think so," she said quickly. "I'm not a fan of cold water."

"I have a wetsuit that will fit you."

"I told you I'm not a great swimmer."

"But you've been in the ocean before. You can swim," he said.

"In warm oceans like in Hawaii, where it's more like a soothing bath than a battle against nature."

"Battling nature can give you a tremendous sense of power, especially when you win. It's a great feeling."

"I don't know," she said, weakening against his eager persistence. She'd been wanting to step outside her usual life, but surfing? And with Jason? She shouldn't even be considering it.

"It will be fun. We could go tomorrow morning," he said. "The Kanes seem eager to watch Lucas whenever you need them to."

"I don't like to take advantage of them," she said, though the Kanes would be thrilled if she called up and said she'd be dropping Lucas off in the morning. "I'm sure they wouldn't be happy to hear we were doing anything together."

"This isn't about them," he said quietly.

"It *is* about them," she corrected. "They're important to me. I couldn't have survived without their support the past five years. Nancy was in the delivery room when Lucas was born; she coached me through the contractions. Every time they'd come to visit, Rick would fix things around the house, Nancy would cook meals, and they'd shower Lucas and me with love. I celebrated every birthday, every holiday with them. In some ways—" She stopped, realizing how much she was revealing.

"What?" he prodded.

"In some ways, I felt more married to them than to Derek," she confessed, feeling a little guilty at the thought. "I would never do anything that would hurt them."

"I wouldn't want to see the Kanes hurt, either. They were my second family growing up. When my father was on one of his depressed benders, they fed me meals and let me sleep over. I thought they were the perfect parents and that Derek was the luckiest guy in the world."

"Is that where your rivalry started—because Derek had what you didn't?"

He shook his head. "No, our rivalry started because we were both highly competitive people,

Derek even more so than me. Maybe it was because his grandfather was so hard on him when it came to his art—perhaps that's why he needed to prove himself in every other area. He always had to win. He had to be the best and have the best."

"The boy you knew sounds different from the man I married," she said with a shake of her head. "Derek had big dreams and ambitions, but I never saw an obsessive drive for material things or any desire to break the law, and I certainly never saw any hint of violence. Even if I could believe that Derek stole those paintings, I could never believe he attacked the security guard. But it's pointless for us to discuss it—we'll never agree."

"Maybe because we each had a different relationship with Derek."

"And you had one that lasted a lot longer," she said. "I know. I get it. Everyone here thinks they knew Derek better than I did." She drew in a breath, then let it out. "Maybe I didn't see him for who he was." Derek had told her as much in the letter he'd left for her. "But it's not even about Derek anymore."

"What do you mean?"

"When you were talking about meeting me in the bar all those years ago, I felt like you were talking about a different girl. Somewhere along the way, I lost myself. Some days I barely recognize my face in the mirror. I don't know who I am anymore."

"Then you should find out who you are. For instance, maybe you're a woman who likes to surf, and you just haven't figured that out yet."

She couldn't help but smile. "Nice segue."

"Just think about it. New experiences can be fun."

"Or they can be horrible."

"It just depends on if you see the glass half full or half empty," he said.

"It hasn't been half full in a long time. I used to be a lot more optimistic. I guess that's part of growing up."

"I don't know about that. My father is one of the most optimistic people I know, and he's in his sixties."

"Speaking of which, has he married Patty yet?"

"Who knows? It's been very quiet."

"A bad sign," she said with a smile.

"Tell me about it."

Lucas returned to the table with a picture he'd drawn. "I made this for you," he told Jason, climbing onto his lap. "It's a picture of you and me and Mommy flying the kite. And there's Digger, too."

The puppy lifted his head and gave a bark.

Jason laughed. "It's great. I love it. Thank you. You're really talented."

"Like my daddy," Lucas said. "Grandma Nancy says Daddy was the best artist in the world."

"He was very good," Jason said. "Can I keep this?"

"Are you going to put it on your refrigerator?"

Before Jason could reply, the front door opened, followed by Nancy's cheerful voice. Brianna's heart filled with dismay.

"Brianna, I know you said you didn't need any

food tonight, but I thought you might have changed your—" Nancy stopped abruptly as she entered the kitchen, her shocked eyes taking in the cozy scene. "What—what's going on here?"

"Jason brought us pizza," Lucas replied, while Brianna was searching for an answer. "And I made him a picture. He's going to put it on his refrigerator."

"No. No." Nancy put up her hand, shaking her head in denial. "This isn't possible. This can't be happening." She whirled around and ran from the room.

Brianna quickly followed her into the living room. "Nancy, wait."

Her mother-in-law looked at her with the shock of betrayal etched in every line of her face. "How could you, Brianna? How could you invite him over here?"

"I didn't invite him. He's house-sitting next door. He pulled up with a pizza, and Lucas invited him in." She could see that her words weren't even getting through. "I'm sorry, Nancy. But there's really nothing to be upset about."

"He hurt Derek. He hurt you. He destroyed our lives. How could you forget that?"

"I haven't forgotten, but—"

"There's no but." Nancy cut her off with an emphatic shake of her head. "You can't be friends with him. Not now. Not ever." She walked out of the house, slamming the door behind her.

*Oh, God.* Hurting Nancy was the last thing she'd

wanted to do. She took a deep breath and returned to the kitchen. Lucas was alone, playing on the floor with Digger.

"Jason said he had to go home," he told her.

Though Brianna was relieved that she didn't have to send him away, the damage had already been done. She just hoped she could find a way to fix it.

# TEN

Charlotte parked her car in front of Joe's house just as the sun was sinking below the horizon. She'd deliberately avoided any situation that would put them in a room alone together, but she had promised to drop off a recipe for chili, and by the time she'd finished with her patients for the day, Joe had already left the station. Since the cook-off was tomorrow, it was now or never.

Joe lived in a one-story house on the ocean side of the street and had a great view from his backyard. The last time she'd been in his house had been purely by chance. She'd been riding her bike and hadn't realized she'd ended up on his street until he pulled into the driveway. He'd invited her in for a drink, and she'd foolishly accepted. She hadn't had more than a sip when his wife, Rachel, had arrived, looking at them as if she'd just caught them in the middle of an affair.

That had been months ago. Joe hadn't invited her

back since, and she'd skipped this particular hill on her bike rides.

Despite her misgivings, she walked up to the house and rang the bell. Rufus, Joe's golden retriever, started barking. There was no sign of Joe, but his car was in the driveway. Hearing activity in the back-yard, she moved down the side of the house, stepped through the back gate, and stopped abruptly at the sight of Joe, bare-chested, swinging an axe at a log next to a huge pile of wood. His tan skin glistened with sweat; his muscles rippled with each powerful swing. She'd thought he was attractive in his uni-form, even hotter in his jeans. But with no shirt and tight, faded jeans, wow . . . Her breath stalled in her chest, and she was torn between a reckless desire to stay and a smarter desire to flee.

Rufus made the choice for her. He ran over and jumped up, his paws landing on her shoulders as he licked her face with happy kisses.

Distracted by the dog, Joe turned around, and the expression on his face wasn't at all welcoming. The raw bleakness in his eyes made a shiver run down her spine. She'd never seen him without his polite veneer.

"I—I just came to drop off the chili recipe," she said, feeling oddly nervous.

Joe dropped the axe and wiped the sweat off his brow with the back of his hand. "Okay," he said fi-nally.

She was almost sorry to see the control come back, but it was probably a good thing. She was a little too fascinated with the glimpse she'd had into a darker part of his soul.

Rufus barked and nuzzled her hand, demanding more attention.

"Rufus, sit," Joe ordered.

"It's fine. He's fine." She felt a little foolish with her inability to find a bigger vocabulary.

"Why don't you come in?" He strode toward the deck without waiting for her answer.

"All right," she muttered to herself. She climbed the stairs and walked through the sliding glass doors into the living room. Rufus ran ahead to the kitchen, while she stood awkwardly in the middle of the room. As she waited for Joe to return from wherever he'd gone, she glanced around.

The brown leather couch and armchair looked supremely comfortable for watching the flat-screen television over the fireplace. There was only one painting on the wall, a large seascape that matched the view outside the room. And that was about it. The simple furnishings suited Joe, but she couldn't help wondering if they suited Rachel. From what little Charlotte knew about his wife, she would have guessed her tastes ran more to sophisticated, modern design.

Joe came out of the bedroom, a button-down shirt now covering his chest. She was a little disappointed but also relieved. "Do you want some water?" he asked as he headed toward the kitchen.

"Uh, sure," she replied, following him to the doorway.

He grabbed two bottles of water from the refrigerator and tossed one to her. Then he unscrewed the top of his and took a long drink. He must have stopped in the bathroom to wash his face, because the beads of sweat had disappeared, but his cheeks still glowed from his recent exertion. "So let's see the recipe."

She set her water on the counter and took out the recipe she'd copied from her mother's collection. "This one won the cook-off four years ago. I took out a couple of ingredients and added some others from another recipe to make it unique. If it works, you'll have a good shot at the trophy."

"There's a trophy?" he asked, raising an eyebrow.

"There's always a trophy," she said with a smile, "especially when my mother is involved in the event. But don't get too excited—it stays in the church hall. You just get your name on it."

"How disappointing. What does it look like?"

"A large bowl with a gold spoon in it."

"Something worth shooting for," he said lightly, but there was no amusement in his eyes.

She frowned. "Are you all right?"

"I'm great."

"Really? Because you looked like you wanted to beat the crap out of that woodpile."

He hesitated for a moment and then walked past her. She followed him into the dining room. He picked up a large envelope, pulled out a thick wad of legal-sized papers, and handed them to her. "I got these today."

It took her a moment to realize what she was looking at. Stunned, she lifted her gaze to his. "Oh my God, Joe. Divorce papers?" They'd been having problems, but Joe had seemed so determined to work things out. She hadn't expected this.

"Apparently, Rachel decided to make this separation permanent," he said tightly.

"She didn't tell you they were coming? I'm sorry, it's none of my business," she added quickly.

"She claims she tried to tell me but I wouldn't listen. That was one of her favorite complaints about me—I never listen." He grabbed the papers out of her hand, stuffing them back into the envelope, as if he regretted having shown them to her. "So, what's involved with this recipe?"

"Joe, you don't have to make the chili. This is clearly not a good night for you."

"I've got nothing else to do, and frankly, I'd prefer to be busy." He took the recipe from her hand and perused it. "I don't think I have any of this stuff in the house."

"I could run down to the store for you."

"I've got a car, Charlotte, and I'm not dying."

"Aren't you just a little?" Her soft words drew his pained gaze. "You were together a long time, weren't you?"

"Since we were fifteen." His jaw tightened. "But that was then; this is now. I'd better get to the market so I can get started on this."

"You really don't have to do it. It's not that important."

"I thought your mother was going to suffer dire consequences if you didn't find her one more chili maker."

"She'll live. I'm more concerned about you."

"Don't be. It's not like this came out of nowhere. We've been having problems for a long time."

"Maybe you should talk to Rachel, see if there's a chance to work things out."

"We've been trying to do that for months—actually, longer than that. I thought the move here would be good for us, but it turns out it was only good for me. Rachel loves Los Angeles. That's where her life is."

"Have you considered going back?"

"I've considered a lot of things." He took a breath. "Let's get back to the chili," he said briskly. "If I'm going to make it, I want it hot."

"You like the spice, huh?"

"Always. My father is Latino. If you're not sweating while you're eating, it's not spicy enough." He tilted his head, giving her a considering look. "What about you, Charlotte? Do you like it hot?"

She drew in a quick breath at the dangerously reckless look in his eyes. She told herself not to encourage him, but she heard herself say, "Absolutely, as long as it's also good."

"Oh, it will be good."

"We should go to the store," she added, knowing that she needed to defuse the situation before they both did something they weren't ready to do.

"You don't have anything better to do—like hanging out with Reverend Schilling?"

"I don't want to talk about Andrew, and I'm guessing you don't want to talk about Rachel, so why don't we just concentrate on making the best chili that Angel's Bay will ever taste?"

"Just chili, huh?"

"Just chili."

"Okay, fine." He reached for his car keys on the side table, and they headed out to his car. "So, you're a good cook, are you?" he asked, as he opened the door for her.

"Heavens no, but I'm a really good shopper. You'll have to do the rest."

"This could quite possibly turn into a disaster."

She had no idea if he was talking about the chili or about them being together. "Well, whatever it is, it will be hot."

It had been a long time since he'd had had a woman cooking in his kitchen, Joe thought as he watched Charlotte chop an onion. Rachel had left town a month earlier, but even before that, she'd rarely cooked. They'd usually grabbed takeout or eaten at one of the restaurants in town.

When he'd first married Rachel, she'd loved trying new recipes out on him. That changed when she went back to school to get a real-estate license and then work full-time. He'd been okay with it, because she was happy, and he couldn't begrudge her a career that she enjoyed. But he'd always thought wistfully about his parents' marriage, all the fun they'd had cooking together. They'd bicker and kiss and cook with the same passion they exhibited in every aspect of their lives. Mealtimes had always been crowded, too, with six kids and whatever friends and family were around. There was always room for one more at the Silveira table.

He'd thought by now he would have his own brood of kids, but he was nearing forty and the vision of children was getting farther away. In the beginning, he'd wanted to put it off. His career was demanding. Then Rachel decided that she wanted to wait because of her career. Since then, it had never been the right time to start a family. Now he had divorce papers.

Sometimes Rachel liked the grand, dramatic gesture. Did she want him to come running to L.A., tell her that he was willing to give up his life for her if she would only rip up the papers? Or did she want him to sign the papers and end it? He didn't like the idea of failing at his marriage. His parents had set a great example and one he'd intended to follow. But he'd screwed up, or maybe Rachel had—or maybe it was both their faults.

He would let the papers sit for a while, give himself some time to think.

Charlotte swore as a chunk of onion flew off the cutting board, and he couldn't help smiling. Since they'd returned from the supermarket, Charlotte had attacked her assignment of chopping up tomatoes and onions with great enthusiasm. He enjoyed watching her go at it, but he was a little concerned that she'd slice off one of her fingers in the process.

"Slow down," he said. "Those are supposed to go into the chili, not on the floor."

"They're a little slippery."

"I hope you're better with a knife when you're doing surgery."

She made a face at him, her eyes blurring with tears. "Well, I'm usually not crying when I'm doing that."

"How do you not know how to cook, when your mother is supplying every ailing or depressed person in town with homemade dinners?"

"That's her, not me. She stopped trying to teach me how to cook a long time ago. It's one of the many ways I disappointed her." She pushed a sweaty strand of hair off her forehead. "You seem to know your way around the kitchen. Was your mom a good cook?"

"She was superb. She could make incredible hearty stews out of nothing, a trick passed down by her frugal Irish grandparents. And my father loved making tamales and enchiladas. Sunday dinners were always a big buffet. My aunts and uncles and cousins would all come over after church, and we'd stuff ourselves for the next four hours."

"Sounds a lot like my Sunday afternoons, only it wasn't so much blood relatives as our church family. But the house was always full. I miss that now.

Never thought I'd say that. At one time, I dreaded the Sunday afternoon command performance. I had to be on my best behavior, which even at its best wasn't all that good." She gathered the onions into a pile and tossed them into the pot. "There. All done."

"I think you were supposed to save some for the garnish."

"Oh, well, you can do those. I've shed enough tears for you." She laughed. "That sounds like the beginning of a country-western song."

"So you noticed my CD collection," he said, enjoying the teasing light in her eyes.

"On the way to the bathroom."

"It's not exactly on the way. You were snooping."

"Guilty." She ran her hands under the water, then dabbed her eyes with a paper towel. "I spied a little. You're not an easy person to get to know."

He'd made it a point not to let her get too close. He was still married, even if there were divorce papers nearby.

"What do you want to know about me?" He picked up a knife and started chopping the next onion.

"Something that no one else in Angel's Bay knows," she replied, leaning against the counter. "Which should be easy, since I'm betting very few people know you at all."

"I'm the chief of police. It helps to keep distance between myself and the community."

She tilted her head thoughtfully. "I appreciate the need for objectivity, but you strike me as someone who always holds his cards close to his chest, even when he's not on duty."

"And you strike me as someone who couldn't bluff her way through a card game to save her life."

Her eyes sparked. "I'm not that bad. I've kept a few secrets over the years."

"Why don't you tell me one of yours?"

"I asked you first."

He finished slicing the onion and then tossed the pieces into a small bowl.

"How did you do that without crying?" Charlotte asked.

"I'm a man."

She rolled her eyes. "Okay, tough guy, so what's one of your deep, dark secrets?"

He wiped his hands on a paper towel. "I can't think of any."

"Sure you can." She picked up the chili powder and tossed another heaping spoonful into the pot.

"Hey, go easy on that," he said.

"I thought you wanted it hot. But I'll go easy if you tell me something about yourself."

"Did anyone ever tell you that you're very stubborn?"

"Almost everyone I've ever met." She gave him an unrepentant smile. "Stop stalling."

"Okay." He thought for a moment, wondering how honest he wanted to be. He wasn't used to sharing his past. But there was something about Charlotte that made him want to talk. "I joined a gang when I was thirteen years old. To show my loyalty, I had to steal a CD player from an electronics store. I wasn't a very good thief, and I got caught."

"What happened to you?" she asked, curiosity and concern on her face.

"The cop who caught me was Latino. He'd grown up in the neighborhood where I lived, and his brother had died in a gang when he was sixteen years old. He took me home and told my parents to lock me up, or else he would. He scared the shit out of me, but he probably saved my life. Fortunately, my parents were able to move a couple of years later, so it was easier for my younger brothers to stay out of trouble."

"And you became a cop so you could return the favor."

"Something like that. I still had a thirst for excitement. I just decided to work on the right side of the law."

"There aren't a lot of gangs here in Angel's Bay."

"Thank God for that. I worked gangs and vice for almost a decade in L.A. I tried to save some kids. Sometimes it worked. Most times it didn't. The problem never went away. For every kid I got out, another one took his place. And the drug situation was just as bad. I never felt like I was making a dent."

He sighed. He might as well tell her the rest since he'd come this far.

"I had a partner who started taking shortcuts, crossing lines that shouldn't have been crossed. If the courts weren't going to put some of these guys away, he would. I started thinking the same way. I beat the crap out of someone one day—justice delivered personally by me. I could have killed him; thank God someone pulled me off him in time. He was a rapist and a murderer, but I wasn't supposed to be his judge or his jury."

"Oh, Joe," Charlotte said, her eyes filled with compassion. "That's terrible, but who could have blamed you?"

"A lot of people. I'm supposed to follow the law, not break it. I realized I'd reached a turning point. I quit the department a few weeks later, took some time to get my head together. I worked construction for my brother-in-law for a while, babysat the nieces and nephews, passed the time. Then my uncle Carlos died and left this house to me, and I drove up here to see the place. I was going to fix it up and sell it, but as soon as I walked through the door, I knew I was home. Luckily, the police department here needed a new chief. It all worked out."

"It must be vastly different to be a police officer here in Angel's Bay."

"Like night and day. I love what I'm doing now. I never stopped wanting to be a cop; I was just overwhelmed with the grimness of it all. It was changing me, and I didn't like who I was becoming, so I made the move. Unfortunately, it wasn't a move Rachel wanted me to make."

"She must have seen what your job was doing to you."

"She was busy building her real-estate business.

Her view of L.A. was mansions in Beverly Hills and beachfront property in Malibu, celebrity parties and designer clothes. We were living in the same town but not the same world."

"Her world doesn't sound that bad."

"It's not bad; it's just not what I want. Okay, your turn."

She thought for a moment. "My favorite color is yellow."

He laughed. "We're sharing secrets here."

A wide grin spread across her face. "That *is* a secret. Everyone else thinks it's blue."

"You're going to leave me out on this ledge all by myself? Come on, Charlotte. Tell me something no one else knows."

She hesitated for a long moment, her smile slowly disappearing. "I really wish you weren't married."

He swallowed hard. He hadn't been expecting her to admit that. "I might not be married for very much longer."

"I know," she whispered.

The air between them sizzled with anticipation . . . then his cell phone rang. He wanted to let it go, but with the festival starting, he'd promised to be on call. He took it out of his pocket, even more disturbed when he saw the number. "It's Rachel."

Charlotte let out a breath. "Talk about perfect timing. You should answer it. And I should go."

"Charlotte, wait." He stepped in front of her. "I'd rather talk to you."

"I don't want to be a reason for you to walk away

from your marriage, Joe. I like you, but I wasn't raised by a minister for nothing. I feel guilty enough for flirting with you. You should call your wife back, because I don't think you're ready to say it's over."

"You don't know what I feel."

Her gaze was direct and steady. "I don't think you do, either. If you were sure, you would have signed the divorce papers."

He wanted to argue, but how could he? "You still don't have to go, Charlotte. We haven't done anything wrong."

"Not yet. Let's keep it that way."

Brianna got up early Friday morning after a restless night of worrying about how she would smooth things over with Nancy. After letting Digger out of his crate and setting Lucas up with cereal and cartoons in the kitchen, she headed into the attached garage where Derek's boxes were stored.

Ever since Jason had told her about Steve Markham's visit and his suggestion that she might have a clue she didn't know she had, she'd been wondering if that was a possibility. It was time to unpack.

An hour later, she'd unearthed very little of personal interest. It was obvious that Nancy had been so rattled by Derek's trial that she'd simply packed up everything in his town house, most of which was of no importance. As Brianna got deeper into one box, however, she found some old, yellowed newspapers dating back twenty or thirty years. The articles seemed to be about Wyatt and his successes as an artist. Some were from the local Angel's Bay newspaper, others from national magazines featuring his art. Apparently, Derek had studied his grandfather's work in great detail. Had Wyatt known how much his grandson had admired him?

Her heart sped up as her gaze fell on a slim packet of letters tied together with an old, faded ribbon. The paper was thin and yellowed and addressed to Francine Kane, Derek's ancestor from the shipwreck. Her heart skipped a beat.

She carefully unwrapped the tie, pulled a letter out, and skimmed the passage. It was short, and the words were a mix of Spanish and English. Fortunately, after years of living aboard, she could read both.

> *My sweet Francine,*
>
> *How sweet our time has been. You brought me out of the dark and into the light, back from the edge of despair to the brink of possibility. I will treasure our nights together for as long as I live. I cannot give you my heart, for it belongs to another, but I give you what is left of me.*
>
> *Victor*

*Victor?* Victor Delgado and Francine Kane had been lovers? Why had she never heard that part of the story? Obviously, Derek had known.

Had Nancy? Nancy had told her all about the

quilt square that Francine had sewn for her dead husband, Marcus. She'd talked about the two boys Francine had raised alone and then with her second husband, George Weller. But Nancy had never mentioned a tie between Victor and Francine.

Brianna opened the second letter, feeling as if Victor wasn't the only one standing on the brink of possibility.

> *Francine,*
>
> > *Why did you run from me? Did I scare you? I am sorry. I drink because Eve haunts me. I have failed her. I cannot paint her as I knew her. I cannot put what I see in my head on the canvas. At night I dream of her and see her tears, her anger, her regret that I didn't know her. You must help me as I have tried to help you. Please, I am desperate. Come to me.*
>
> > > > *Victor*

Brianna could feel his desperation in her soul. He was the tormented artist, forever haunted by his dead lover. It had never seemed so real before. Had Derek felt the same incredibly strong link to the past when he'd read these letters? Had the paintings captivated him so much that he had to have them?

Her heart thumped in her chest. She didn't want to believe he'd lied to her for five long years, but he'd certainly never shared the connection between Francine Kane and Victor Delgado. Why hide that? It could only be because it would have meant something to someone.

Turning her attention back to the packet, she realized there was only one letter left, and the handwriting was different, more precise, neat, feminine.

> *Victor,*
>
>     *No amount of passion can replace the love you felt for Eve, just as nothing can ease my grief over Marcus. We were wrong to run away from our pain. We must face it, fight it, cherish it, for it is all we have left of them. We must not speak again. Already there is suspicion. No one can ever know about the baby. I will say that Marcus left me with this precious gift before he died in the shipwreck. Please know that I will love our son well, and he will be our hope for the future.*
>
>     *Eve loved you, Victor, as you loved her. Don't ever doubt that. And I loved you, too.*
>
>                                    *Francine*

Brianna's head spun. Not only had Victor and Francine had an affair after the wreck, but they'd conceived a child.

Had Francine sent this letter to Victor? If she had, why would it be in the pile with those she'd received from him? Perhaps she hadn't found the courage to tell him. Maybe the secret had never been revealed—at least, not to Victor.

And what had become of their son?

Her breath caught in her throat. Was Derek descended from Victor and Francine? Had Delgado blood run through his veins?

She drew in a quick breath, terrified by that thought. Had the blood connection given Derek an even stronger, more personal motivation to steal the paintings? Was that why he'd kept the tie a secret, so that he wouldn't give the police more ammunition against him?

But the value of the paintings was in the money they were worth, not in any relationship Victor Delgado might have had to Francine Kane. These letters didn't prove anything, except that Derek had been holding back information. They'd all spent months wondering who had the most motivation to want those paintings. And never in all that time had Derek mentioned the family tie to Victor Delgado.

Nancy and Rick couldn't have known. They would have told her.

That left Wyatt. Had Derek shared the information with his grandfather? Or was that where Derek had gotten the information in the first place? Katherine Markham had told her that Wyatt was obsessed with Delgado's work. Was this why? Did he have a blood tie to the dead painter? Had she actually stumbled on a new piece of information?

And if so, would the information clear Derek's name or make him look more guilty?

The doorbell rang, shocking her out of the past. Scrambling to her feet, she went to answer it, Lucas and Digger following close behind.

Katherine Markham stood on the porch, dressed

in a beautiful blue suit, her hair pulled back from her face. Brianna was suddenly very aware of her pajamas and bathrobe. A quick glance at the clock in the living room told her it was after ten. She'd lost all track of time.

"I'm sorry to bother you," Katherine said. "I'm on my way to work, and I wanted to drop this off." She held up a large gray sketch pad.

"Please, come in," Brianna told her.

"Hi, Lucas," Katherine said with a smile. "I brought you something." She sat down on the couch and put the pad on the coffee table. "This was your dad's. He used to draw in it when he was in high school. I thought you might want it."

Lucas gave a vigorous nod. Brianna sat next to Katherine, pulling Lucas onto her lap. She felt a little tense at the idea of looking at Derek's art book. The pad reminded her that she needed to spend some time going through the sketches Derek had done in prison, but for some reason, she hadn't been able to open that envelope again. His words had made her afraid, because he'd hinted that there were things she didn't know, maybe things she didn't want to know.

"Look, a sea monster," Lucas said, calling her attention to the drawing Katherine had opened up to.

Brianna was surprised by the lighthearted sketch of a sea monster appearing before a boatload of shocked tourists. From everything she'd heard about

Wyatt training Derek to be a superb artist, she'd never expected to see such whimsy.

"These were for fun," Katherine said, answering her unspoken question. "The art colony runs a summer day camp for kids. Derek and I used to teach there. This kind of art was like a day off, something just for the kids."

Finally, a sweeter side of Derek, Brianna thought, gazing down at the sea monster with genuine appreciation. She'd been doubting herself, wondering if she'd seen traits in Derek that simply weren't there, but he *had* had a sense of humor, a love of fun. This was proof of that.

"Thank you," she said to Katherine. "This means a lot."

"Just some silly sketches," Katherine said with a shrug. "I wish you could have seen some of Derek's really brilliant work. Even at the sketch stage, he had an eye for detail, an interesting viewpoint."

"Actually, I do have some sketches. Derek did them in prison. I just received them from his attorney. I haven't really had a chance to study them yet."

"Really? What kinds of sketches?"

"Memories of his life."

"I'd love to see them. If you don't mind sharing, of course."

"Uh, sure," she said slowly, wondering if she shouldn't keep them private. Derek had chosen not to share them with anyone but her. She cleared her throat, stalling. "But not today. I have to take Lucas to the Kanes and go to work. I've taken on a shift at the quilt shop."

"That's great. The quilt shop is the heart of the town."

"Do you quilt?"

"No. I've designed a few for my friends, but I don't sew. My art is strictly canvas-based." Katherine got to her feet. "I'd better get to my own job."

"Thanks again. I really appreciate it. Aside from Nancy and Rick, there aren't a lot of people around here who remember Derek fondly." She walked Katherine to the door. "By the way, I heard your uncle came to see me yesterday, but I wasn't home. Do you know what he wanted?"

"Uncle Steve was here?" Katherine asked in surprise. "I have to say that shocks me a little."

"Me, too."

"I can ask him what he wanted, but I'm not sure he'll tell me. We're not all that close."

"That's fine. I'm sure he'll be back if he wants something." Should she ask Katherine about the Wyatt-Victor connection? she wondered. But she didn't know how much information Katherine shared with the Markhams, and she didn't want to tip Wyatt off if the blood tie might be an important clue in finding the paintings. So she simply said good-bye.

As she shut the door, it occurred to her that she'd been putting all of her attention on Wyatt, thinking he was the one who hadn't wanted to donate the paintings, but there were two other people involved:

Gloria and Steve Markham. Perhaps one of them had wanted to keep the paintings.

Still, if Wyatt was the blood descendant, then he had the purest motive. Or Derek had found the perfect way to get back at his grandfather . . .

She sighed. So far, everything she learned made Derek seem more guilty. Maybe finding the truth would only bring more pain.

# ELEVEN

"I upset Nancy," Brianna told Rick when she dropped Lucas off at the Kanes' house on her way to work later that day. Lucas had already taken Digger inside, so it was just the two of them on the front step.

"She just had to run an errand; she'll be right back," Rick said, clearing his throat somewhat awkwardly.

Brianna didn't buy that for a second. Nancy hadn't wanted to see her; that's why she'd been conveniently absent. "Jason is house-sitting next door to me. He's run into us a few times and made friends with Lucas. That's why he was at the house last night."

"That's what Nancy said. Lucas told us Jason made him the kite, too. Nancy and I didn't like it, but we figured it was just something you couldn't get out of. Lucas gets his mind set on things, and he probably pushed you into letting Jason help."

Rick was giving her an excuse, but she knew it wasn't all Lucas's fault.

"But when Nancy saw Jason having dinner with you," Rick continued, "well, it hurt her. She said he was sitting in Derek's place. It made her cry."

Brianna drew in a breath, seeing the pain in her father-in-law's eyes. "I'm sorry. It wasn't planned. Jason came by with a pizza, and it was a spur-of-the-moment thing."

"How long is he going to be next door?"

"Just a few more days."

"Well, let's hope those will pass quickly. Unless you're changing your mind about him?" he asked with a worried look.

She had to take a second to think about that. "It was easy to blame Jason for everything, but he wasn't the only one who sent Derek to jail," she said slowly.

"He was the only one who was a friend," Rick reminded her. "Derek felt betrayed by Jason. And if you become friends with him, it's like you're turning your back on Derek. Do you think Derek would be happy that you and Lucas had dinner with Jason?"

"No, I don't think he would be," she said quietly.

His gaze softened. "I know it's hard on you, Brianna, moving to a new place, trying to raise that little boy on your own. There are a lot of people in this town you can be friends with—perhaps Jason shouldn't be one of them." He paused. "Now, I'd better go see what Lucas is up to. Oh, and we're going to the chili cook-off tonight if you and Lucas want to come with us."

"I'll think about it." Jason might be there, and she wasn't up to another scene, especially in front of the entire town. She needed to take a step back, consider her options.

When she was with Jason—when he smiled at her, when he kissed her—it was easy to forget all the reasons why they couldn't be friends or more. But when she was with the Kanes, she was reminded of how much they had gone through together, how Rick and Nancy had supported her through some very dark days. They were her family. They loved her, and there weren't many people who did. How could she choose Jason over them? She shouldn't even be thinking about making such a choice, but she was, and that scared her the most.

Her husband was avoiding her, Kara thought with a sigh. She'd once known Colin inside and out, but ever since he'd awoken from his coma, he'd changed. He was no longer the happy, gregarious, adoring Irishman who couldn't keep his hands off her. Now he was impatient, short-tempered, and distant. As soon as they'd arrived at the church auditorium for the chili cook-off, he'd disappeared, making some excuse about helping his cop buddies set up their stations. But the truth was that he just wanted to get away from her.

He'd even slept on the couch the last few nights, claiming he was restless and didn't want to wake her up. Colin, who once couldn't sleep without touching her, now wanted to be in another room. He could barely bring himself to give her a quick peck on the lips, and he only held the baby when he had no other choice. She didn't know if he was afraid or if something had turned off in his brain.

What if he didn't want her anymore? How could she live without him? He'd been her whole life since she was a child.

A wave of panic ran through her, and her daughter began to fuss in her arms, obviously sensing her mother's distress. "It's okay," Kara crooned. "Everything will be fine. I didn't come this far to give up on him now. I hope he's not giving up on me, either."

Faith blinked a few times and then drifted back to sleep, reassured that all was well with her world.

"What a little angel," Charlotte commented as she joined Kara at the back of the room. "I bet she doesn't look this sweet at two o'clock in the morning, though."

"Actually, she does. I spend a lot of time just staring at her. I never imagined I'd feel so close to another human being. I thought it would be like loving Colin, but it's even deeper than that."

Charlotte gave her a soft smile. "You sound like a new mother."

"I know," Kara said with a helpless smile. "I'm totally in love with her."

"Where's the new daddy?"

"Over there talking to Joe and Warren." She

tipped her head toward the far side of the room. "They're hoping to beat the fire department this year. I guess the chief put in an entry."

Charlotte flushed a little. "Yeah, he did."

Kara gave her a curious look. "Did you have something to do with that?"

"We were short on cops since Colin bowed out this year."

Another example of how Colin had changed. There had been a time when he would have died before giving up his spot in the chili cook-off. He'd always taken pride in his chili, even when it wasn't all that good. But this year, he'd begged off early. She'd offered to do all the chopping and prep work, but he'd insisted that he wasn't up to it.

"Colin is not himself," she said.

"I hope you don't think I was complaining," Charlotte said quickly. "No one expected Colin to enter, after everything the two of you have gone through. The last thing you need to worry about is the chili cook-off."

"It might have been good for him. He stresses over not being able to do his normal activities, yet sometimes when he has the opportunity, he ignores it. I don't get it."

Charlotte put her arm around her shoulders for a quick hug. "Things are rough, huh?"

"I'm that transparent?"

"Your brave soldier face is beginning to crack. What's going on?"

Kara lowered her voice so they wouldn't be overheard. "You know how you told me I could have sex anytime now? Well, Colin wasn't as excited about the idea as I was. He hasn't come near me since."

"That's not uncommon. You just had his baby. You're breastfeeding. Some men feel a little jealous of the baby, and they have trouble adapting to their wives being mothers. Those breasts used to be his territory, and where you and Colin are concerned, *only* his territory. You've never slept with anyone else, and vice versa, right?"

"And what if that's what's bothering him? What if he looked his mortality in the eye and wondered what the hell he was thinking only having sex with one woman in his lifetime?"

"Wow, you are flipping out, Kara," Charlotte said, shaking her head in amazement. "I'm sure that's not what he's thinking."

"I am going a little crazy," she admitted. "Colin won't talk to me. He won't touch me. And it's not like I'm dying to have sex, it's just that I—I miss him. I miss *us*. I miss the way things were. I thought everything would be the same when he woke up."

Charlotte gave her another hug. "You'll work things out. You and Colin are a matched set; there's no breaking you up. Just give him some time. Colin loves you more than anyone in this world, and I know you feel the same. Frankly, the two of you have set a really high standard for the rest of us. I can't imagine having what you have. You're so connected, so honest with each other."

"We used to be. But we'll get it back," Kara said with renewed determination.

"Of course you will. Shall we try out some chili? I'm starving."

"Sounds good." Kara put Faith in her stroller, and they made their way down the aisles, debating which chili looked the most interesting.

Their progress was slow, as they were constantly stopped by friends and neighbors eager to see the baby and to say hello. Despite Charlotte's declaration of hunger, she didn't seem to be in a hurry to sample chili, instead leading the way toward Colin and Joe.

"I know what you're doing," Kara told her. "But you can't matchmake when I'm already married to the guy." She stopped to let some people go in front of them. She wasn't ready for everyone to see how disconnected she and Colin were.

"Maybe this isn't about you," Charlotte said with a mischievous sparkle in her eyes.

For a moment, Kara was confused, then she realized the focus of Charlotte's attention. "Oh, Charlie, not Joe! He's married."

"I know that. We're just friends."

"Are you?" she asked worriedly.

"Yes, we are," Charlotte said, but she didn't quite look Kara in the eye.

"Joe and Rachel have been having problems, but do you really want to get in the middle of a marriage?"

"I'm not in the middle. I just enjoy his company."

"And he's hot."

"Well, there is that," Charlotte conceded with a laugh. "Relax, Kara, I'm not breaking any rules."

"I'm more concerned about your heart. You like to keep things light and casual, but you're more vulnerable than you let on. If you want to get involved with someone, why not Andrew? He's just as good-looking and has a lot less baggage."

"Not where I'm concerned. Our history follows us around—not to mention all the other single women in town. Look at him now. He's surrounded."

Andrew was in the middle of a group of women ranging from their twenties to their late fifties. "He does have a lot of groupies," Kara admitted. "Chicks and cougars."

"He has that holy charisma thing going. It's very powerful. My father had women lusting after him, too, but my mother always ran them off."

"You could do the same for Andrew. He likes you. Did you ever find out why he canceled dinner?"

"No, he made some vague excuse about something coming up, and he hasn't asked me out again. Typical man. As soon as they hook you, they don't want you anymore."

"I don't think that's true," Kara said.

"Well, it's just as well. I'm happy being single. So stop stalling. Let's go see what the guys are up to."

The guys were eating chili and talking about basketball. Colin gave Kara a smile, and she felt some of her tension dissipate. He looked like the old Colin. He'd just needed to get out of the house and be around people.

"Hey, Charlotte," Colin said. "Try some of that chili over there. You're going to love it."

Kara wondered about the smile Joe and Colin exchanged—obviously, something was up. Joe ladled some chili into two small bowls, handing one to her and the other to Charlotte.

"Uh, Kara, hang on," Colin said.

But he was too late. The fiery burn was already sweeping down her throat. Colin handed her his bottle of water, and she took a long gulp. "Oh, my God," she said when she could talk again. "That's so hot."

"It can't be that hot," Charlotte said.

"Try it, then," Kara suggested.

"Yeah, try it," Joe echoed.

Charlotte took a much smaller bite than Kara, grimacing as she swallowed. "That's awful. How did that happen? I barely put any pepper in."

"*You* made this chili, Charlotte?" Kara asked.

"I helped Joe, but he did most of it," Charlotte declared, flushing a little under the scrutiny.

Kara turned to Joe. "You let her cook? Do you have a death wish? Everyone knows Charlotte can't cook."

"I told him that," Charlotte said.

Joe's eyes sparkled as he looked at Charlotte. "I thought you were being modest."

"I'm never modest."

"What got into you, Charlotte?" Colin asked. "I've never known you to pick up a knife unless you were cutting someone open."

"I was trying to be helpful," Charlotte repeated. "Didn't you taste this before you brought it here, Joe?"

"No. I had it in the refrigerator all night. I just heated it up when I got here. But don't worry; I haven't let anyone else get close to it. I was just about to take it away when Colin thought it might be fun to let you try it."

"Nice," Kara said, giving her husband a playful slap on the arm.

Colin laughed. "I tried to warn you, but you jumped in too fast."

Joe grabbed the pot. "I'll take this out to the car,"

"Good idea," Charlotte said. "I'll bring the rest of this stuff." She picked up the condiment bowls and followed Joe out of the auditorium.

When they were gone, Kara turned to Colin, happy to see the smile on his face. She almost asked him how he was doing, if he was tired and needed to go home, but stopped herself. He was frustrated with her constantly watching over him. He was an adult; he could decide when he'd had enough. "I think Charlotte has a crush on Joe," she said.

Colin's eyes widened. "No way. She wouldn't get involved with a married man."

"I didn't say they were involved, but there are definitely sparks between those two. Didn't you see the way they looked at each other?"

"I was too busy looking at you." He moved in closer, his arm tightening around her waist. "I'm sorry, Kara."

"You don't have to apologize," she began, but he cut her off with a shake of his head.

"I do. You've been incredible the last few weeks,

and I've been an ass. Will you let me make it up to you?"

Her eyes blurred with tears as she looked into Colin's eyes and saw him really present for the first time. "There's nothing to make up. I love you, even when you're an ass."

"I love you back." He gazed at her with the tender smile she'd always adored. "I've been in a weird space, like when you take a nap and wake up disoriented and you don't know what time it is or even if you were really asleep. That's how I've felt almost every day. I haven't handled it very well."

"I'm glad you told me." She put her hand against his solid chest, then stood on her tiptoes and kissed him lovingly on the lips.

"I can't believe Jason was right," Colin said.

"About what?"

"He said if I told you how I felt, you'd get all hot for me. I didn't think it was that easy."

She smiled. "Where you're concerned, I've always been easy. You know that."

"I wanted to tell you how I felt for a while. But I couldn't quite put it into words," he said on a more serious note. "I knew I was pissing you off, but I couldn't stop myself. It was a little easier to breathe when you weren't around. You always had your eyes on me. You caught every little screwup. I couldn't get anything past you. I felt a little ashamed."

His words stung a bit, but she appreciated the honesty. "I spent three months watching you sleep, Colin—waiting for some flicker of your eyelid, some twitch of your fingers, something that would tell me you were still there. I guess I watch you now because I'm afraid you'll slip away from me when I'm not looking. I'll try to back off."

"I'm not going anywhere, Kara. I'm healing. I'm not leaving you." He kissed her again. "Want to go home and make out?"

She laughed at the familiar question. Ever since they were thirteen, he'd been asking her to go somewhere and make out. "Absolutely."

Before they could move, Jason came up to them. He looked tired, and there was a hard note in his eyes, an irritated set to his jaw.

"Hey," he said shortly.

"What's wrong?" she asked.

"Nothing. I'm just hungry. Any chili recommendations?"

"The only one I tasted was really bad," Kara said. "What about you, Colin?"

"Warren's is good, but Dan McCarthy has a line out the door, so I think there's a good chance the fire boys are going to whip our butts this year."

Jason nodded, but he seemed distracted.

"Have you talked to Brianna again?" Kara asked, sure that this mood had something to do with Derek's widow.

"I saw her last night. Is she here?"

"I don't think so," Kara replied.

"What happened last night?" Colin asked.

Jason didn't answer, his gaze on someone approaching. Kara turned around and saw Nancy Kane heading toward them like a woman with a mission, which was surprising, since the Kanes had avoided Jason for the past five years.

"I have just one thing to say to you, Jason," Nancy said abruptly. She didn't seem to be aware that anyone else was there. "Brianna and Lucas are all I have left of the child you took from me." Her voice shook with rage. "I treated you like my own son, and you turned on Derek. Now, you stay away from them. Do you hear me? You stay away."

Jason turned pale as she left. The people around them had gone silent during the brief confrontation. Kara exchanged a quick glance with Colin and saw the concern in his eyes.

Colin turned to the crowd. "So who has a chili recommendation for me?" he asked, drawing the attention away from Jason. That was Colin, always the protector.

Kara put her hand on Jason's arm as the quiet broke. "What the heck did you do?"

"I had dinner with Brianna and Lucas," he said tightly. "Nancy walked in on us."

"You need to leave Brianna alone." Too many people could get hurt, including him.

"I'm trying," he said.

"Try harder."


"Sorry I ruined your chili," Charlotte told Joe as he stuck the pot in the trunk of his car. "You must have distracted me."

"At least we didn't poison anyone. That wouldn't have sat well with your mother."

She laughed. "True, but she'd blame it on me, not you. She has a weakness for good-looking men who stand up for truth and justice."

"I need to get to know your mother a little better. You have me intrigued."

"She'd be perfectly lovely to you. It's just me she doesn't get along with. We're very different, and we've never understood each other. I don't think we ever will. Are you going back inside?"

"No. My mouth is still burning."

"Mine, too. We could go for ice cream." She saw the hesitation in his eyes and realized she'd over-stepped. "But I should probably stay here and help tabulate the votes."

"It's just that it's a small town, Charlotte."

"I know. It was a dumb idea." She drew in a breath. "I think I'll take a little walk before I go back inside. I've always loved the church grounds at night. I used to climb out my bedroom window after my parents went to sleep and come over here."

"To fool around with Andrew?"

She smiled. "On a few occasions, but mostly I just wandered. I could be myself in the dark shad-ows. I was out from under my mother's watchful eye, so I was free."

"Show me where you used to go," he suggested.

If going out for ice cream in a public place was a bad idea, then wandering around the church grounds in the dark was even worse. But she nodded and led the way through the trees. They walked in silence. Joe wasn't much of a talker unless he had something to say, and she kind of liked that.

She paused under a tree with sprawling branches that provided a thick, protective canopy over the grass. "This was my favorite tree for climbing. I was quite the tomboy. I once made it all the way to the top."

"You like high places, don't you? That's why I always see you running or biking up the hills around town."

"I guess I do." She was a little surprised that he'd noticed that about her. "There's something about a view that opens up the world to me. Another favorite spot of mine is the bell tower. Want to see?"

"Sure."

She headed back toward the empty church, taking him in through the side door, then led him up a narrow, winding staircase to the top of the tower. The old bell had been removed years ago, but the open windows provided a great view.

"In the daytime, you can see the ocean and the ships coming in and out of the harbor," she said. "At night, this place is great for stargazing."

As Joe moved next to her, her breath caught in her chest. She'd forgotten about the cozy, intimate nature of the tower.

"Did you come up here with Andrew?" he asked.

"You're very curious about what Andrew and I did together. Should I start asking you about your old girlfriends?"

"There aren't any. I began dating Rachel when I was fifteen. We had a couple of brief breakups during college, but I never went out with anyone else on a long-term basis."

She was surprised that he hadn't had more relationships, but his words also reminded her that Rachel had always been the one for him and probably always would be.

"What about you, Charlotte? Any other guys besides Andrew?"

"Dozens," she said lightly.

"I'm talking serious boyfriends."

"I don't do serious." Even in the shadows, she could see his curious look and regretted her impulsive choice of words. "I've been busy with college, medical school, internship, residency, then moving back here. When would I have had the time?"

"I don't think it's just about time. What happened to make you not want to do serious? Broken heart?"

"Oh, please, everyone's heart breaks in high school. Some on a weekly basis."

"I told you one of my secrets," he reminded her. "You still owe me. Tell me why you left Angel's Bay."

"I wanted to be a doctor."

"Always?"

She sighed at his persistence. No wonder everyone in town thought he was a good interrogator. "Well, not always," she conceded.

"Why medicine?"

No one had ever asked her why she'd become

a doctor. And in the quiet of the dark night, she found herself wanting to tell him. "I had a miscarriage a long time ago. I didn't get medical care when I should have, and the baby died. I wanted to find a way to make up for it, to save someone else's child. Since I was good at science, I went into medicine."

"I'm sorry, Charlotte."

His quiet words brought an unexpected tear to her eyes.

"You don't have to be. I'm fine."

Joe held out his arms, and after a moment, she moved into his embrace. She rested her head against his chest, listening to the steady beat of his heart. When she'd lost her baby, she'd desperately wanted someone to comfort her, but she'd had to go through it alone. Her mother had made sure of that.

She reluctantly pulled away, knowing that she couldn't use the old tragedy to create more trouble. "Thanks, Joe."

He tilted his head, gazing down at her. "Does Andrew know?"

"I never said he was the father."

"You haven't said he wasn't."

"The only person who knew I was pregnant was my mother, and, believe me, she didn't tell anyone. I was a disgrace. I had shamed the family."

"She didn't tell your father?"

"Oh, no. She thought my mistake would reflect poorly on her."

"What would she have done if you hadn't miscarried?"

"She was planning to send me away, to create some fake trip to the other end of the country. I probably would have gone, too, because I was confused and scared, and she was very formidable."

"Now I understand why there's so much anger between you. If one of my sisters had gotten pregnant in high school, my mother would have been there rocking her in her arms. She wouldn't have considered sending her away."

Charlotte fought back tears at the image. "Your mom sounds very kind. Now I know where you get it from. We should go, Joe. It's getting late." And she was starting to like him way too much.

"All right. But just so you know, Charlotte, your secret is safe with me."

She smiled softly. "I wouldn't have told you if I didn't know that."

# TWELVE

"Won't Jason be mad if I don't go kite flying with him?" Lucas asked worriedly as they waited in the living room for Rick to arrive late Saturday morning.

"I'm sure he won't be," Brianna replied, sitting next to him on the couch. Rick had called the night before to set up the kite-flying expedition. He'd made it clear that kite flying was a family tradition he wanted to share with his grandson, and she'd agreed, hoping to smooth the waters.

"But Jason is going to come and see me fly in the contest tomorrow, isn't he?" Lucas persisted

"I'm not sure," she said.

Lucas's face fell. "He doesn't like me anymore, does he?"

She was shocked by the question. "Of course he does. Why would you say that?"

"Daddy got mad at me and didn't want me to see him. I heard you telling Grandma on the phone."

"No, no, honey," she said, pulling him onto her

lap. "Your daddy loved you very much. He didn't want you to visit him because he wanted you to have more time to play with your friends. He wasn't mad at all." She kissed away the tears on his cheeks. "Your father adored you. Don't ever think that he didn't."

"How come he couldn't live with us?"

"He just couldn't," she said, knowing he was too young to understand.

"What if *you* do something wrong, and they make you go live in the big ugly house?"

She wished she could erase the fear from his eyes—with time, she hoped he'd stop worrying that she might leave him, too. "That won't ever happen. We are always going to be together. There's no splitting us up."

Lucas smiled. "I love you, Mommy."

"I love you, too." The doorbell rang. "There's Grandpa. Go get your jacket," she said as she got up.

Rick had on jeans and a windbreaker, and excitement lit his brown eyes. "Is my boy ready to go?"

"Yes, he is," she said as Lucas struggled into his jacket. "He's really excited about this."

"Me, too. It's been a while since I flew a kite."

She turned to Lucas. "Be good for Grandpa, okay? Stay with him, and listen to whatever he says."

"I will, Mommy. I promise."

"He's always good with me," Rick told her.

"I'm glad. Thanks for taking him out. He loves spending time with you."

Rick gave a small nod, his lips tightening with emotion. "We love him, too. We thank God every day we have him in our lives." He paused. "Nancy was sorry she missed you yesterday. But we'll see you tonight at the picnic in the park, right?"

"You bet." Brianna walked them out to the porch, watching as they got into Rick's car and drove down the street. Jason's Jeep was in the next driveway. She hadn't seen him since the night Nancy had interrupted their dinner.

And she wasn't going to see him now, she told herself firmly as she headed back inside.

She shut the door and turned the dead bolt for good measure. She needed to concentrate on unpacking, to think about Derek. But it was Jason's image that had been playing in her mind lately, and she couldn't seem to get it out.

The doorbell rang again, and her heart leaped. She knew it was him even before she opened the door.

Jason wore faded blue jeans and a T-shirt that clung to his broad shoulders. His brown hair was curling and damp, either from the ocean surf or from a recent shower. His face was cleanly shaven, his mouth so . . . so sexy. She really needed to see him in his cop's uniform again. She wanted that ruthless, unyielding guy in her head, not this one.

Clearing her throat, she realized he was checking her out, too. She was casually dressed in jeans and a knit top. She hadn't done much with her hair or makeup, thinking she'd be spending most of the day unpacking the last few boxes in the garage. Now she wished she'd thrown on a little lip gloss.

The silence lengthened between them, crackling

with tension. She wanted to invite him in but was afraid to do so. There was something burning in his eyes, something that looked like anger . . . or was it hunger? A shiver ran down her spine.

"Nancy came up to me at the cook-off last night," he said, breaking the silence. "She told me to stay the hell away from you."

Rick had said nothing about a confrontation between them. "So why are you here?" she asked warily.

"Because I *can't* stay away from you." He stepped into her living room, kicked the door shut behind him, and hauled her into his arms.

His mouth on hers was hard and demanding, forcing her lips open so he could sweep the inside of her mouth with his tongue. He groaned with pleasure, sending the spark between them into a raging flame. Any thought she had of pushing him away went up in smoke. It was crazy, it was reckless, it was probably wrong, but God, it felt right. She didn't want to fight him, didn't want to fight herself. She leaned into his kiss, sliding her hand under his shirt, feeling the heat of his skin warm her from the outside in. She'd been cold for so long, and Jason was deliciously hot.

He lifted his head, his eyes dark and filled with promise. "I want you."

"Then have me," she said, giving in to the inevitable.

They stumbled into the bedroom, stopping every now and then to shed an article of clothing. Jason's body was beautiful, tan from the sun, his muscles honed, his arms and hands strong and rough and passionate for her. She hadn't felt so desired in a long time.

He backed her up against the edge of the bed, then reached around behind her and unhooked her bra straps, peeling away the lacy cups. She felt vulnerable under his eyes yet so very feminine. He kissed her lips, then his mouth slid down to her collarbone, the valley between her breasts, his tongue finally swirling around her nipples, sending liquid fire to her core.

When his hands pulled her hips to his, she could feel his erection through his boxers. They tumbled onto the bed together. He stripped off her thong. She pushed his shorts down to his knees, and he kicked them off.

He cupped the back of her head with one hand as she fell against the pillows. His other hand slid between her thighs, touching, teasing, slipping inside her. She moved her legs restlessly, wanting more than his wicked fingers. But Jason was tormenting her with his mouth and his hands, creating a deep, driving need for release.

"It's not enough." She gasped. "I want all of you."

That was all the encouragement he needed. He straddled her body, parted her thighs, and slid inside, filling the emptiness in her soul, chasing every thought out of her head, making her feel as if she was a part of him and he was a part of her and she'd never be alone again. It was exhilarating and terrifying, and she never wanted it to end.

* * *

Jason's heart took a long time to slow down. He didn't want to slide out of Brianna, didn't want to break the connection between them. He'd never felt so completely in sync with a woman—not just physically but emotionally.

*Shit!* What the hell was he thinking? He sounded like a woman.

He rolled over onto his back, taking long, deep breaths, then pulled Brianna into his arms. She laid her head on his chest and wrapped her arm around his waist. He closed his eyes, enjoying her sweet scent, the brush of her hair against his chest. Making love to her had been more than he'd ever imagined. There was so much passion between them, so much heat. She'd wanted him as badly as he'd wanted her.

Or maybe she was just lonely . . .

The thought drove the smile from his lips.

Maybe she was just trying to find a way to stop feeling so numb . . .

Tension crept into his limbs, and his eyes flew open. Maybe this wasn't the beginning of something but just the surrender to a reckless impulse, a basic physical need . . .

Brianna sat up, her eyes unsure as she pulled the sheet up over her breasts.

"A little late," he drawled. "I've already seen everything."

She stared at him for a minute. He wanted her

to say something, but not just anything—the right thing.

Suddenly, she was off the bed, retrieving her clothes, slipping them back on as fast as she'd taken them off. Then she was tossing his clothes at him, his boxers, his jeans, his shirt. He was too stunned to move. He'd jumped out of a few beds before, but never this fast. And he couldn't remember when a woman had beaten him off the mattress.

"Whoa, what's the hurry?" he asked.

"You have to get dressed. Lucas could come back anytime."

"You're not worried about Lucas. What's wrong?"

"You can't stay. We can't do that again," she said in a rush, running a hand through the tangled waves of her hair.

"We could definitely do that again. It was great."

"Jason, you need to *go.*"

"That's not what I need—or you, either. Slow down, Brianna, and talk to me."

She left the room. He got up and slowly put his clothes on, buying some time. She intended to throw him out and never let him back in again, and it wasn't going to end like that between them.

When he entered the living room, she was waiting by the door, her arms wrapped around her waist, fear in her eyes.

"What are you afraid of?" he asked

"You know what I'm afraid of—you and me, we can't be together."

"We were fantastic together."

"It was just sex, Jason. I needed to be with a man, and you were willing. That's all."

He didn't want to believe there was a speck of truth in what she'd said, but his own doubts were beginning to take hold. She'd told him that she was tired, that she was lonely, that she was cold, and he'd wanted to make all that go away. But she'd never said she cared about him. Maybe it *had* just been about scratching an itch. Her husband had been in jail a long time. She was a single mother. How much action could she have had?

His heart hardened. He had put himself on the line with her. He'd told her that he had wanted her from the first minute he'd seen her, and he'd never said that to anyone before. He'd watched his father make a fool of himself over women more times than he could count and wasn't about to follow in his footsteps.

"Who said it was anything more than sex?" he challenged.

"Then I guess we're good," she retorted.

He put his hand on the back of her neck and pulled her mouth to his, crushing her lips in a kiss neither of them would forget for a while. "We *are* good. And one of these days, you're not going to tell me to go. You're going to beg me stay."

As if *that* would happen. Brianna slammed the door behind him, but her tingling lips called her a liar.

It had taken all of her willpower to throw him out while her body was begging for more.

What on earth had she done? As she raised her hand to tuck her hair behind her ear, the light caught her diamond ring.

She drew in a long, slow breath. It felt like a lifetime since Derek had put that ring on her finger. She walked into the bedroom, slipped it off, and set it inside her jewelry box. Immediately tempted to snatch it back, she resisted the urge. She wasn't married anymore.

She wasn't married anymore.

The idea shocked her, made her so dizzy that she had to sit down on the bed. The tangled sheets still felt warm, and the scent of Jason's aftershave lingered in the air. It had been a long time since a man had shared her bed. Five years, if she didn't count the few conjugal visits.

The passion between her and Jason had gone way beyond the physical. She'd felt connected to him in a way she hadn't expected. There hadn't been any awkwardness between them while they were making love. Afterward was a different story, and that was mainly her fault. She'd totally freaked. The wonderful thrill she'd felt had scared the hell out of her, because she wanted to do it again and again and again. And how could she?

Guilt had followed terror. She couldn't want Jason in her bed, in her house, in her life. The Kanes hated him. He was their enemy; he was supposed to be hers. But wasn't it time to stop worrying about what everyone else thought and focus on what *she* wanted for herself and her son?

But was Jason truly what she wanted?

"You know you want to, Charlotte."

Charlotte eyed the rope in Andrew's hands with misgiving. She had no intention of participating in the three-legged race; she'd only come to the festival to drop off her mother's baked goods for the cake-walk. "No way."

"I need a partner." Andrew gave her the same smile that used to make her want to say yes to anything he suggested.

"Find someone else. I'm not good at that game."

"All you have to do is hold on to me." Andrew leaned forward, his blue eyes begging. "Please, Charlotte, take pity on me. If it's not you, it's going to be Margaret Wells, and she might kill me."

Margaret Wells was a very tall, very large woman in her early forties, who probably had a good thirty pounds on Andrew. She'd just divorced her second husband and was looking for number three.

"Where's your generosity of spirit?" she asked. "You know she likes you."

"She's at least twelve years older than me."

"You know what they say about experienced women."

"It's not a race down the aisle, Charlotte, just across the grass," he teased. "What are you afraid of?"

"I'm not afraid."

"Sure you are. You're scared of being in a relationship."

"Just because I don't want one with you doesn't mean I'm scared of relationships."

"When was your last one?"

She shrugged. "Last year."

"What was his name?" he asked skeptically. "What did he look like? What did he do for a living?"

She grabbed the rope out of his hand. "Fine, I'll do the race with you, if only to shut you up." She marched over to the starting line, where the other contestants were tying their legs together. The park was packed with festival goers and picnickers, but this stretch of grass in front of the gazebo had been cleared for the games. The mayor stood on the steps of the gazebo with a megaphone in his hand, prepared to start the race. Andrew knelt down to tie their legs together.

As he rose, Margaret walked by, dragging Butch, the forty-five-year-old owner of the local market. Margaret shot Charlotte a dirty look as she and Butch headed to the other end of the line.

"Did you see that?" Charlotte asked, socking Andrew in the arm. "Margaret hates me now. She'll never give me a good table at the Blue Pelican." Margaret had inherited one of the hottest restaurants in town from her second husband, and there was usually a wait for tables on Friday and Saturday nights.

"If you go with me, she will," Andrew said, a cocky light in his eyes.

"I *was* supposed to go with you," she reminded him.

Discomfort flashed in his eyes. "Right. I need to make that up to you."

"You never told me what came up."

"It's nothing I can share."

Which made her wonder even more. "Who says I'll give you another chance?"

"Contestants ready?" the mayor called.

"Time to put your arms around me." Andrew smiled down at her.

"Ah, now we get to the heart of your evil plan."

"The best part." He put his arm around her, pulling her up tight against him.

She put her arm around his waist and was reminded of how well they fit together, how having his arms around her had once been all she could think about.

The whistle blew, and they were off. Despite their tight embrace, their legs soon got tangled up together, and they fell down in a laughing heap halfway across the grass. Andrew tried to pull her up, but after one more step, they were down again. They couldn't get in sync, which was pretty much how their relationship had always gone—one step forward, two steps back, then utter collapse.

"I don't think we're going to make it," she said, laughing helplessly.

"Oh, we will," he promised, gazing into her eyes. "You just have to trust me." He held out his hand.

And suddenly, they weren't talking about the race anymore.

Joe's gut clenched at the sight of Andrew and Charlotte tangled up in the grass. Her blond hair was flying around her face, her eyes sparkling with laughter. She looked happy; so did Andrew. They seemed to be a good match. She'd liked Andrew once, maybe even loved him. So why was she resisting Andrew?

Was it because of him? He hadn't imagined the heat between them in his kitchen the other night or the emotional connection he'd felt when she confided in him about the baby she'd lost.

The fact that she'd trusted him that much had touched him. Despite Charlotte's outgoing personality, he sensed there were very few people she trusted completely. She'd spent most of her life in the shadow of her father's heavenly spotlight, afraid to be herself for fear of being judged. But she'd let down her guard with him for a few minutes—then it had gone back up.

Because he was married. Because they both knew they were walking a dangerous line.

As if on cue, his cell phone rang. It was Rachel again. His gut clenched. This was the fourth time she'd called since the divorce papers had arrived, and he had yet to call her back, because what the hell would he say? He didn't know what he was going to do. Sign the papers and free her up to move to another man, probably to her good pal Mark Devlin? If he didn't sign the papers, if he prolonged things, where would that get him?

The ringing stopped, followed by the message that he had a new voice-mail. He pushed the button, because he'd been her husband too long to ignore her. If something was really wrong, he'd never forgive himself.

"Joe, it's Rachel. You have to call me. Your silence is making me crazy. I know I should have told you the papers were coming, but I had to do it. One of us had to force the issue. We can't just live in limbo, the way we've been doing the last year. Call me, please."

He deleted the message and then hit redial, drawing in a deep breath as Rachel's voice came over the phone. "What do you want me to do?" he asked her. "Do you really want me to sign the papers without trying to save this thing?"

"This *thing* is called a marriage," Rachel said. "And we've been trying to save it for a long time, Joe."

"Have we? You've been gone for more than a month. Why don't you come back here so we can talk?"

"You've been gone longer that that," she countered. "I'm not coming back. I realize now that I'm just not willing to move to Angel's Bay. I have a life here that I like, a life I don't want to give up."

"So you're willing to walk away from me for your L.A. friends?"

"Aren't you doing the same thing, for a place you never even heard of until a year ago? How can the people there mean more to you than I do? It's not just *me* that's here—there's your family, your friends, the men you worked with for more than a decade. I'm not the one who's ripping apart an entire life. That's you."

His stomach churned with the truth of her words.

She paused for a long moment. "If you'll move back to L.A., Joe, I'll give it another shot."

"Otherwise it's over?" he asked, his heart pounding against his chest. "All or nothing?"

"You could be happy here. You were for a long time. I know you needed to get away to clear your head, but you've done that. Now come home."

"I'll think about it," he said tersely, ending the call. He drew in a deep breath and slowly let it out.

Rachel had finally drawn the line in the sand. He could have her or Angel's Bay, but he couldn't have both. Why was he fighting so hard to stay in this place? Rachel was right. There were a lot of people in Los Angeles whom he loved.

He just didn't know if he loved *her* the way he should. If he did, would it really be this difficult to leave? And if she loved him as much as she should, would she have filed for divorce? Was it really about Angel's Bay, or were they just trying to find a simple reason for why they didn't work anymore?

The mayor got on his megaphone again, announcing the winners of the three-legged race. Andrew and Charlotte had been soundly beaten—but Andrew, with his arm flung around Charlotte's shoulders, didn't look unhappy at all.

"Andrew, you can let go of me now," Charlotte said pointedly. "The race is over, and people are staring at us."

"Just wait until Margaret leaves," he said.

He was just using Margaret as an excuse to flirt with her, but he was so damn charming she couldn't get mad at him. "I'll give you one more minute, but after that, you'll have to ward off the cougars on your own."

"I thought you two would make it a closer race," Rabbi Ziegler said as he stopped by, proudly holding the gold cup. "Your father and mother never would have let me and Louise beat them," he told Charlotte.

"I'm sure that's true," Charlotte said. "My mother has a very strong will to win."

"How is she? I haven't seen her much in recent weeks."

"She's all right," Charlotte said, noting the kindness in his eyes. The rabbi had spent many evenings conversing with her parents about religion and other interests they shared.

"Good. She's a wonderful woman. This town wouldn't be the same without her." He paused. "Andrew, did you have a chance to meet with the Goldmans about the possible adoption?"

"Annie is going to meet them next week."

"Very good. Will I see you two in the water-balloon toss?"

"Not a chance," Charlotte said as the rabbi laughed and walked away. "Don't even think about it, Andrew. I've done my duty."

"You have," he said, sounding distracted.

She gave him a curious look. "Something wrong?"

"I was just thinking about Annie. Suddenly, there are a bunch of couples interested in adopting her baby, but she needs to tell the biological father before we can proceed. I don't want to put anyone in the position of thinking they're going to get the baby, then at the last minute they don't."

"I agree."

"You need to persuade Annie to do the right thing. She looks up to you. She listens to you."

"Telling the father might be more complicated than we know. I think he's probably married or involved with someone else. Annie might be protecting him or protecting his family. Maybe that feels more right to her than telling the truth and ruining a marriage."

"I can see your point, but in the end, the truth always comes out."

"Sometimes the truth doesn't matter."

"You don't really believe that," he said.

"It doesn't always change things. Sometimes it just hurts."

His eyes flickered with curiosity. "Are we still

talking about Annie? Is there something you want to tell me?"

"No. I have to run. I have a bunch of stuff to do today."

"Charlotte, wait. Every time we get a little close, you pull away. Are you ever going to let me back into your life?" he asked seriously.

"I'm not sure."

"I'm going to try to change your mind, Charlie. I believe in second chances."

But there wasn't always a second chance. Some mistakes lasted forever.

# THIRTEEN

The park was pretty at night, with white lights strung between the trees, local bands playing on the stage, couples on the makeshift dance floor, and buffet tables laden with food and drinks. Brianna had skipped most of the Harvest Festival events, but the Kanes had insisted she join them for a picnic supper. She'd been happy to get out of the house. Her bedroom reminded her of Jason, and the boxes in the garage reminded her of Derek. She'd been caught between the two men for a long time.

"This is so much fun." Nancy smiled, sliding down the bench seat to nudge Brianna with her shoulder. "Aren't you glad you came?"

"I am," she admitted. "The food was excellent. I'm stuffed."

"Everyone goes all out for these things. We're lucky the weather cooperated. In a few weeks, we'll all be inside and wishing for lovely nights like this."

It *was* a nice night, crisp, cool, and deliciously

aromatic, with the nearby dessert table offering up pumpkin pie, apple tarts, peanut brittle, and oatmeal-raisin cookies.

"Lucas and Kyle are getting along well," Nancy added. "Every time Kyle sees me now, he asks me if Lucas is coming over."

Kyle lived next door to the Kanes and was only three months older than Lucas. They'd become fast friends, and today they were kicking a soccer ball back and forth with a third boy. Lucas was having the time of his life, laughing, running, and throwing himself on the ground. Little boys certainly were physical, at least her little boy.

"I can't believe he has so much energy," Nancy continued. "Rick said Lucas ran him up and down the beach today with that kite. He came home and took a two-hour nap. They had a lot of fun, though. Rick has become a new man since Lucas's arrival. He's got more energy, more hope." Nancy shot Brianna a quick look. "You're quiet tonight."

"Just enjoying the atmosphere."

"It's too bad we can't bottle the innocence of youth," Nancy said, her focus back on Lucas, who was now turning cartwheels with his friends. "The days of childhood go so fast." She turned back to Brianna, the hint of tears in her eyes. "When Rick and I first got married, we wanted to have four children. I have three sisters and a brother, and I enjoyed growing up in a big family. But we had trouble getting pregnant. It took almost six years. Derek was like a miracle. After he was born, I got pregnant once move but had a miscarriage, and then nothing. We felt so lucky to have Derek, we spoiled him with love. We couldn't help ourselves.

"I never thought I could love someone as much as I loved my son," Nancy continued. "I miss Derek so much, it hurts like an open wound. It's not right for a mother to outlive her child. He should have been here to enjoy this picnic and watch his son play with the other children. He should have been sitting here with you, his arm around your shoulders."

Nancy's words tugged at Brianna's heart. For a moment, she could see the picture exactly as Nancy had set it up. She could almost feel Derek's arms around her . . . but then the whisper of warmth fled away. She'd never had that kind of moment with Derek. It was just part of a dream that had never come to life.

"I know you're angry with me," Nancy said. "You probably think I overreacted to Jason being in your house. But look at that little boy playing with Lucas. If you saw Kyle knock Lucas to the ground, would you be able to look at him the same way?"

"Probably not," Brianna admitted. It wasn't nearly the same situation, but she couldn't imagine forgiving anyone who hurt Lucas. There was nothing more primal than a mother protecting her child.

But Derek and Jason had stood against each other as men, not as children. And what had once seemed black and white was now filled with endless shades of gray. She'd been blinded by love and swept up in the Kanes' devotion to their son, their unyielding belief in Derek's innocence. But Derek himself had told her that he'd done things he wasn't proud of, that she didn't really know him. Perhaps his parents didn't know him, either.

"I know you'll run into Jason around town, but I hope you won't let him into your life," Nancy added. "You're like my daughter, Brianna, and I couldn't stand to see him hurt you, too. Rick and I love you."

Brianna melted. Her parents had rarely told her they loved her, and she doubted they'd ever worried about her. But with Nancy's love came strings and expectations. No matter how hard they tried, she and Lucas could never replace Derek. And while the Kanes might look at her as their daughter, she was a grown woman, and she needed to make her own decisions about who was or wasn't going to be in her life.

"I love you, too," she said, seeing the worry in Nancy's eyes. For the moment, she would leave it at that.

She reached for her diet soda, only to realize it was empty. "I need another drink. Can I get you something?" At the sudden look of shock on Nancy's face, she stopped abruptly. "What's wrong?"

"Your wedding ring. Where is it?" Nancy asked in alarm. "Did you lose it?"

"Oh, no." She pulled her hand out of view. "It—it slipped off. I've lost some weight." In light of Nancy's obvious distress, she couldn't say she'd felt driven to take it off and that not wearing it had brought a sense of freedom she'd never expected.

"You have lost weight, dear. You need to eat more."

"With your cooking, that won't be difficult," Brianna said. "Shall I take Lucas with me?"

"Oh, no, he's having fun. I won't let him out of my sight."

Brianna had no worries about that. Nancy would guard Lucas with her life.

She wandered across the grass, looking for some decaf coffee. As she joined the line, she realized she was right behind Gloria Markham. The dark-haired woman had on a colorful orange and red scarf over her black coat and pants. When she saw Brianna, surprise and discomfort flitted across her eyes.

"Hello," Gloria said. "It's a long line," she added, clearing her throat.

"Yes, it is." She knew she should use this opportunity to quiz Gloria, but she didn't know where to start.

They stood for a moment in silence, and then Gloria turned to her. "The other day, I wanted to tell you how sorry I was about Derek. I never imagined that he would die in prison. It was tragic."

Brianna saw real pain in Gloria's expression. She'd thought that Wyatt and the Markhams were united in their dislike of Derek, but it seemed not. "Do you think we could talk for a minute?" she asked impulsively. Maybe Gloria would speak more freely without her husband or Wyatt around.

Gloria hesitated. "I suppose so. Let's step over there."

They moved away from the crowd to stand under the canopy of a large tree. "Your husband came to my house the other day," Brianna said. "I missed him. Do you know what he wanted?"

"No. I didn't know he'd gone to your house," Gloria said slowly. "I suppose he wanted to ask you if Derek had left you any clue to where the paintings are. We'd like to get them back."

"Do you think I'd hang on to them if I had them?"

"I don't know. I don't know anything about you."

Brianna stiffened. Gloria wasn't the first person to believe she'd known what Derek was up to, but it still stung. "Well, I wouldn't. I'd love to find those paintings and prove that Derek wasn't the one who stole them." She paused, debating her next words, then decided to go for it. "Did you know that Victor Delgado had a son?"

Gloria started, then reached up to adjust her scarf as she stalled for time.

"You don't have to answer. I can see it in your eyes." Brianna felt a rush of adrenaline. "Wyatt and Derek are descendants of Victor."

"Where did you hear that?" Gloria asked.

"I found some old letters in Derek's things. So why would Wyatt be willing to donate those paintings to the museum? Why didn't he want to keep them in the family?"

"Wyatt always believed that art should be seen by the masses," Gloria replied. "He's spent a lifetime encouraging private collectors to share their pieces with the world by lending them to museums and galleries. He would never keep important paintings hidden away in his studio. It's not who he is. But Derek was different—or at least, he changed over the years. When Derek stopped painting, he traded his soul for cash. He no longer cared about the art, only about what someone was willing to pay for it. You didn't know that about him, did you? How could you? You barely knew him."

She didn't like Gloria's sneering tone. "You don't know anything about my relationship with Derek."

"No? Derek and I had a long talk when he brought you to Angel's Bay. I wasn't surprised that he had picked you, because you were beautiful in the way that Derek liked. In fact, he said just that."

Brianna frowned. "I don't think—"

Gloria cut her off. "He told me that you had a cool, untouched innocence about you, like a canvas begging for paint. Derek wanted to color you, to finish you, to make you his."

The words didn't make sense to her. "I don't understand."

"Of course you don't. With you, Derek could be whoever he wanted to be. You didn't know his heart, his soul, because you didn't know him as an artist. That's where he poured it out. That's where he was himself."

"Then why did he stop painting? Because Wyatt told him he was no good? Why didn't he fight if art was so important to him?" Brianna demanded.

"Derek was consumed by fear. He was scared of

success and terrified of failure. So he ran away, and he married a woman who would never pick at that part of his soul, never demand something of him that he didn't want to give." There was anger in Gloria's voice, bitterness burning in her eyes.

"You wanted him to pick someone else," Brianna said, sure of her words.

"Yes—someone who wouldn't let him run from his talent."

"Did you tell him that?"

"I did," Gloria said, with no apology in her voice. "But I was too late. Derek had already gone to the dark side. He'd chosen a path from which there was no recovery." She took a breath. "I never thought he would die in prison though. That was never supposed to happen."

As Gloria left, Brianna's stomach churned. What *was* supposed to have happened? Was Derek supposed to get out of jail and do something besides go back to her and Lucas? Had there been another woman in his life? Someone he was supposed to have been with?

The Kanes had told her that Derek had never introduced them to anyone else, but that didn't mean anything. He'd been living in L.A. for eight years. His parents had known next to nothing about his life there, and neither had she.

"Brianna?"

Startled, she whipped around to see Jason come out of the shadows. He had on his uniform tonight, the moonlight glinting off his badge. She'd wanted to remind herself that he was the cop who'd put Derek behind bars, but now, all she could see was the man who'd made love to her that morning, whose kisses had driven her wild, whose touch had made her scream with pleasure. The man she'd thrown out of her house because she was scared—not of him, but of herself.

He moved closer, quiet and quick as if about to pounce. Her heart skipped a beat as she looked into his eyes and saw that he was remembering, too.

Why was it suddenly so hard to breathe?

"Brianna," he murmured, her name sounding like a caress. "Are you all right?"

"Yes," she said, gazing into his eyes. She cleared her throat, realizing she was getting lost in a glance that was far too intimate for their surroundings. "I just had an interesting conversation with Gloria."

"I saw. What was that about?"

"I found something out earlier. I didn't get a chance to tell you before, but I discovered some old letters in one of Derek's boxes. They were from Victor Delgado to Francine Kane, and vice versa."

His eyes widened. "There was a connection between Delgado and the Kanes? What did the letters say?"

"Apparently, Victor and Francine had an affair. They'd both lost their lovers when the ship went down, and they turned to each other in grief. But that's not all. There was a baby. Francine passed it off as the child of her late husband, Marcus Kane." She waited, letting the words sink in.

A light sparked in his eyes. "So Derek—"

"Was a descendant, and Wyatt, too. I told Gloria. She didn't deny it, and she didn't act surprised. What I want to know is why no one ever mentioned this before."

Jason stared at her for a long moment. "The family connection probably wouldn't have played in Derek's favor. It would have give him a stronger motive to want those paintings."

"It also would have given Wyatt a stronger reason to steal the paintings back from the museum." She paused. "You and Joe Silveira both told me to come up with something new. I think I have."

"We'll talk about it later. I'm on duty now. I've got to take a swing through the park."

"All right," she said. He didn't move. "Was there something else you wanted?"

His lips tightened. "I didn't like the way things ended this morning."

She stared back at him. "I didn't, either," she admitted.

He nodded. "Okay. I know it's complicated, but shutting me out isn't the answer."

"You say that now, but you were having second thoughts this morning, too. I might have acted before you did, but I could feel you tensing up. We both know that the two of us together is a crazy idea. It could never work."

"*Never* is a strong word."

"It's the only one that makes sense." She paused as a gust of wind blew her hair across her face. As she pushed the strands away, she saw Jason's gaze narrow.

"Where's your wedding ring?" he asked abruptly.

She drew in a deep breath. "I took it off. I did it for me, not for you, and it's no one's business whether I wear it or not. I was married to Derek, not the rest of you. It's my choice. My life." She wished she'd said the same words to Nancy, but like a coward she'd run.

"I agree," Jason said. "It is your life, your choice to be with whoever you want to be with."

She saw the challenge in his eyes. "That doesn't mean I'll choose you. As I said before, the two of us together doesn't make sense, and any friendship between us hurts people I care about. I don't just have myself to consider, but also Lucas. I can't put him in the middle of a battle between you and his grandparents. We have to stop this now. It's the right thing to do."

"The right thing—or the easy thing? I know you're a fighter, Brianna. Is Derek the only one you can fight for?"

She didn't have a chance to answer as a sudden commotion in the beer garden took Jason's attention away from her.

People were yelling, and two men were shoving each other, knocking over chairs and tables, sending people fleeing for cover.

"Shit! The Harlan boys are at it again." He took off toward the action.

"What are you going to do?" she asked, running next to him.

"Stop them."

A siren blared in the distance; help was on the way. She hoped Jason would wait for it. The two men were quite large, very drunk, and completely out of control. She glanced over her shoulder, making sure Lucas was still with the Kanes and out of harm's way.

Jason's demands that the men stop fighting went unheeded. Brianna gasped as one of the men picked up a chair and hurled it past his opponent, almost taking out a light stand and a couple of bystanders. Jason jumped into the fray, trying to drag one man off the other, but his face got in the way of the other guy's fist.

He staggered backward, blood dripping from his nose, but he recovered quickly, grabbing one of the men by the waist and wrestling him to the ground. The other man sank to his knees, either exhausted from the fight or too drunk to continue. Jason got his cuffs on the one guy just as two other officers ran in to help, and a few moments later, the men were being led to a police car.

Jason was rewarded by applause, which he quickly waved off. Brianna wanted to go to him, but she was acutely aware that the Kanes and her son were watching the action. Jason wasn't left alone for long, as Kara and a big blond guy ran up to him.

"A little late, as always," Jason told his friend.

"I was on the other side of the park," the man replied. "I can't believe you took that sucker punch. Your reflexes have slowed way down, dude."

"Up yours, Colin."

Kara handed Jason some napkins to soak up the blood. "Do you need to go to the hospital?" she asked with concern.

"He's fine. He has a bloody nose," Colin said.

"He can talk for himself," Kara argued.

"I'm all right, Kara. I just need to get a towel and some ice." He glanced away from them, his gaze meeting Brianna's.

One of the servers from the beer garden brought Jason a bag of ice, and more people gathered around him until he was completely lost to Brianna's view. Shaking her head, she turned around and walked back to the table where the Kanes sat.

Lucas came running up to her, his eyes lit up with excitement. "Mommy, did you see that? Did you see Jason fight that big guy?"

"I did," she said.

"He was cool," Lucas added, swinging his own fists in the air. "I want to learn how to fight like that."

"Jason was *stopping* the fight," she told him. "He's a police officer. He was trying to prevent anyone else from getting hurt."

Her reasonable explanation fell on the deaf ears of a four-year-old boy who now thought Jason was a superhero.

She hadn't wanted to see Jason like this—brave

and courageous and willing to put his life on the line to protect others.

"Mommy, Kyle wants me to sleep over at his house tonight. Can I?"

"What?" Brianna asked, refocusing her attention on Lucas.

"Can I do a sleepover, please? Kyle has bunk beds."

She smiled, as it was Lucas's greatest wish to sleep in a bunk bed. "I don't know, honey."

"Please, please, please," he begged. "Kyle's parents are really nice. His mom makes hot chocolate with marshmallows."

"It's a good family, in case you're worried," Rick interjected. "We've known them for ten years."

"Maybe she'd rather not be alone," Nancy suggested. "Don't feel pressured, Brianna."

She wondered if Nancy was worried about her being on her own or being alone with Jason.

"Say yes," Lucas begged.

"Yes." She smiled.

He jumped up and down with excitement. "I've never done a sleepover. I'm a big kid now!"

"I guess you are. Let's go home and get your pajamas."

After packing up Lucas and spending a half hour with Kyle's parents before saying good-bye, Brianna returned home. Jason's car wasn't in the driveway; he was probably still working. It would be strange when he wasn't house-sitting anymore. She'd gotten used to thinking about him being next door.

Though it would probably be better to put more distance between them. Then she wouldn't be so tempted . . .

As she entered the house, Digger came running to greet her, barking with delight. She let him out in the backyard, hoping he'd run off his energy.

Wispy clouds floated around the moon, and the wind blew colder. She felt a shiver run down her spine, not sure where it had come from. There was nothing but peaceful quiet surrounding her, yet she felt on edge.

She called to Digger, took him back into the house, and locked the door. She put him in his crate and headed toward her bedroom. Her sense of uneasiness increased as she entered the room. Nothing looked out of the ordinary, but something felt different.

She just needed to get hold of herself. It had been a very long time since she'd been completely alone; she'd always had Lucas with her.

Too restless to sleep, she wandered back into the living room and glanced out the window. Her heart skipped a beat at the sight of Jason's car. She debated for a minute, then grabbed her keys and slipped out the front door.

She would just see how he was feeling after the fight, offer some neighborly support. She was still thinking of ways to rationalize her visit when Jason opened the front door.

"Thank God. I thought I was going to have to knock on your door." He grabbed her hand and pulled her into the house, his mouth coming down on hers before she could say a word.

She sank into his kiss, cupping his face with her hands, her fingers threading through his hair as he angled his mouth one way and then the other, not giving her a chance to breathe or to think.

As her fingers slid down the side of his face, she felt the swelling around his eye, heard his quick intake of breath. She pulled away. "You're hurt." His right eye was already turning black and was swollen halfway shut. His nose looked puffy, too.

"Kiss me and make me feel better," he teased.

"I can't believe you didn't wait until the other officers came."

"I didn't want anyone to get hurt."

"*You* got hurt."

"Roger Harlan can't usually get off that good of a punch." He paused. "Is that why you came over here? To see if I was okay?"

"It was one of my reasons."

"And?"

"I couldn't stop thinking about you, about us," she whispered. "It's so wrong."

"No, it's not," he said with a definitive shake of his head.

"I'm going to hurt everyone I care about, the only people who care about me."

"Don't you think the Kanes want you to be happy?"

"They don't want me to be happy with you." She stepped back, putting her palms against the door.

She needed to steady herself and also to stop herself from jumping back into his arms.

"What do *you* want?" he asked quietly, his gaze meetings hers.

"I don't know, Jason."

"You do know—you're just scared."

"Scared that I don't want to mess up my life again—hell, yes. Since I came back here, everything I thought I knew is changing. I'm doubting Derek. I know you're happy to hear that, but it doesn't make me feel good. Because if I was wrong about him, what else was I wrong about?" She gave him a worried look. "And are you going to be another bad decision?"

"No, I'm not. I am what you see, Brianna. I had no hidden agenda five years ago, and I have none now. I told you before that the first time I saw you, I knew you were it."

"But I didn't think that about you. Doesn't that bother you?"

"Well, I would have preferred you to dump Derek on the spot and run into my arms, but we can't change the past. Now we have another chance to get it right. And even though you didn't dump Derek, I think you liked me, too. You just didn't have a chance to figure it out."

She shook her head, his cocky smile way too appealing. "You do know how to put a good spin on things."

"Is Lucas asleep?" Jason asked, suddenly moving closer.

"No, he's, uh . . ." She stalled, realizing that taking Lucas out of the equation was like waving a red flag in front of a bull.

"He's what?" Jason prodded. "It's late for him to be awake."

"He's sleeping over at his friend Kyle's house."

Jason's eyes sparked. "Really? So you don't have to get home?"

"I wouldn't say that. I left Digger in the crate, but he doesn't do well alone for long."

"So we'll go back to your house. We don't have to do anything you don't want to do. We can . . . talk."

She smiled. "The last thing I want to do with you is talk." She stepped forward, grabbed his shirt by the hem, and pulled it over his head. "Digger can wait."

# FOURTEEN

Brianna had never been so impatient to have a man. With Jason, there was no slow build-up to romance, no candles or mood music, no soft words of affection. There was no pretense between them, only raw, honest passion. He'd said that when he first saw her, he'd known she was it ... and she wanted to be his *it* girl, the woman who could make him crazy.

She stripped off his clothes with eager enthusiasm, enjoying every bare inch of him. He was a gorgeous man, rugged, tan, muscled, a man of earth and fire and the sea. He was all the elements wrapped into one. And when he was kissing her and touching her, she felt like a different person.

Jason pulled her out of her head. There was no thinking, no planning, no rule books. He urged her to explore his body while he did the same with her, no holding back. It was scary and exhilarating to put so much on the line.

Every nerve ending tingled as their hands,

mouths, and bodies tangled. They made it onto the narrow couch, Jason pulling her on top of him, letting her set the pace, the rhythm, while his eyes burned with pleasure. She felt as if she was flying. Every slide of their bodies, every tense, delicious place of friction, was unbearably good. She wanted to stay up in the clouds forever, but the tension built, fast and furious, until she cried out with release. Jason held on to her until they both floated down to earth.

Long minutes passed before she could breathe, then she lifted her head and met his gaze.

He put his hand on the back of her head and stole another kiss, long and tender. Her emotions threatened to spill over with the sweet caress, because it didn't feel like sex anymore; it felt like love.

A tiny frisson of fear went through her. She wanted to get up, to run again, but Jason was holding on to her.

"You can go home," he said, meeting her gaze, "but I'm going with you. I want us to spend the night together—you and me." He paused, giving her a slow grin. "And Digger."

She smiled back. "You'll have competition, then. He likes me."

"I like you, too."

She sat back, grabbing an afghan off the back of the couch as she searched for her clothes. "What about the pets here? I thought you were supposed to stay with them at night."

"The cats pretty much hate me, the bird doesn't

care, and Princess is asleep in the middle of Patty's bed, which is the most uncomfortable bed I've ever slept in. Thank God my father is coming back soon."

"Did you hear from him? Did he get married?" she asked as she pulled on her bra and panties.

"I don't know. He texted me that he'd be back tomorrow." Jason pulled on his jeans and grabbed his shirt off the floor.

"So you might have a new stepmother?"

"It's possible."

She gave him a thoughtful look. "You don't sound quite as upset about it as you did before."

"I've got another woman on my mind," he said, kissing her forehead. "Are you ready?"

She gave a nod and tossed the blanket back onto the couch. When they got back to her house, all was quiet; Digger had gone to sleep. She went into her bedroom, Jason right behind her. He slipped his arms around her waist, nuzzling her neck.

"What side of the bed do you sleep on?" he asked.

"I pretty much take over the middle," she said, turning in his arms. "I haven't had to share."

"That's going to change."

"Jason—"

"I know, it's too fast," he said. "But you don't want to talk. You don't want to think. So how shall we pass the time?"

She liked his smile now, liked how easy it was between them. Jason could be intense and passionate but also teasing and playful. "You could tell me about yourself," she suggested, knowing that wasn't what he had in mind. "Stories that don't involve Derek, preferably." She moved out of his arms and sat down on the bed, scooting up to lean against the headboard and stretch out her legs.

Jason sat across from her. "What do you want to know?"

"Tell me about your last girlfriend."

"I don't think so," he said.

"Okay, when did you decide to become a cop?"

"I had the idea in my head for a while—because of my mom."

"What do you mean?" she asked in surprise.

"She didn't just die; she was killed," he said somberly. "A bank robbery. She was in the wrong place at the wrong time. She died on the way to the hospital."

She put her hand on his knee. "I'm so sorry, Jason."

"I never got to say good-bye. My dad didn't, either, and it made him nuts. We had no closure. One minute she was there, and the next she wasn't."

Brianna could relate; Derek's death had also been shocking and unexpected. But she didn't want to bring him or her feelings into Jason's story. "What do you remember about her?"

He thought for a moment. "Her laugh. She had one of those all-body laughs. Her shoulders would shake, and tears would stream out of her eyes, and she'd tell my dad that he was just too funny for words."

"So your dad's a funny guy?"

"He can be, especially after a few beers. But he's also an emotional man; whatever he's feeling is always right there on his face. And believe me, he feels everything."

She stared at Jason, understanding him a little bit better. His mother's death had shut him down. His father had been able to express his grief, and in doing so had maybe overwhelmed Jason even more. "So you're not big on feelings?"

"Not when they hurt, and they usually do." He paused. "I don't need to tell you that, do I? Look what love got you."

"A lot of pain," she admitted. "But a lot more, too, including Lucas. I'll never regret loving Derek. I might be sorry I stood by him, but I won't be sorry that I was with him." She paused. "I think your mother would be really proud of what you've done with your life."

"I hope so. When I first became a cop, I saw everything as black or white, right or wrong, good guys on one side, bad guys on the other. I pursued justice for the victims of crime, but I didn't realize there were victims on both sides of the equation—people like you and Lucas, who got caught up in a situation that wasn't of your making. I never thought I'd have to arrest one of my closest friends or that I'd be responsible for ruining your life. It might not have looked like I cared, because I had to keep that professional distance, but it ate me up inside."

She was touched by his admission. "I didn't want to see your side of it. I just wanted you to be wrong," she admitted.

"I can understand that. Look, if you want to talk about Derek, I'll listen. I might not agree, but I'll hear you out."

She thought about that. "Okay—then there is something I want to share. I told you about Derek's letter. He said a bit more than that he loved me and he was innocent."

"I figured."

"He said that while he hadn't taken the paintings, he wasn't completely innocent, either, and that I didn't know who he really was. The more I learn about him, the more I realize that he was right."

"Did he give you anything more concrete?" Jason asked.

"He was very cryptic, but he also left me some sketches." She went over to the dresser to retrieve the envelope. As she picked it up, her eye caught on the framed photograph of Derek and her that had been taken on the Angel's Bay beach for their engagement shot. The glass was broken, tiny pieces lying on the dresser. "That's weird. How did this break?"

Jason got up from the bed. "Maybe Lucas was throwing a ball around in here."

"I think he would have told me." She remembered the eerie sensation she'd had earlier when she'd first come into the house. But her doors had all been locked—at least, she'd thought they were. She'd gotten into the habit of leaving the back door open for Lucas and Digger to go in and out.

"What's wrong?" Jason asked. "Is it that the photo is damaged? Or that you don't know how it happened?"

She hadn't thought about the meaning of the picture being broken. "I don't know."

"I'm going to look around," Jason said.

"I let Digger into the yard earlier, and I locked the door when I came back in. But I can't remember if it was unlocked when I first went out there."

"I'll be back."

While Jason was gone, she took the envelope back to the bed and sat down. Pulling out the letter she read through it again. It was easier the second time; she had more distance now. And Derek's voice in her head was nowhere near as loud. She hoped to see some new clue in his words, but nothing jumped out at her. She set the photos aside and leafed through the sketches.

"Everything looks fine," Jason said, returning to the bedroom. He sat down on the bed and picked up the sketch of her in the L.A. gallery. "Did Derek do this?"

"In prison," she said. "These sketches were with the letter. I had no idea he was drawing. I used to bring him books and magazines; he never asked for a sketch pad or pencils. I don't know where he got the materials."

"They're really good," Jason said quietly as they looked through the pictures.

"He drew you, I think." Brianna held up a sketch of two boys climbing on rocks in front of a cave that looked very much like the one Jason had shown her at Shelter Cove.

"I wonder why. He even made me look good, no devil's pitchfork in my hand," he said wryly.

"I guess he was remembering the good times." She liked the ones of Lucas. Derek had captured all the details of his face: his eyes, his brows that quirked with curiosity, his big smile.

Setting those drawings aside, she picked up another sketch. "Derek liked to draw the coast, and this looks like an art studio." She paused, noting the shadowy silhouettes of a man and a woman in a passionate embrace. "Who do you think these two are?"

Jason's gaze followed hers. "Derek, maybe?"

"I wonder who the woman is." She tilted her head. "There's something off about some of the pictures. Like things aren't in the right spot."

"I agree," Jason said, puzzlement in his eyes. He studied the sketch for another moment, then said, "I've got it. It's a mirror image. He's sketching what he sees through the mirror."

He was right. "Katherine said Derek liked to use unique perspectives when he painted. He saw the world in a different way from most artists." She sighed and put the sketches aside.

"I wish he'd just told me what he did or didn't do. I keep thinking I'm missing a clue."

"Maybe you are," Jason said, surprising her.

"But you've always thought Derek was guilty," she reminded him.

"I've also always thought he had a partner, someone here in Angel's Bay."

She thought about her earlier conversation with Gloria. "When I spoke to Gloria, she said she'd never thought that Derek would die in prison. She'd never imagined that it would end that way. That doesn't sound like much, but if you'd heard the note in her voice . . . I got the feeling there was some plan Derek had screwed up by dying in prison."

"That sounds like a stretch."

"I could be reading more than was there," she admitted. "But taking Derek out of it for a moment, someone else was involved, and it was probably an individual well connected to the art world. The Markhams, Wyatt—we keep coming back to them."

"I talked to them all several times."

"Do you think you asked the right questions?"

Anger flashed in his eyes, but she wasn't going to back down. He wanted her to face some hard truths; perhaps he needed to do the same thing.

"I thought I did, but you've given me some doubts," he said finally.

"Then we're even. Because you've given me some doubts, too."

"We'll figure it out," he promised.

"Together? Even if it means uncovering a mistake in the investigation?"

His jaw hardened. "I hope that doesn't happen,

but I'd rather admit a mistake than let a guilty person continue to go free."

She nodded, biting her bottom lip as she was caught off guard by a rush of emotion.

"What's wrong?" he asked, scooting across the bed. "Why are you crying?"

"You're on my side," she said simply. "Even though you don't really believe me, you're still willing to help me. That means a lot. I'm not feeling all that strong on my own."

"You've got amazing strength, Brianna. It pissed me off that you stood by Derek, but I couldn't help admiring your loyalty, your devotion, your determination to fight for him."

"Even if I was fighting the wrong fight?"

He smiled. "Let's wait and see how this ends before we make any judgments. Since there's not a lot we can do this second, how do you feel about . . . getting a little more comfortable?"

"Hmm, sounds perfect. Maybe I'll take off a few things," she said teasingly.

"I'll help," he offered.

"I bet you will."

He stole a kiss, then pulled back. "You'd better set your alarm first."

"Why? I don't have to pick up Lucas until eleven."

"But you'll be up at six, because that's when the waves will be the calmest."

"I'm not going surfing with you."

"It's perfect timing. Lucas is occupied. It will be just you and me."

"But—"

He kissed her again, and as his tongue slid along her lips, she decided to let the argument wait until later . . . much later.

"I can't believe I'm doing this," Brianna said early the next morning as she stood in a wetsuit on the sand, shivering in the cold morning air. Jason had taken her to the beach behind his condo, and they were completely alone. The waves were gentle, but the ocean was still vast, deep, and scary.

"You'll have fun, I promise," Jason said reassuringly.

"I liked the fun we were having before you dragged me out of bed," she said grumpily.

"You told me that you've spent too much of your life as a spectator. Here's your chance to get your feet wet," he added with a laugh.

"Very funny. But I'm a mother; I can't do risky things. I'm all Lucas has left."

"I would never let anything happen to you. You can trust me, Brianna. But more important, you can trust yourself. You can do this. I know you can."

It *was* past time to step outside the lines that had limited her life. "All right. Let's do it."

He slung the board under his arm and took her hand. "We'll go together the first couple of times. Then you can try your own board."

Her toes hit the freezing water, and her teeth

began to chatter. She almost backed out, but Jason had her hand, and he wasn't letting go. As they got deeper, the wetsuit soaked up the cold, but she could still feel the sting of the water as they paddled out to the waves.

She gripped the sides of the board tightly as Jason turned it toward the shore.

"When I say go, start paddling," he said. "I'm going to be with you the whole time, hanging on to the back. Just stay on your stomach the first time. Next time, we'll get you up on your feet."

"I didn't think we'd be this far out," she said, panic running through her.

"The waves will take you home." He kissed her cheek. Then he slid toward the back of the board and said, "Go."

She started paddling, feeling the wave rise beneath her. Suddenly, the ocean was doing all the work, and she was flying toward the shore. She hung on for dear life, but she managed to swallow a few mouthfuls of seawater that left her spluttering when the board hit the sand. Still, she felt supremely triumphant. "Let's do it again!" she said, coughing out the words.

Jason grinned. "You're on."

On her second ride, she tried standing up, lasting about three seconds before she slid off the board. Jason was instantly by her side, pulling her up to the surface.

"Do you want to take a break?" he asked as she grabbed the board again.

She shook her head. "Not until I can ride a wave all the way in. I want to do it, Jason. I want to beat Mother Nature at her own game."

He laughed. "I thought you weren't a competitor."

"I guess I am," she said with a smile. "And maybe a surfer, too."

It took three more tries to ride a wave all the way to the shore, but when it happened, she was giddy with joy. She jumped up and down in the knee-deep water, flinging her arms around Jason's neck and giving him a long, wet kiss. "Thank you," she said, gazing into his eyes. "That was amazing."

He tucked a strand of wet hair behind her ear. "I think you found that girl in the bar again."

"I think I did."

As a man called to his dog, she turned her head. The beach was waking up. An older couple was coming down the steps to the beach, and a car full of young guys was unloading their surfboards in the nearby lot.

"We should go." It was one thing to be with Jason when it was just the two of them, another to be out in public together. She wasn't quite ready to announce to the world that they were friends.

"Yeah, we should," he echoed, a grim look on his face.

"Jason, I need some time to figure out how to handle this—us. I don't even know what we are exactly, and it's complicated."

"I understand." He dragged the board up to the beach.

"You don't sound like you do," she said, following him out of the water.

"What do you want me to say, Brianna? I don't care who sees us together, but you do."

"That's true for now, not forever. I just need time to figure things out."

"Take all the time you need. I'm not going anywhere. But I will be at the kite festival today. I promised Lucas, and I won't let him down."

"He would be crushed if you did," she said, appreciating his concern for her son. "But I don't want to put him in the middle of your battle with the Kanes."

"It's not my battle; it's theirs. And I don't think it's just Lucas you're worried about."

"I love them, Jason. I don't want to have to choose between you."

"It might come to that, Brianna."

"Well, it's not there yet." And she hoped it never would be.

"How am I going to pick?" Annie asked Charlotte, desperation in her voice.

Charlotte had stopped in the doorway to ask Annie if she was ready to go to church and found her sitting in the middle of her bed with a bunch of file folders in front of her.

"They're all good people," Annie said. "Way better than me. One of the ladies is a teacher. Another is a nurse. This guy is a doctor. They're all smart with money. They're married and in love." She choked back a sob.

"Oh, honey, are you all right?" Charlotte sat down next to Annie, putting her arm around her shoulders.

"I didn't think it would be this hard," Annie said. "It wasn't supposed to happen like this. I wasn't supposed to get pregnant or end up alone. I'm dependent on you and your mother, and we're not even related."

"My mother and I love having you here, and we have no intention of putting you or the baby out. Mom already pulled out Jamie's old crib and some of the clothes she kept from when we were babies."

"She's being very nice. But Reverend Schilling said I need to think about what's best for my child long-term."

"Do any of these couples stand out?" Charlotte asked, glancing at the photos attached to each file.

Annie's shoulders started to shake, and Charlotte saw not just worry on her teary cheeks but also fear.

"Okay, what's going on?" she asked, softly.

*"He* wants to adopt the baby. He's in one of these pictures."

It took a moment for Annie's words to sink in. *"He?* You mean the father?" Charlotte's gaze flew back to the pictures. There were five possibilities, all of them married.

"He doesn't want his wife to know that he's the father. He wants to pretend that it's just a straight adoption."

"That is wrong on so many levels. Did you talk to him, Annie?"

"He called me before I met him and his wife. He told me not to say anything, that this was the perfect way for him to help. He'd take the child and raise it as his own, and his wife would be a good mother, and no one would ever have to know that he was really the biological father."

"And what did you say?"

"I didn't say anything when I met with him and his wife and Reverend Schilling, but it was hard. I was afraid to look at him or her, scared I might give something away."

"Who is he, Annie?"

"I can't tell you yet. I don't know if I can give up my baby and watch my child being raised by his wife." Another tear slid down her cheek. "I know it was wrong of me to have sex with him. He was just so nice to me. He made me feel special, and I loved him."

"I know you did, honey."

"I shouldn't have done it."

All five of the men were at least a decade older than Annie. "You didn't do it alone, and this guy knew how young and innocent you were. He took advantage of you, Annie."

"It wasn't like that. We talked. He was sad; things weren't going well in his marriage. I was sad, too. My father rarely let me leave the house, and I was hungry for someone to listen to me. And now my baby will grow up without its parents being together." She looked at Charlotte through pain-filled eyes. "I never wanted that to happen. I know what it's like not to have two parents. My mother died a few years ago, and my father has pretty much always been gone, at least in his head."

"You're not in the ideal situation, Annie, but families come in all shapes and sizes. Single mothers and single fathers can still be great parents. As long as there is love, understanding, and commitment to parenting, your baby can thrive. This is a big decision, one you need to consider very carefully."

"I thought there was a chance that . . ." Her voice trailed off with another sob.

"That he might leave his wife and marry you?"

"Pretty stupid, huh? What should I do, Charlotte? Should I give him my baby?"

"What do you *want* to do, Annie?"

Annie put a hand to her abdomen. "I can't imagine giving my child up. He or she is the only family I have left. My father barely remembers I exist, and when he does remember, I'm sure he hates me. But then I think, How selfish is that? If I give my baby to his father, that's something, I guess."

Charlotte didn't want to put her own opinions into the mix, but she was very troubled by this new development. The baby would have his biological father, but he would be raised with a secret hanging over his head. What if the wife found out at some point about the deception and walked out? Did this child deserve to be put in the middle of what had to be a turbulent marriage since the husband had decided to cheat?

Her gaze strayed back to the pictures of the happy couples. One of their marriages was a sham.

"I don't like the idea of this being a secret," she said. "Secrets have a way of coming out. And think about yourself, Annie. You'd be living in the same town. Knowing what you know, could you really do that?"

"But how could I give my baby to another couple when *he* wants it?"

It was a difficult point to argue. "The most important thing is what's good for the baby. Your needs and the father's needs should be taken into consideration as well, but don't make your decision based on him. I really wish you'd tell me who it was."

Annie gave her a half smile. "So you can yell at him?"

"He deserves a little yelling. He cheated on his wife." As she said the words, Charlotte felt a little guilty about flirting with Joe. She'd told herself she'd never take it any further, but maybe she'd already taken it too far. Joe hadn't signed his divorce papers yet, and his hesitation was a telling sign.

"He's sorry," Annie said with a sigh, referring to the father of her baby. Her gaze drifted toward the photos, but then she quickly looked up, probably afraid she would give something away.

"I'll bet he is sorry. But that doesn't excuse what he did then or what he's doing now by staying silent and not supporting you." Charlotte got up from the bed. "We'd better go to church before my mother sends a search party for us."

"You won't tell Reverend Schilling that one of these men is the father, will you?"

She really wanted to, but since Annie had entrusted her with the information, she'd keep it to herself. "I won't tell Andrew, but you have to tell anyone involved in the adoption. For the baby's sake, they'd need to know his medical background. I understand that you want to protect this man, Annie. But sometimes you have to tell the truth, even if it hurts."

"He could lose his wife."

"Maybe that's the price he has to pay."

Annie sighed. "I wish I knew what to do."

"You know," Charlotte told her. "You just have to find the courage to do it."

# FIFTEEN

"Where's Jason?" Lucas asked, for the tenth time since they'd arrived at the bluffs.

"He'll be here," Brianna said. "And so will your grandparents, and Kyle, too." She was hoping for a huge crowd so that the Kanes and Jason could coexist without a scene.

"Jason!" Lucas cried.

She turned her head to see Jason approaching, wearing jeans, a T-shirt, and a black leather jacket. His eye was still swollen and bruised, but it had improved considerably in the past few hours. He gave her a sexy smile, silently reminding her of all they'd shared in the past twenty-four hours. A rush of heat burned her cheeks, and she was extremely glad that the Kanes hadn't arrived yet.

"Hey, buddy. You ready to make that thing fly?" Jason put one knee on the ground to take a look at the kite. "Looks good to go."

Lucas gave a vigorous nod of his head. "Are you going to watch me?"

"You bet I am. I'm going to go down toward the other end of the bluff so I can see you better."

"Do you think I'll win?"

Brianna saw the need in Lucas's eyes, but she didn't think it was as much about winning as about gaining Jason's approval. He'd certainly made an impact on Lucas's life in a short period of time—hers, too.

"Just remember to have fun," Jason said.

"Does your face hurt?" Lucas asked curiously.

"Not as much as the other guy's."

"Can you teach me how to fight?"

"I can teach you how to stay *out* of a fight. That's more important. But right now, it's all about the kites, buddy. And . . ." He leaned over and whispered something in Lucas's ear.

Lucas gave a happy giggle. "Okay."

Jason stood up, the grin still lingering on his face, as Kyle came running over, grabbing Lucas's attention.

"What did you tell him?" Brianna asked.

"Run fast, and hold on tight."

"Sounds like good advice." She shifted her feet, wishing she didn't feel the need to walk away, but the Kanes would be arriving any moment.

His smile dimmed, a shadow entering his eyes. "Don't worry, I'm going."

"It's not that I want you to."

"Isn't it?" he asked. "There's always a choice."

"Not always."

"You just tell yourself that because it's easier than having to make one."

"We've had one night together. Don't push me."

Jason nodded, then left. He didn't get far, though, as a couple of attractive women stopped him. One very pretty woman put her hand on his bruised face, and he didn't seem in a hurry to shrug her away. What did she expect? He was an attractive guy, a town hero, and single. Even if she didn't want him, a lot of other women did.

Only she *did* want him. She just wasn't sure she could have him.

Forcing herself to look away, she turned to Lucas. A moment later, Rick and Nancy joined them.

"This is going to be so much fun," Nancy said with a smile. Rick looked equally delighted. "It's been a long time since we had someone to root for in this contest," she added.

"I'm going to win, Grandma," Lucas declared.

"I bet you will," Nancy said.

"I'll take you over to the starting line," Rick offered, grabbing Lucas's hand.

"Just stay with the others, Lucas, and remember to watch where you're going," Brianna called, concerned that Lucas might get swallowed up in the big crowd.

"He'll be fine," Nancy said. "They let the little kids go first, and two adults run alongside them."

"That's good. There are so many people here. I didn't expect it to be so crowded."

"It's the last event of the festival. Wait until you see the adult kites—they're spectacular. Professional kite flyers from all over the world come to participate."

"I didn't know one could be a professional kite flyer."

Nancy laughed. "I guess there's something for everyone. At least we have a good wind today. Some say this bluff is where the angels play. One year, we had a bright blue sky, then out of nowhere, wispy clouds started blowing in. The angels wanted to dance among the colorful kites." She lifted her gaze toward the sky, where there wasn't a cloud in sight. "I wonder if that will happen today. Even if it doesn't, I know that Derek is up there watching his son."

Rick returned, announcing that the kids were about to start. The starter blew a whistle, and Lucas and three other children took off running. Lucas was by the far the shortest and the youngest, and the look of excitement on his face reminded Brianna so much of Derek. The comparison didn't make her feel sad today but happy. Derek might be gone, but he'd left a piece of himself behind in his son.

As Lucas's kite leaped into the air, Brianna started running along the sidelines. She didn't know if Rick and Nancy followed; she was too caught up in sharing the moment with her son. She shouted encouragement but doubted he could hear her; he was too busy having the time of his life.

At the finish line, Lucas dropped the kite at her feet and ran straight to Jason. Jason swung him up in his arms and gave him a high five, and it was all Brianna could do not to fling herself into their huddle.

Jason set Lucas down, and the little boy ran back to her. "Do you think I won, Mommy?"

"I don't know. They'll announce the winners soon; we'll have to wait and see."

"My kite went really high!"

"It did," she agreed, happy to see the joy in his face. "Did you have fun?"

He gave a vigorous nod and took off again, running into his grandfather's arms this time. "Grandpa, did you see how good I did?"

Brianna suddenly realized she was exactly where she hadn't wanted to be—caught between Jason and the Kanes. She took a surreptitious glance over her shoulder and saw that Jason was gone. She wished she felt relieved instead of disappointed.

They returned to the staging area to await the announcement of the awards. Lucas came in second and was given a red ribbon for his efforts. Unfortunately, he was not a gracious loser. "I should have won, Mommy!" he declared angrily. "My kite was better than the other one."

"You did your best, and that's what counts."

"But I want a blue ribbon," he said stubbornly. "Not this stupid red one."

"Your dad would be proud of you," Rick told Lucas. "He got second place a few times, too."

"He did?" Lucas wavered, clearly torn between wanting to be like his dad and wanting to be first and best.

"Absolutely. Now, why don't you and I take a look at the big fancy kites over there?"

"Okay. Will you hold my ribbon, Mommy? I want to show it to Jason later."

"I've got it." She didn't have to look at Nancy's face to feel the sudden tension between them, and she was relieved when Nancy was distracted by one of her friends.

Alone in the crowd for a few minutes, she enjoyed the spectacle in front of her. Angel's Bay had come to life in full, vibrant color, and she felt much the same way. The thick fog of uncertainty and despair that had surrounded her life had slowly been lifting. She was feeling lighter, more in the mood to look up instead of down, to stop thinking so much about where she'd been and more about where she was going.

"Brianna, hi," Kara said as she pushed a baby stroller up to her. "I saw your little boy. He was having a blast."

"I've never seen him have so much fun. Look at your sweet little girl," she added, peering down at the tiny baby who was bundled up in blankets, awake, her wide gaze taking in the scene.

"She loves being outside," Kara said. "In a few years, she'll be running with the kites, too. I thought I saw Jason with you, but then he disappeared."

Brianna knew the curious look in Kara's eyes had more to do with Jason's relationship with her than his whereabouts. "I don't know where he went."

"It's none of my business," Kara began, then

stopped with a rueful smile. "I should leave it at that, shouldn't I?"

It was difficult not to like such a friendly, warm-spirited person who obviously cared about her friend. "It's probably best that you do," Brianna said lightly. "I don't think I could give you the answers you'd want to hear, anyway."

"I don't want to see anyone get hurt, and I'm not just talking about Jason, but about you, too. The history between you will be difficult to get past. Just be careful."

"It might be too late for that," Brianna murmured.

Kara gave her a sympathetic smile. "I was afraid of that."

An hour later, Brianna and Lucas returned home. She'd managed to get out of Sunday dinner with the Kanes, claiming that Lucas needed time to decompress and get ready for his first day of preschool on Monday. Which was all true but not the reason she wanted to skip dinner.

She found Nancy's intense scrutiny disconcerting. Her mother-in-law couldn't seem to keep from staring at her empty ring finger. Nancy obviously felt as if she were slipping away, which wasn't the case, but Brianna did need space. While she hadn't been trapped behind steel bars the past five years, she'd been stuck in one place for too long—physically and emotionally—and the Kanes had been trapped there with her. They needed to forge a relationship that would work now that Derek was gone.

Digger jumped out of his crate with an eager bark, and Lucas played happily with the puppy for a few minutes, but she knew it was only a momentary respite. He wanted to show Jason his ribbon. Jason's car wasn't next door, and she knew his father and Patty were returning today, so his house-sitting duties were over. He'd no doubt gone home.

"Can we go to Jason's now?" Lucas asked again, the ribbon back in his hand. He'd gotten over the fact that it was for second place. It was the first ribbon he'd ever won, and he was proud of that.

She hesitated one last second and then gave in. "All right, but we can't stay long."

"Can Digger come, too? He's tired of being in the crate."

"Sure." The more chaperones she had, the better.

When they arrived at the condo, Lucas ran ahead of her to press the doorbell. When Brianna reached the door, she heard multiple voices. Damn, this really was a bad idea. What if he was entertaining a woman? How awkward would that be?

But it was too late to retreat. The door opened, and Jason's jaw dropped in surprise when he saw them. "Brianna, Lucas. I didn't expect to see you here."

"I got second place," Lucas proclaimed. "We came to show you my ribbon."

Jason took the ribbon from in his hand. "Wow, that's a big one."

"I didn't get the blue one," Lucas said, anxious to see Jason's reaction.

"Red is my favorite color," Jason said.

"I like it, too," Lucas decided.

The puppy barked in agreement, straining at the leash to get to Jason.

Jason smiled, gave the puppy a quick scratch, and stepped back. "Why don't you come in?"

"Thanks, but you have company," Brianna said.

"Not company—my father and Patty. You can meet your neighbor."

Brianna smiled. "Is she still his girlfriend, or does she have a new title?" she asked as they stepped inside.

"So far, they've held off on any announcements, but who knows what's coming? I could use some backup."

Hal Marlow was an older version of Jason, with the same dark eyes and light brown hair, but he had slivers of gray at the sideburns and was a little shorter and stockier than his son. Nearly six feet tall, Patty Pease had brassy blond hair and the biggest breasts Brianna had ever seen. Her tight knit top emphasized her cleavage, and her leggings showed off her long legs. She had on a good deal of makeup, and Brianna guessed her to be in her late forties. In her arms was Princess, who didn't look at all happy to see Digger. Brianna kept a tight hold on Digger's leash.

Jason made the introductions. Patty gave her a wide, welcoming smile and a big hug. Hal's friendliness turned a bit cool as he made note of her last name, but he gave her a nod and said hello to Lucas.

"We didn't mean to interrupt," Brianna said. "Lucas was excited about his ribbon, and he wanted to show it to Jason."

"You won a ribbon today?" Hal asked Lucas.

"My kite came in second." Lucas proudly showed off his ribbon to Hal and Patty. "Jason helped me make it."

"He did, did he?" Hal gave Jason a questioning look. "How did that happen?"

"Brianna moved into the house next to Patty's," Jason explained.

"Really? We're neighbors?" Patty asked in surprise. "That's wonderful."

"I hope you still think so when you see the hole her puppy dug under your fence," Jason added.

"Oh, well, that's a puppy for you," Patty said with a wave of her hand. "I think he likes Princess. Isn't that sweet?"

"Princess doesn't return his feelings," Brianna said wryly.

"Well, they'll have to get to know each other," Patty replied. "Why don't you two stay for dinner? Hal and I brought tons of food, and we can all get better acquainted. Hal and I were just going to take Princess for a walk on the beach. Why don't you and Digger come with us, Lucas? While we're gone, you two can make us some margaritas. The fixings are in the kitchen."

"I don't know if Lucas can handle Digger on his own," Brianna said.

"I'll take the leash," Hal said, extending his hand. "He needs to burn off some energy. We'll be back shortly."

They were through the sliding glass doors that led to the deck before she could stop them.

"Patty likes to matchmake," Jason said with a grin. "She thinks if she can find me a woman, I'll be too busy to watch out for my dad."

"She seems nice."

"With a heart of gold. Or maybe her heart is set on getting some gold." His smile turned cynical.

"Is your father rich?"

"Not wealthy, but he has some money. His construction firm built these condos. That's how I got this sweet deal on the beach."

She'd only gotten a quick glimpse of his condo when they'd gone surfing, and now she took a longer look. His condo was indeed sweet, with hardwood floors covered by colorful throw rugs, antique tables, brown leather couches, and a stone fireplace for cold winter nights. One wall was made of floor-to-ceiling windows, with a view of the beach and the sparkling ocean beyond.

"Did someone help you with the interior design?" she asked.

"My father's third wife was a designer. She picked out the rugs, the pictures, the lamps, and the couches. Some of the tables I found, others I made."

Brianne ran her fingers along the exquisitely curved edge of a side table. "Did you make this?"

"I did," he said, folding his arms across his chest.

"Really? It's beautiful."

He shrugged. "My father taught me carpentry as soon as I was old enough to hold a hammer. I was supposed to go into the family business, but I liked police work better. I still do cabinetry and carpentry work as a hobby."

"Is this your mother?" she asked, picking up a family photograph from an end table. The woman was a slightly plump blonde with a wide smile and laughing eyes. At her side were her husband and son; Jason looked about six in the picture.

"Yes. It was taken a few weeks before she was killed—our last family photo."

Her heart broke for the little boy in the picture. No wonder he had such an affinity for Lucas. She put a hand on his arm, went up on her tiptoes, and kissed his lips. As she pulled away, Jason grabbed her arms and hauled her back for another, deeper kiss.

Breathless, she said, "I think we're supposed to be making margaritas."

"You distracted me."

"Likewise."

"I'm glad you came by. I thought you might have dinner with the Kanes. Sunday dinners used to be a tradition with them."

"They wanted to, but I begged off."

"They couldn't have been happy about that. Even less happy if they knew where you were now."

"They don't know."

He looked as if he wanted to say more but let the subject drop. "Let's make those drinks. I know I could use one."

They tossed together a pitcher of margaritas and took them out to the back deck, which stepped down to the beach.

The afternoon wind had died down, and the sun was setting. It would be dark shortly. Brianna took a sip of her salty margarita and set it on the railing. Hal, Patty, and Lucas were at the far end of the beach, keeping a good distance from the water. Hal and Patty sat shoulder to shoulder, while Lucas and Digger dug a good hole in the middle of the beach. Princess was still in Patty's arms, and everyone seemed to be enjoying the moment.

Brianna glanced toward the sky, watching streaks of orange and pink shimmer across the horizon. "If I lived here, I don't think I could take my eyes off the view. I'd never get anything done." She glanced over at Jason. "The waves are bigger now. Do you think I could handle them?"

"Maybe not yet, but practice makes perfect."

"I would like to go out again."

"Just say when." Jason came up behind her, sliding his arms around her waist, pulling her back against his chest.

She felt too relaxed and comfortable to move away. In a few minutes, everyone would be back, and they'd have to pretend that there was nothing between them, but for now she would enjoy the moment.

"Your dad seems happy," she commented. "And I don't think you dislike Patty as much as you want to."

"She's growing on me."

"She's just not your mom."

"I'm not worried about someone taking my mother's place. I don't want to see my dad get hurt again. It takes him a long time to recover."

"He's the reason you don't put yourself out there, isn't he?"

"When you see someone get stabbed in the heart a few times, it's easier to stay away from the knife."

"That's a rather grisly description," she said, turning in his arms. "Have you ever been in love?"

"Until a few days ago, I would have said no," he said quietly, his dark eyes reflective.

She swallowed a knot of emotion. "Jason, I have feelings for you, too, but it's all happening so fast. I feel like a wishbone, the Kanes on one side, you on the other, and . . . and then there's Derek. I still hear the pain his voice when he told me you didn't believe him. He might not have showed it, but he was devastated when you testified against him."

The pulse in Jason's neck began to pound. "Derek should have told me a better story. Then I wouldn't have had to arrest him."

She sighed. "Apparently, he didn't have one. But the trial aside, being with you and letting you do things with Lucas that a father would do seems like betrayal."

"You already gave Derek five years of your life. How many more does he get?"

"When I married him, I promised to give him my whole life."

"He's gone," Jason said in frustration. "You need to live *your* life, not his."

"I'm starting to do that," she said firmly. "I just don't know if I'm going to be able to do that with you."

Jason let her go and stepped away.

"I'm sorry. You wanted nothing but truth between us," she said, "and that's where I am."

"I'm not taking that as your final answer, because I think you're going to change your mind. Perhaps finding out who was working with Derek will bring a new perspective to you and the Kanes. In the meantime, I'm going to light the grill."

While Jason was tending the barbecue, the others came back. Brianna took Digger's leash from Hal and tied it around the deck railing.

Patty and Jason headed inside to get the food going, Lucas tagging along. Patty waved off her offer to help, leaving Brianna and Hal alone on the deck. Jason's father poured himself a margarita and sat in the deck chair across from her, regarding her with a contemplative look. "I was sorry to hear about Derek. When news came back here that he'd died in prison, none of us could believe it. I don't think Jason has had a good night's sleep since then. It reminded me of how he was during the trial."

She didn't want to talk about Derek or the trial, but Hal seemed determined to have his say. She expected him to tell her how hard Jason had worked and how Derek was guilty in spite of what she thought, but his words surprised her.

"I always thought Jason's worry had as much to do with you as with Derek."

Had Jason told his father about their first meeting, how he'd supposedly felt about her? "We barely knew each other," she said, treading carefully.

"My son never looked at a woman the way he looked at you then—the way he looked at you tonight." He paused, letting his words sink in. "So you're friends now. I can't imagine the Kanes are too happy."

"They're not, no." She finished her margarita. She was drinking too fast, but she felt very much on the hot seat.

"So you've got a mind of your own."

"Not many people think so. I did stand by a convicted felon."

"Which shows you have a tremendous sense of loyalty—not easy to find these days. I've got just one more question."

"What's that?" she asked warily.

"Are you interested in Jason, or do you want to get back at him for what he did to Derek?"

She was shocked at the suggestion. "You think I'm playing Jason for some type of revenge? I would never do that. I'm not that kind of person."

"Sorry, but I had to ask. He's my son. I wasn't always a good parent. I let others raise him for me, including the Kanes. It's too late to make up for that, but I try to watch out for him now when I can."

"You don't have to worry about me."

"Good. By the way, you've got a great kid. Lucas sure talks up a storm."

"Yes, he does," she said a little stiffly, still rattled by his accusations.

Jason returned a moment later with a platter of meat ready for the grill. He gave them a curious look. "Everything okay out here?"

Hal smiled. "I was just telling Brianna not to hurt you."

Jason sighed. "I can take care of myself, Dad."

"That's what I always tell *you*, but it doesn't stop you from butting into my life."

"That's because you constantly screw your life up."

"I don't see you doing much better. And don't burn the steaks this time. They're supposed to be pink in the middle, otherwise all the juice dries up."

As Hal got up to bicker with Jason about the grilling strategy, Patty brought out a tray of vegetables and dip. "Lucas is in the kitchen stirring the brownie mix for me," Pattty said. "I hope that's okay."

"I'd better get him before it's all over the kitchen."

"You just sit. I love children, and since my daughter grew up and moved across country, I rarely get to spend time with any. Lucas is a friendly little boy."

"He's never met a stranger," Brianna agreed. "Sometimes it worries me, how trusting he is."

"Well, around here, there's nothing to fear." Patty cast a quick glance over her shoulder at the two men who were caught up in the fine art of barbecuing. "I've known a lot of shady guys in my time, but those are two of the finest men I've ever met. A girl couldn't do any better—in case you were wondering."

"I wasn't."

Patty gave her a knowing smile. "Well, just in case."

# SIXTEEN

After Hal's initial inquisition, he'd turned into an amicable host, treating Brianna to a number of stories. Between's Hal's tall tales about fishing and Patty's hilarious anecdotes from life in the stripper lane, there was no lag in the conversation. The stories got more risqué after Lucas left the dinner table and curled up on the living-room couch to watch television, soon falling asleep with Digger at his feet.

Patty and Hal made a quick exit after dinner. Brianna didn't know if they were in a hurry to be alone or to leave her and Jason alone, but either way, she and Jason ended up on the deck with nothing but the stars to watch over them.

"My father is anything but subtle," Jason said, sitting next to her on the love seat.

"I wasn't sure he liked me at first, but he seemed to warm up as the night went on. Maybe it was the margaritas."

"Or you. You're fairly likable."

"As is your father. No wonder he's been able to find so many women to marry him."

"Yeah, he's a real charmer. I can't quite believe that he got out of Vegas without tying the knot. I thought for sure Patty would get him down the aisle."

"I think she's the one resisting," Brianna said. "She told me that she really loves your dad, and she wants to go slow, to make sure it's right."

Jason looked surprised. "Interesting. We'll see what happens."

"I'm glad she's going to be my neighbor. I'll have a chance to get to know her better."

"You won't miss having me right next door?"

"Maybe just a little."

He nudged her shoulder with his. "So, is Lucas a heavy sleeper?"

"Not going to happen," she said with a laugh.

"Yeah, I figured." He took her hand and leaned back against the cushions. "A lot of stars out tonight."

In Angel's Bay, far away from big-city lights, the stars were brilliant. "It's amazing that exploding balls of hydrogen and helium can create such a spectacular sight," she said.

Jason laughed. "Well, that's romantic."

"Sorry. I have a lot of trivia in my brain."

"All those days spent in the library."

"I do like to read," she admitted. "I should find the Angel's Bay library and take Lucas there. So far, he hasn't shown much interest in books. He'd rather play with his trucks or balls or anything that moves."

"He's a boy."

"And I have little experience with boys. I didn't grow up with brothers, and my father was an intellectual. I don't think he played with a monster truck in his life."

"Well, I did, so if you need any tips, you know who to call."

She glanced over at him. "Lucas is crazy about you. It worries me. He's sensitive about people not liking him, especially men. It all ties into Derek not living with us. On some level, Lucas feels that was his fault."

"He'll understand as he gets older. And I think you should stop worrying for tonight. There's always tomorrow."

"You're right." Her gaze swept across the sky. "I wish we had a telescope. Imagine what we could see.

Jason sat up. "I have one. It's in the garage." He shook his head, an odd expression flashing across his face.

"What?"

"Everything always comes back to Derek. We found the telescope together at a flea market, and we used to set it up on the bluffs at night. A few times, we turned it on some of the neighbors' windows." He smiled. "Shauna Huxley used to undress with her curtains open. That was a lot better than the stars."

"Ah, now we get to your true love of the telescope," she teased.

He got to his feet. "I'll get it. We can try it out."

"I'll come with you."

She checked on Lucas before following Jason into the garage. As she stepped through the door, she realized this was Jason's workshop. A large work-table was set up in the middle of the room, and there were tools and wood shavings on the floor. A delicately carved rocking chair called to her, and she stroked the wood with her fingers. "This is gorgeous, Jason."

"It's my first attempt at a rocking chair."

"I can't believe how talented you are." She glanced back at him. "If you ever decide to stop being a cop, you could do this."

"I don't think that will happen." He pulled away some boxes from the corner of the garage, digging behind them. "Here it is." He took out a black cylindrical case. "I hope it still works." He set the case on the table and opened it.

She got out of the chair to take a closer look.

"What's this?" Jason asked in surprise.

Inside the case was a roll of what appeared to be thick, heavy paper. Jason pulled it out and unrolled it.

Brianna's pulse quickened as the first hint of color appeared, the lingering scent of oil paint. Her heart pounded as a woman's face began to form: the dark red hair, the widow's peak on the hairline, the mysterious violet eyes . . .

"Oh, my God!" She put a hand to her racing heart. She knew this face almost better than her own, because she'd spent five years searching for it. Eve—and not just one vision of her, but three.

Blood pounded through her veins, followed by disbelief and shock. Finally, she tore her gaze away from the paintings to look at Jason. His face was white, his eyes huge, stunned.

"This isn't possible," he murmured in confusion.

"The paintings were here. In *your* house."

"I didn't know they were here, Brianna." Jason shook his head in disbelief. "I had no idea."

Her head spun with questions. "You arrested Derek for stealing the paintings, but you had them all the time."

"Derek must have stashed them here."

"Why would he do that?"

"Hell if I know, but that's the only explanation that makes sense." He ran a hand through his hair as he looked at her, and anger hardened his eyes as he read her expression. "I did not set Derek up, Brianna. You know I didn't."

"Do I?" Her voice was shaky. She'd had so many doubts about Derek in the past few days and far fewer about Jason. They'd switched places in her mind, who was good and who was bad. Now she felt bewildered.

"Dammit, Brianna, *think*. Why would I have opened this case in front of you if I'd hidden the paintings here?"

"I don't know. Maybe you forgot."

"I wouldn't have forgotten where I hid million-dollar paintings." His gaze was penetrating, demanding that she listen to him. "But it's not about logic; it's about what you know—and you know me."

She stared back at him. "I don't know if I can trust my instincts anymore."

Disappointment darkened his eyes. "Then I guess I'll just have to prove it. Because I did not know these paintings were here."

He picked up one of the rolls and stretched it out, anchoring it down with blocks of wood. The wicked face of Eve gazed back at them—the one with the amused, sardonic expression and the cynical eyes that had made Victor try again and again to get her right. This woman was at the root of all of Brianna's problems.

"I *hate* her," she said. "I hate everything about her. I don't give a damn who she was, and I don't care if Victor Delgado came close to getting her right or not. She ruined all of our lives." She paced around the room, trying to release some of the adrenaline surging through her body.

"Derek was here the day before the robbery. He stood in this garage while I refinished a table," Jason added. "After the robbery, Derek had to hide the paintings somewhere. He couldn't do it at his parents' house. And he couldn't put them anywhere that could be traced to you or to him, because all of those locations would be searched." Jason paused, thinking . . . "This was the perfect place. I was the one investigating him. I wouldn't search my own garage. And Derek had access; he knew where I kept the spare key."

"How would he know that?"

"Because everywhere I've lived, I've always kept

a key outside. Derek must have figured that hadn't changed. It's not that tough to find; I leave it under a rock by the back door so I can get in after I surf."

"Derek said he didn't take the paintings, Jason. Who else could have put them here?"

"No one. I wasn't friends with any of the art people."

"What about another cop?"

"No one had a motive, Brianna. And if a cop had stolen these paintings, they would have fenced them a long time ago. What kind of thief would sit on paintings worth millions of dollars?"

"The kind of thief who did just that. What are we going to do now?"

"We're going to take the paintings down to the station and turn them over to the chief. He can re-open the investigation."

"You'll be part of that investigation," she pointed out. "You're in possession of the stolen paintings."

"Maybe this time you can take the stand and testify against me. Think how great that would feel," he said sarcastically. He released the blocks and rolled the paintings back up.

"Jason, that wouldn't feel great."

He gazed back at her, his face a cold, hard mask. Now he looked like the ruthless cop who'd taken the stand and testified against Derek. At the time, she'd thought it was ambition that had made him look so determined, but it wasn't that then or now—it was pain. She'd hurt him with her doubts. But there was no way to take them back.

"Do you want to come with me to the station?" he asked.

"I'll let you do that on your own," she said quietly. She'd finally found the paintings, but she still didn't know the truth.


Brianna awoke tired on Monday morning, exhausted from endless nightmarish questions that had plagued her dreams, her mind conjuring up every possible scenario for how the paintings could have ended up in Jason's garage. None of them made sense.

Putting her focus on the present, she got Lucas dressed and out the door for his first day of pre-school. He was so excited to be going to school with his best friend, Kyle, that he had no problem leaving her at the door of the classroom with a quick wave and a hug.

After dropping him off, she drove to the police station. Joe Silveira had called her earlier that morning, asking her to come in, and she wondered if Jason would be there, too. As she left her car, she zipped up her jacket, thankful she'd thrown on a heavier sweater. Storm clouds were brewing over the bay, and a cold wind was blowing through town. Change was definitely in the air—a big change for her.

She didn't know how the paintings had gotten into Jason's garage, but at least she had something new to work with.

Upon entering the station, she was surprised to

see Wyatt Kane and the Markhams. They weren't giving away much by their expressions, but Brianna could feel the barely suppressed excitement in the room. A few minutes later, they were ushered into a conference room. On the long rectangular table were the three paintings, unrolled and anchored by paperweights and books. Joe Silveira and Jason stood at either end of the table.

"Thanks for coming," Joe said. "As I told each of you on the phone, these paintings were discovered late last night, and I want to make sure that they are, in fact, the paintings that were hanging in the museum five years ago."

Wyatt, Gloria, and Steve crowded around the table. The three art experts studied the minute details of the paintings through magnifying glasses. Brianna found her gaze drifting away from the paintings to Jason. She couldn't read his mood, except that he was tense and not interested in looking at her. Joe Silveira's expression was guarded as well.

The minutes ticked by as Gloria, Steve, and Wyatt exchanged a few descriptive sentences about brushstrokes and paint thickness and other technical terms.

"Excellent," Wyatt said finally, but the light in his eyes had dimmed. He stepped back from the paintings, and a silent look passed among the three of them. "Excellent copies," Wyatt finished.

Jason started. "What are you talking about?"

"These are fakes," Wyatt proclaimed.

"Very good fakes," Steve Markham added.

"How can you be sure?" Brianna asked, shocked. "They look exactly like the photographs. The signature is the same." She turned to Gloria, whose gaze was still focused on the pictures. "Gloria?"

The older woman nodded her head. "Wyatt is correct. These were painted by a talented forger, not by Victor Delgado."

"Someone want to explain how you know that?" Joe cut in. "I thought we might have to do some forensic testing."

"You suspected these were fakes?" Jason asked the chief.

"Let's just say I was keeping an open mind."

"This mark." Wyatt pointed to a spot in the lower left-hand corner of the painting that depicted Eve's last moments—the stormy sea, the ship breaking apart, her outstretched hands. "It's the artist's mark. He couldn't allow himself to complete the painting without leaving some evidence of his own brilliance. That was his one and only mistake."

Gloria sat down abruptly, her face pale. "It's not possible," she muttered.

"It's obvious," Steve told his wife.

"Not to me," Brianna interrupted. "What are you all talking about?"

"This swirl of paint and this one," Wyatt continued. "They're not part of the original paintings. You have the photographs, yes?"

Joe opened the file on the table and pulled out the pictures.

Wyatt put one of the pictures next to the painting, then offered his magnifying glass to Joe.

There was a very faint difference, Brianna thought when she got her turn with the glass, although she still had doubts. "Are you sure it's not just the texture of the oil compared with a photograph?"

"Absolutely sure," Wyatt said.

There was something in his expression that she didn't understand, a mixture of anger and . . . pride? Her heart sank. "You know who forged these paintings, don't you?" She willed him not to say the name on the tip of her tongue, but her wish was in vain.

"Derek," Wyatt said.

She couldn't breathe for a second.

"This is Derek's work?" Jason asked, stepping closer to the table. "He painted these fakes? And that mark is supposed to be his signature?"

"His initials, D and K," Gloria mumbled, looking shattered.

"He practiced them on all of his art," Steve added. "He wanted his signature to become part of the painting, so he worked hard to make the initials look like brushstrokes."

"You said he wasn't a good artist," Brianna told Wyatt. "Now you're telling me that Derek was able to paint *The Three Faces of Eve* to such perfection that the only thing separating the fakes from the real paintings are his own carefully crafted initials? How is that possible?"

"Derek was very good at copying. It was originality that escaped him," Wyatt said bitingly. "He couldn't produce anything on his own. He could only take what was great and replicate it. He was just a hack."

Brianna turned to Joe. "What do you think?"

"We need to have a thorough appraisal conducted by an independent party," Joe replied.

"Where did you find the paintings?" Gloria asked the chief.

"I'm not at liberty to say at the moment."

Was he protecting Jason, or did he not want to compromise the investigation?

Brianna thought about Derek's final words to her—that he hadn't stolen the paintings but wasn't completely innocent, either. Had he been referring to the fact that he'd produced copies of the paintings?

"Why would Derek have done this?" she asked aloud. "Why would he have made these fakes?"

For a moment, no one answered, and then Wyatt said, "Derek must have meant to switch the forgeries with the originals, so that no one would realize they were missing—at least, not right away."

"When the security guard interrupted him, he didn't have time to make the switch," Steve added.

"There's no other possible explanation?" Brianna asked. "There's no one else besides Derek who could have taken the paintings?" She'd been defending Derek for so long it was difficult to stop. But even if Derek hadn't stolen the paintings himself, he'd known someone wanted them. Otherwise, he wouldn't have painted the fakes.

"Derek wanted to prove something to you, Wyatt," Gloria said wearily. "He wanted you to know these were his, that he was better than you thought. If he hadn't tried to show you that, these copies would have been perfect, and you would never have known."

"They would still have been copies," Wyatt said harshly. "A true artist creates his own art, something that's real, something that matters. He doesn't knock off someone else's work."

Brianna could only imagine how Derek must have felt to know that his grandfather thought so little of him. But what she couldn't imagine was Derek working so diligently on forgeries. He would have had to have been painting them during the time they'd been together, yet he'd never spoken of it. She'd never seen any trace of paint at his town house. He'd done it all in secret.

What else had he done in secret?

Anger ran through her, blinding her with impotent rage. Seeing the pity in the others' eyes made her even more furious. She ran from the room. How stupid she was to have put her trust, her love, her loyalty in a man who'd been as phony as his paintings.

# SEVENTEEN

Jason wanted to go after Brianna, but he was too stunned to move. He'd truly believed the paintings were the originals.

As Joe ushered Wyatt and the Markhams out of the room, Jason moved around the table to take another look at the art. The paintings were beautiful—the colors, the detail, the light. Derek had been brilliant.

Had he created the fakes to get back at his grandfather? Was that the master plan—steal the paintings his grandfather loved the most and replace them with fakes? Derek would have loved having that kind of secret. He would have finally gotten the best of his grandfather. Knowing about the blood tie between the Kanes and Victor Delgado would have made his revenge even sweeter.

Joe returned to the room. "I have some personal business to attend to, but I'll be back this afternoon. I've asked Betty to set up an independent appraisal."

"You don't trust Wyatt Kane or the Markhams?" Jason asked.

"Do you?" Joe countered. "I don't think our skilled forger could have made fakes this good without some help."

"I agree. Derek would have needed time and access to the paintings. They were kept in the Markham Gallery for several weeks before the official donation to the museum."

"And all three of our art experts knew about Derek's talent. Who else would have had that knowledge?"

"Possibly Katherine Markham. She works at the gallery—hell, maybe all of the local artists knew Derek's skill in that area. He was a big part of the art scene, growing up here. I questioned a lot of people during the investigation, but forgery was never a consideration." Jason shook his head, anger and disappointment in himself leaving a bitter taste in his mouth. "I didn't ask the right questions. I might have solved part of the crime but not all of it. And there's a chance now that Derek really didn't take the paintings. He could have been set up by someone else to take the fall, just like he said."

"Before you drown in guilt," Joe said sharply, "let's not forget the forgeries. Your old pal was in the thick of this, even if he didn't do it by himself."

"Right." Jason gave himself a mental shake. Whatever Derek had done, he'd done it with his eyes open.

"So let's find out who he was working with. Start with Wyatt Kane and the Markhams."

"There's a possibility Wyatt Kane actually shares a bloodline with Victor Delgado. Brianna found some letters in Derek's things that weren't definitive but suggested a connection. I was going to follow up that angle, but then the paintings appeared."

"In your house," Joe said. "You're in the thick of this, too, Marlow. Let's get some answers."

"I thought you wanted me off this case."

"Since these are fakes and you're no longer in possession of stolen property, you're back on and, I'm assuming, highly motivated. Check with me before you make any big moves." Joe paused in the doorway. "If one of our three art experts was part of a double-cross with Derek, then the other two might already be figuring that out. Someone might make a move. You've got to get there first."

"I will," Jason promised, but he had no idea how he would do that. He gazed at the paintings for a long minute, his mind racing through what he now knew.

Derek had forged the paintings. That was clear, but what else? Had he broken into the museum, assaulted the security guard, and stolen the originals? If he had done that, why hadn't he inserted the fakes in their place? No time?

Or had something else happened? Had someone gotten there before him?

Was it possible Derek didn't know who had set him up? Or had one of his friends stabbed him in the back—the same friend who had let him sit in a prison cell for five years? That didn't sound like friendship, more like revenge.

Maybe he'd finally come up with the right question: Who would have wanted Derek to suffer?


*The paintings were fakes. Her husband was a forger.* The thoughts filled Brianna's head as she drove home.

Derek had to have known the paintings were going to be stolen from the museum, either by himself or by someone else. He wouldn't have made copies for any other reason than that they would be used in a cover-up or passed along as the real thing. That was why he'd said he wasn't completely innocent. Why hadn't he taken his partner down with him? Because he was protecting her and Lucas? Or was he protecting himself? Had he remained quiet because he had other secrets to keep?

Nausea rolled through her stomach. What else could he possibly have been hiding?

She was almost sorry they'd found the forgeries. If they were still hidden away, she wouldn't be facing new and disturbing revelations about her husband. But her eyes were finally all the way open. She would get the truth, and she would face it. She would protect Lucas as much as she could.

The Kanes were another story. The news of the forgeries would spread across Angel's Bay like wildfire, and she had to tell them before someone else did. Only one thing worried her more than telling them about the fake paintings: the idea that they might already know. She didn't think she could handle learning that *they'd* lied to her, too.

She glanced at her watch as she pulled up in front of the Kanes' house. Lucas would be at preschool for another hour, thank goodness. By then, maybe she could get a handle on what needed to happen next.

Rick was in the driveway, checking the oil in his car. He gave her a friendly wave, but his smile dimmed as she marched across the lawn.

"What's wrong, Brianna?" He wiped his hands on a rag.

"I need to speak to you and Nancy."

"It's not Lucas, is it?"

"No, it's Derek. It's always Derek, isn't it?" she asked somewhat wearily.

"Nancy is in the house."

"Good, because I can't do this twice." She followed him up the steps and into the kitchen, where Nancy was making cookies. The room was warm and smelled like chocolate. Nancy had a peaceful, happy expression on her face; that wouldn't last long.

"Hi, Brianna," she said happily. "I'm making Lucas his favorite cookies for his first day of school. I hope he'll like them." She stopped abruptly, taking in the mood in the room. "Oh, dear. Something has happened."

"Brianna has some news about Derek," Rick said.

Nancy turned her gaze on Brianna, waiting and obviously worrying.

Brianna wasn't quite sure where to start. The Kanes were innocent victims, too. At least, she hoped they were; she loved them so much. But their total devotion to Derek had never been a secret. They'd wanted their boy to have everything. How far would they have gone to ensure that?

"Brianna, please, whatever you have to say, say it," Nancy implored. "I'm imagining the worst."

"What would that even be?" she asked helplessly.

"You're right. The worst happened when Derek died," Nancy replied. "So whatever this is can't be that bad."

"Last night, I thought I found the paintings, *The Three Faces of Eve*," she said, the words finally getting past her lips.

Nancy's gasp of surprise seemed genuine. She reached out a hand to the kitchen counter to steady herself. Rick moved next to her and took her hand in his.

"But this morning, Wyatt and the Markhams said the paintings were expert forgeries," Brianna continued. "They said that Derek painted them, that he'd left his signature."

"I don't understand," Rick said in confusion. "There are fake paintings now?"

"Yes, but they were so cleverly done they could have passed as the originals if Derek hadn't decided to leave his mark on them."

"You can't believe anything Wyatt says," Nancy interjected. "He was jealous of Derek's talent. He couldn't bear that his grandson was a better artist than him." She shot her husband a quick glance. "I'm sorry, Rick. I know he's your father, but it's true."

Rick's jaw tightened. "I still don't understand why Derek would paint fakes."

"To swap them for the originals during the robbery," Brianna explained. "Everyone seems to think that Derek was interrupted before he could do so." She paused for a moment, taking in their mystified expressions. "Derek wouldn't have made the copies if he didn't plan to use them."

"He could have just done it for fun. He liked to copy art. He was good at it," Nancy said. "What's the harm?"

"It's fraud," Rick said flatly.

"Only if you try to sell them," Nancy said. "Brianna, you're not losing faith in Derek, are you?"

Nancy's words cut to the core and made Brianna's heart ache, because she wasn't losing faith—she'd already lost it.

"He never told me anything about his art, Nancy. He never showed me that part of his life. Yet, I know now that Derek had to have painted those fakes when we were together." She took a breath. "He had a secret life that he didn't share with me."

"Maybe he didn't want you to judge him. When he was a small boy, he wouldn't show me his art, either. He'd get embarrassed and hide it away."

"Stop making excuses for him," Rick said sharply. "Let the girl talk. What else, Brianna? There's more, isn't there?"

She could see that Nancy didn't want to hear more, but she had to finish it. "Mr. Isaacs brought me a letter from Derek. In it, Derek said that he'd done things he was ashamed of, that he'd lied and created a false life that he'd started to believe in. He'd lost track of what was fake and what was real. It was all so cryptic I couldn't make sense of it until now."

Nancy sat down at the kitchen table. "You could be wrong, Brianna. He could have been talking about other mistakes, simple errors that we all make." She twisted her hands together. "Where did you find the paintings?"

Brianna didn't want to answer, but she had no choice. "They were hidden at Jason's house."

"Jason!" Nancy exclaimed. "He's still setting Derek up. He's making you doubt Derek. He's the reason you're confused. He's an evil, evil man."

Brianna sat down across from her mother-in-law and put her hand over Nancy's. "I love you, Nancy. You and Rick have been like parents to me. I've been incredibly touched by your generosity and your love. You are two of the most wonderful people I have ever met in my life, and the last thing I want to do is hurt you." She fought back tears at the sorrow and fear in Nancy's eyes. It wasn't fair that she had to suffer more pain, but they all needed to find their way to the truth. "This isn't about Jason. It's about Derek. I need to know who he really was."

"You do know. He was the man who loved you."

"But who else was he?"

"Are you sure you want to find out?" Rick interjected, his expression bleak. "I doubt it will make any of us happy."

"I am sure," she answered. "I'm never going to regret loving Derek, because I wouldn't have Lucas if I hadn't fallen for your son. And I wouldn't have you, either. I don't want to lose you."

"We don't want to lose you, either," Nancy said. "But Jason is poisoning your mind. He wants to take Derek's place in your life. It's not right."

"I'm making my own decisions. Jason may have made mistakes, but we both know now he couldn't have been completely wrong."

"How can we help?" Rick asked quietly.

"Would you mind picking up Lucas from school? I want to take one last pass through all the boxes that came from Derek's house, and then I need to talk to some people, starting with Wyatt. I don't think he's been as forthcoming as he could be." She didn't want to get into the Kane-Delgado connection at this point; she'd already dumped enough on Nancy and Rick.

"Take all the time you need, Brianna," Rick said. "We must have the truth, whatever it is."

The Markham Gallery was crowded when Jason stopped in. He hadn't been in the gallery in quite a few years, but it was exactly as he remembered, with floor-to-ceiling windows and an array of mirrors and lights that added to the atmosphere of importance and grandeur.

"Jason," Katherine said, coming up to him. "Can I help you?"

"I'd like to talk to your aunt and uncle."

"They're out, but they told me about the paintings. I was blown away." She tipped her head toward a quieter alcove. "Let's step over there."

He followed her across the room. "Did you know that Derek was a skilled forger?" he asked when they were alone.

"I knew he was a fabulous artist," she said, her dark eyes concerned. "I didn't realize he'd gone in that direction. Was this a one-time thing? Had he done it before?"

"I don't know. Right now, I'm just concerned about *The Three Faces of Eve*. Derek had to have access to the paintings in order to copy them, and the paintings were here before they were moved to the museum."

She nodded. "They were in the vault. I saw them right before I left on my trip."

"Who has access to the vault?"

"My aunt and uncle, my cousin Dane . . ." She thought for a moment. "Wyatt, of course. He's an investor in the gallery. I assume he has all the keys and codes. Maybe George Randall. He works here part-time and often does the close late at night. That's it. You don't think my aunt or uncle had something to do with this, do you?"

"I'd like to talk to them. When will they be back?"

"They didn't say, but I'll tell them you're looking for them."

"Thanks." He could see in her eyes that she had something else she wanted to ask him. "What?"

"My aunt said she didn't know where the forgeries were found. Care to enlighten me?"

"Sorry, it's an ongoing investigation."

"It seems strange that they'd suddenly be found now. It must have something to do with Brianna coming to town."

He could see the curiosity in her eyes, but he wasn't about to share the fact that the forged paintings had been in his garage all along. He had no idea what kind of relationship she had with her aunt and uncle and Wyatt, but since she worked with them, he had to assume that she was in their camp.

"Do you still think Derek stole the paintings?" she asked. "Or has this changed your mind?"

"Let's just say my mind is open, and I'd appreciate any help you can give me."

"My suggestion would be to talk to my aunt first," Katherine said. "She knew Derek a lot better than my uncle or Wyatt did." She paused. "It hasn't been easy for her to be the woman between two strong and powerful men. She sometimes gets tired of their shadows."

"Are you trying to tell me something?" he asked sharply.

"I think I just did," she replied. Then she walked away.

\* \* \*

Jason stopped off at Wyatt's studio next, but he was also out. He needed a new angle, and aside from Katherine's cryptic remarks about Gloria, the only lead he had was Wyatt's blood tie to Delgado. He had to know if that was real.

He thought about calling Brianna, but he'd rather talk to her when he had something definitive to say. And she had no way of proving the blood link beyond the letters she'd found. He needed someone who was up on Angel's Bay history . . .

Making a sharp turn, he headed to Kara's house. The Murrays were one of the founding families of Angel's Bay, and they knew more about the bloodlines of the original twenty-four shipwreck survivors than anyone.

After parking in front of the house, he jogged up the steps and rang the bell. He pushed it again when no one immediately answered, then felt guilty. The baby was probably sleeping, and Kara was going to be pissed at him for waking her up. He shouldn't be adding more stress to their lives when he knew they'd been having trouble connecting in the past few weeks.

He was just about to leave when Kara threw the door open. Her red hair was mussed and tangled, and she was scrambling to secure the tie around her silk bathrobe. Her legs were bare, and her lipstick was smudged. He saw Colin coming out of the bedroom wearing just a pair of sweatpants and realized he'd interrupted more than the baby's nap. But at least there was a grin on Colin's face and not a scowl. In fact, they both looked happier than they had in a long time.

"Well, well," he drawled. "What have we here?"

"We were taking a nap," Kara said hastily, a sparkle in her eyes."

"Is that what you're calling it these days? Sorry to interrupt. Get back to doing what you were doing."

"Did you want something?" Kara asked. "Because we're . . . done."

"Speak for yourself," Colin teased, coming up behind her and sliding his arms around her waist. "This is intermission."

"Don't you two have a baby somewhere?" Jason asked.

"At Grandma's," Colin replied.

Jason nodded approvingly. "Way to fully utilize the babysitting time."

"So what's up?" Colin asked. "You rang the doorbell with a hell of a lot of purpose."

"I need some information, Kara. Do you have any of those family trees your grandmother made up for Founders Day?"

"I do. Why would you want them?"

"I need to see the line of descendants from Francine Kane. A lot has happened. I can't get into it right now, but I'd love your help."

"Come in," she said, stepping aside. "I'll get it."

"What's this all about?" Colin asked when they were alone.

"We found forgeries of *The Three Faces of Eve*. Derek painted them. It's quite probable he was planning to switch them for the originals during the robbery, but he either didn't have time or changed his mind."

"I guess the case isn't closed anymore," Colin said with concern in his eyes.

"It's wide open. I missed something, Colin. Something important."

"Are you sure? If he painted forgeries, he's still looking guilty to me."

"I need to know *how* guilty." Jason glanced over his shoulder to make sure Kara was nowhere in sight. "So it looks like you got over your little problem, huh?"

Colin's grin widened. "It turned out not to be so much of a problem. I took your advice. I spilled my guts to Kara, and it turned her on. She practically jumped me, and well . . . you know how I like it when she does that."

"Glad I could help," he said, happy the two of them had found their way back to each other.

Kara returned a moment later with a notebook. "Okay, what do you want to know?"

"Which one of Francine's sons was Wyatt descended from?" he asked.

"That would have been David, the younger son." She lifted her gaze to his. "Why does that matter?"

"Because I think Francine and Victor Delgado had an affair after the wreck, and she had his baby—the baby she passed off as her youngest child."

Kara looked back down at the chart. "He was born nine months after the wreck. The dates are close if the affair happened quickly, but I thought Victor was obsessed with Eve."

"Apparently, he found some comfort elsewhere."

"That's amazing," Colin cut in with surprise. "Wyatt and Derek were related to Victor. Did they know?"

"Derek did, and I'm guessing Wyatt did, too. What about Ramón Delgado?" he asked impulsively. "Did he have any children?"

"You know, the funny thing is that Ramón and the other two survivors who ended up at Shelter Cove weren't part of the original twenty-four survivors. Their stories weren't depicted in the quilt, because it was made before they found their way up the coast. They're often not even mentioned at Founders Day." Kara turned the page over. "Let's see. Yes, here it is, Ramón had a daughter named Ava. Pretty close to Eve, isn't it?"

"What happened to her?"

"She married a man by the name of Douglas Tanner. They had one girl, Jane, who married Randolph Hillman. She had a daughter named Elizabeth, who then had a daughter named Rhea. Nothing but girls in that line. It ends with Rhea, born in 1941, married to John Lawrence in 1965, daughter Gloria."

His pulse leaped in excitement. "Gloria?"

Kara looked back at him with the same surprise in her eyes.

"As in Gloria Markham?" he added.

"It doesn't say, but it's an odd coincidence."

"I don't think it's a coincidence at all," he said. It wasn't just Wyatt who was tied to the Delgado brothers. Gloria was related to Ramón, the much maligned younger brother and quite possibly the original thief of the paintings. Had she repeated history? Had she decided that Victor's paintings of Eve would never see the light of day? Katherine had told him to talk to Gloria first. Did she know? Was she trying to hint without completely giving up her aunt? "I have to go," he said abruptly.

"Go where?" Colin asked.

"I'll let you know when I get there."

"You can't leave us hanging, dude," Colin said. "We'll worry about you."

"I think you'll find some way to distract yourselves. I'll explain everything later. By then, I should know who took the paintings."

"I thought it was Derek," Kara said.

"So did I, but I don't anymore."

As he left the house, his cell phone rang. His body tightened at the gruff voice on the other end. "Wyatt, I'm glad you called me back. I'll be at your studio in ten minutes." He felt a surge of adrenaline as he got back into his car. Someone was finally ready to talk.

# EIGHTEEN

Brianna sat on her couch and spread out Derek's sketches on the coffee table. Now that she knew about the forgeries, about the way he'd slipped his initials into the art because he just had to let someone know what he'd done, she couldn't help thinking that he'd left her a clue as well.

She put aside the scenes of her or Lucas; she was interested in the sketches he'd done of the town. Three stood out: the caves in Shelter Cove, the art studio, and the Markham Gallery with its wall of mirrors. There were no distinct people in any of the scenes, just shadows and shapes that implied some sort of energy, and a lot of that energy felt hostile. Was she feeling Derek's anger or someone else's?

Why had Derek drawn these particular scenes? They were places that were important to him in some way, but was there more to it than that? Was he trying to tell her something?

She didn't know why Derek hadn't switched the

fakes for the originals. But hiding them at Jason's condo had been deliberate. As Jason had said, what better place to hide something incriminating than in the garage of the man who was investigating him?

But where were the originals? She was convinced Derek didn't have them. She wasn't sure he even knew where they were. Perhaps someone had turned on him—there had been a plan, but something had happened. Derek had taken the fall, and his partner in crime had let him sit in that jail cell for five years.

She heard footsteps coming up the porch steps and jumped to her feet. When she opened the door, she expected to see Jason, but it was Katherine Markham.

"Hi," Katherine said tentatively. "Can I talk to you?"

"Come in," Brianna said, stepping back.

"I spoke to Jason earlier, as well as my aunt and uncle. I know about the forgeries," Katherine said as she walked around the coffee table. Her gaze fell on the sketches. Surprise flashed across her face. "Are these the sketches Derek did in prison?"

"Some of them."

Katherine sat down on the couch, her gaze moving from one sketch to the next.

"Those are the ones of Angel's Bay," Brianna said, taking a seat in the chair across from her. "I feel like Derek is trying to tell me something, but I'm not getting it."

Katherine didn't answer right away. It seemed to take some effort for her to drag her attention away from the sketches. Finally, she lifted her head, gazing at Brianna. "He's trying to tell you where the paintings are."

"I think so, too, but where? I thought he'd incorporate some pieces of the Eve paintings into these, like a trail of bread crumbs, but nothing jumps out at me."

Katherine looked back down at the sketches. Then she turned to the other stack. "What are these?"

"Those are of me and Lucas. That one is the first time we met," she said, following Katherine's gaze.

"He always loved looking at a woman in a mirror," Katherine murmured. "He used to tell me that while most people think the glass doesn't lie, because a mirror is the purest form of reflection, variations in the glass can still shape the truth in a way that's almost unrecognizable. That's why he used to paint objects through the perspective of a mirror."

"He did seem to have a fascination with them," Brianna said. The more she talked with Katherine, the closer she felt she was coming to something, but it was just out of reach. "I know the answer is right in front of me. I just have to figure it out."

Katherine cleared her throat. "Maybe I can help. I came here to tell you that I think you're on the wrong track, suspecting Wyatt. I feel like I'm betraying my family, but I feel so bad for you and Lucas. And for Derek most of all. I think his partner was my aunt Gloria."

Her heart skipped a beat. "Why do you think that?"

Katherine gave her a steady gaze. "Because they

had an affair—a long-running affair over several years. Derek broke it off after the two of you got engaged."

Brianna swallowed hard, a knot growing in her throat. Gloria was married and at least fifteen years older than Derek.

"I saw them together once at my aunt's art studio. She told me later that Derek had asked her to pose for him, and one thing led to another. She said she was sorry, and maybe she was, but she was also crazy about Derek. I'm sure they came up with the plan to steal the paintings together." She paused. "I didn't want to tell Jason this, because I didn't want to be his source of information. It's my family we're talking about, and my job. My mother is ill. I need the money. No one can know that I tipped you off."

"I understand. So if your aunt and Derek were in it together, where are the paintings now?"

Katherine looked down again. She picked one sketch up and smiled to herself. "I don't know why I didn't think of this before. It's so clear. And Jason should have figured it out, too, because they used to go there all the time."

"Shelter Cove?" Brianna asked in confusion.

"The caves," Katherine replied, a light in her eyes. "They go way back under the bluffs, where it's completely dry and very secluded, and no one ever goes there anymore." She jumped to her feet and glanced down at her watch. "The tide won't be coming in yet. I'm going to check it out. I'll let you know if I find anything."

"Wait," Brianna said. "I'll come with you."

"Lucas isn't here?"

"No, his grandparents are watching him today."

"Great. Do you have a flashlight? We'll probably need it."

"I'll get one," Brianna said. It felt good to take some action, and with a little luck, maybe Katherine's hunch would pay off.

During the drive to the cove, Brianna was caught up in her thoughts. She couldn't imagine Gloria and Derek together, but they did share a passion for art, as well as, apparently, each other.

"If Gloria was Derek's partner," Brianna began, "why wouldn't Derek have told the authorities about her?"

"I don't think you're going to like my answer," Katherine said. "Derek did some shady stuff. I suspect that if he'd turned the spotlight on Gloria, she would have done the same back. He might have had to spend a few more years in prison."

"Okay, I don't need to hear any more," Brianna said quickly. One crime at a time was all she could deal with.

"I figure Derek hid the paintings where no one could find them, so that when he got out, he could reap the rewards for his prison time."

"If Gloria was his partner, why didn't she just sell them?"

"They must have had a falling-out. Something

went wrong with the plan. She let him take the fall because he didn't hand over the paintings. And he took the fall, because she had too much on him. I'd always wondered if she was involved, but I didn't know until today—until I realized there were forgeries, and only a handful of people could have given Derek access to the paintings."

Katherine parked along the bluff, and they made their way down to the beach. The waves seemed bigger today as they came around the point. There were tall clouds blowing in off the ocean, mixed with some lower-level fog. In an hour or so, the beach would be completely socked in. As they approached the caves, Brianna felt trepidation. The water wasn't near the entrance, but she had no idea how fast the tide came in.

"I can do it alone," Katherine said, sensing her hesitation. "I've been in there a dozen times. I know how to get to the back. You can wait here."

She didn't like the fact that Katherine was so eager to go in on her own. While she'd been nothing but helpful, she was still a Markham. Maybe she wanted to get the paintings for herself. She could lie and say the paintings weren't there, then come back to get them on her own later. "I'll go, too," she said.

"Great. It is a little less scary when there's two people."

As they made their way into the rocks, Brianna was surprised by how large the caves were. She didn't feel as claustrophobic as she'd expected. Jason had said that several survivors had lived within these caves for months. "This is where Ramón Delgado landed, right?"

"That's right," Katherine said, turning down a dark tunnel. She flashed the light on, the beam bouncing off the rocky walls. "Ramón wrote on the walls about losing his beloved Eve not only to the sea but also to his evil brother, Victor."

Brianna grew more curious as they moved deeper into the cliff. The passageway narrowed and twisted and turned. She was glad to have Katherine leading the way, since she seemed to know exactly which shadowy passages to go through.

Eventually, the tunnel opened out onto a wider, more open space. Katherine pointed out the deep scratchings on a nearby wall. There were names, dates, and figures, as if the men were trying to tell their story with all they had left.

Katherine motioned her toward another passageway. As they walked, the space got smaller and narrower. Brianna began to feel a little panicky. "Are we almost there?"

"We're there." Katherine stepped back, motioning Brianna to go in front of her.

Brianna couldn't see a thing. She turned back around and found the light shining in her eyes, blinding her.

She put up a hand. "Can you turn the light away?"

Katherine pointed the light toward the ceiling so they were facing each other again. Brianna didn't like the look in Katherine's eyes.

"This was almost too easy," Katherine murmured.

Brianna suddenly realized she'd made a big mistake. "The paintings aren't here, are they?"

"You're way too trusting, Brianna. First Derek, then me."

"Why did you bring me here?"

"Because you were getting too close to where the paintings really are. Derek figured it out and left you clues in his sketches. I guess it was some type of insurance. As soon as you told me he'd started drawing again, I knew I had to see those sketches."

Brianna remembered the broken picture on her dresser. "Did you go into my house?"

"That was easy, too. The back door was open."

"Why did you break my engagement photo?"

"Because it disgusted me," she said, an angry light in her eyes.

"*You* have the paintings, don't you, Katherine? It wasn't Gloria who was Derek's partner, it was you." It was suddenly all so clear.

"Bingo. But Gloria and Derek did have an affair. Derek loved women and slept with almost everyone he met. But he and I had a special connection. We painted together. We used the mirrors on each other; we were naked, bare, with no secrets between us and no lies. He and I were supposed to end up together. And then you came along." Her lips tightened. "He wasn't supposed to get engaged. He wasn't supposed to bring you to Angel's Bay to get married. He was flaunting you right in my face. It wasn't love; you were just his trophy. The beautiful girl in the mirror that he had to have."

"So you set him up," Brianna said, everything clicking into place.

"It didn't start out that way, but when I realized he intended to marry you, he had to pay."

"But you were out of town during the robbery."

"I came back without anyone knowing. I got into the museum before Derek and took the paintings. When he arrived to swap the fakes, the originals were already gone. The security guard surprised him and had him cornered, so Derek knocked him out with his flashlight. That was a mistake."

Brianna couldn't believe how pragmatically Katherine spoke about the crime. "You say you loved Derek, but you betrayed him, and you let him sit in prison. You're the reason he's dead, Katherine. How does that make you feel?"

For just a moment, Brianna saw a flicker of guilt in the other woman's eyes. Then she straightened and threw her head back.

"I didn't know that would happen," she said. "I was holding the paintings until he got out. I had decided to split it all with him like we planned, to make up for the time he'd spent in jail. And also because Derek had the right contacts. I would have had a lot of trouble selling them on my own. Then Derek had to go and die. I didn't know what I was going to do. But you forced my hand—you and your questions."

Brianna shook her head. "You did all this out of spite? You're crazy."

"Not crazy, just determined to get what's rightfully mine. My aunt and uncle treat me like dirt. They pay me nothing. They never respected my talent. Not like Derek did. We were both misunderstood artists."

"So what now?" Brianna asked, feeling moisture seeping in at her toes. Katherine was between her and the entrance, and she had the only flashlight.

"Now we part company. I need to get the paintings, and I can't have you getting there before me."

"But I don't know where they are."

"Yes, you do."

Brianna thought back to the sketches she'd looked at. "Are they at the gallery?"

"Good guess. I put the paintings in a place Derek would have appreciated, where people were looking at them each and every day but didn't know it. Gloria and Steve and Wyatt thought they were so much smarter than Derek and me, so much more talented, more capable. The three of them were fools. I'll have the last laugh." She switched off the light.

Brianna blinked in terror, surrounded by darkness.

"I know these caves like the back of my hand," Katherine said, her voice echoing off the walls. "Derek and I used to make out down here. We even made love here once."

Brianna followed Katherine's voice, creeping forward, her hand sliding along the wall next to her. "Katherine, turn the light on. I won't tell anyone. I don't care anymore about the paintings. I just want to get back to my son."

Katherine laughed. "Like you'd let me walk away now. Don't worry about your little boy; the Kanes will raise him. They'll spoil him just like they did Derek. But if you get out before the caves flood, maybe you'll be able to catch me in time. I always did like a challenge. So did Derek. He never would have fallen for this."

"Jason will figure it out," Brianna said, trying to keep Katherine talking. She stumbled and felt water seep through her shoes. Panic rose in her throat. Had she taken a wrong turn?

"Jason has had five years to figure it out. He thought the crime was about money, but it was always about revenge. Money was just icing on the cake. Jason will probably miss you, though. You've got him wrapped around your little finger, just like Derek, but then Jason and Derek always competed for the same thing. That's why he wants you—because he always wanted what Derek had."

"Katherine, come on," Brianna pleaded. She hated to beg, but she had to fight—not just for herself but for Lucas.

"I hope you can swim, because I lied about the tide. And when the waves start crashing over the rocks, the water comes in through all the cracks. It doesn't take long to fill up the caves. Colin almost died here when we were kids. He said an angel saved him. Maybe one will come and save you," she mocked.

"Katherine, stop. Come back." Her words were

met with silence this time. Only the taunting sound of Katherine's laugh echoed in the caves.

Brianna tried to keep moving, but she kept running into rocks. Battered and bruised, she had no idea if she was going in the right direction. Her feet were freezing, and there seemed to be more and more water swishing over her feet. Was the tide coming in?

She told herself to stay calm, to think. She couldn't afford to panic. She could get out. Katherine didn't have that much of a head start on her, and she'd probably turn her flashlight back on once she got farther away. She'd be able to catch some stray light from that.

But there was nothing but inky blackness, damp moisture coating her face, icy water licking up her legs. Something brushed against her face, and she screamed. A flurry of pebbles fell from above her.

Maybe screaming wasn't such a good idea; she had no idea how stable the earth above her was. The shipwreck survivors had spent days in these caves, so there had to be someplace the ocean couldn't reach. She just had to find it.

Why the hell had she followed Katherine? She should have known something was off, that Derek wouldn't have kept paintings in a damp cave. But Katherine had been so excited and sure and had played it so casually, as if she didn't care if Brianna came or not. And she'd been so hell-bent on finding those paintings, on proving Derek's innocence, she'd lost track of the big picture. Those paintings wouldn't change her life. In fact, she didn't need her life to be changed. She had Lucas. She might even have Jason, if she gave him a chance.

She stumbled again and landed in water up to her knees. She heard the rumble of the ocean. She was getting closer to the sea—but was she was going to make it in time?

Jason left the gallery as dusk settled over the town. He'd just finished a long meeting with the Markhams and Wyatt, and he'd finally gotten some answers. He needed to fill Brianna in. He'd tried her cell phone, but it had gone straight to voice-mail. He was hoping she'd be home.

Her car was in the driveway, but when he rang the bell, she didn't answer. A bad feeling shot down his spine when he realized the front door was slightly ajar. He pushed it open, calling her name. There was no reply: no Brianna, no Lucas, no puppy. He glanced at the coffee table and saw Derek's sketches.

Had Derek left her a clue that she'd gone to investigate? The three drawings that had been pulled out of the pile were of the gallery, Wyatt's studio, and the beach. He'd been to two of those locations, and Brianna hadn't been there, which left only one: Shelter Cove.

He drove like a maniac to the beach. As he neared the spot where he usually parked, he saw another car peeling out, leaving a cloud of dust behind. Katherine was behind the wheel, and she was alone. Damn. He'd never thought Katherine would go straight to Brianna. What had she done?

He parked the car and jumped out, taking off on a dead run toward the beach and the caves. Fog and clouds made visibility difficult, and when he reached the entrance, the water was up to his ankles, and the current was surging.

He saw a flashlight by the entrance. The front was bashed in as if someone had tossed it against the rocks on their way out. Brianna had to be inside.

*Shit!* He pulled out his cell phone. There was no signal. He tried the flashlight, but it didn't work. Fortunately, he had a light on his key chain. It wasn't much of a beam, but he turned it on as he jogged into the cave.

"Brianna!" he shouted, his voice lost in the rushing sound of water.

A rush of terrified adrenaline ran through his body as the narrow beam from his penlight danced off the black walls like a laser beam. He hadn't been in the caves in years. If he took the wrong turn, he could easily get lost.

The water rose higher with each passing second.

"Brianna!" he yelled again. "Where are you?" The icy water swirled around his legs. It was difficult to fight the strong current and the cold. A new wave rolled in, pushing him further into the cave. "Brianna!"

"Help!"

His heart stopped at the sound of her voice. "I'm coming, Brianna!"

"Jason!" she yelled.

"Where are you?"

"I don't know. I can't see anything."

Her voice was loud now. He stumbled and fell against the wall, then slid down as a cascade of dirt and rocks showered on him.

"Jason, where are you?"

"I'm here!" he yelled, trying to pull his foot loose, but the rocks had shifted, pinning his leg.

He heard more scrambling. He tried to point the light toward where he had heard her voice, hoping she'd see it.

She appeared like an angel in the night, her blond hair standing out in the darkness.

"Jason!" Tears streamed down her face as she threw her arms around his neck. "Thank God. I didn't think I was going to make it."

"We're not that far from the entrance." He kissed her quickly.

"Let's go, then," she said.

"I can't. My leg is pinned under a rock. Take the light." He held out the light to her. In the shadow, he could see the fear on her face. "You hold it while I figure out what to do."

Brianna couldn't see what was holding him down, because the water had risen to their thighs. She leaned over, digging with her hands, trying to move the large, heavy rocks that now seemed immovable. Jason kicked out, hoping to free himself, but all he could feel was the jagged edges of the rocks cutting through his jeans.

"You've got to get out of here now," he said. "Call nine-one-one when you get to the beach."

"I'm not leaving you, Jason."

"You have to. You've got Lucas to worry about."

She struggled harder to move the rocks.

"Brianna, *go*. We're running out of time."

"Then shut up and let me do this, dammit."

She gritted her teeth and pulled with all her might. The rock budged ever so slightly. She squatted down in the water, grappling with the rocks. Another wave came rolling in, dousing them with a chilling spray, but Brianna didn't give up. She could die trying to save him, and he couldn't let that happen. *Save her*, he prayed to the angels.

A wave splashed over them, and for a second there was nothing but dark, swirling water. Then the water receded, and new bright streams of light flowed through the cracks in the walls, as if the sun had come out.

Brianna shoved at the boulder again, and it lifted just enough for him to slide his leg free.

"You did it," he said in amazement.

She smiled back at him. "Let's get out of here."

He grabbed her hand as they splashed back toward the entrance. They were almost out when the current enveloped them, lifting them off their feet.

"Don't let go of my hand!" he cried. "We're going to ride the wave just like I taught you."

Then they were swept out to sea.

He knew the ocean well, knew how to swim parallel to the coast until they could fight the current.

Brianna struggled to keep her head above water. She was terrified, but she was fighting for all she was worth.

Fifty yards down the beach, they finally made it onto the sand, collapsing from the effort. For a few moments, all he could do was breathe in and out, searching Brianna's face for any sign of injury or pain. She was soaking wet. Her skin was white, her eyes a dark, dark blue.

Unable to speak, she pointed toward the caves, and he followed her gaze. The black storm clouds had parted directly over the rocks and beams of light streamed down from the heavens, illuminating the cave as if it were onstage, and the rest of the world was in the dark.

Maybe the angels had heard his prayer, or maybe Derek had been watching out for Brianna. Whatever the reason, he was immensely grateful that they'd made it out alive and together.

Brianna crawled across the sand and fell into his arms. She cupped his face and kissed his lips, her mouth cold but joyful. "We made it," she said. "I wasn't sure we would. You saved my life, Jason. I was lost in those caves. Then I heard your voice, and I knew where to go. I wouldn't have made it out if you hadn't come for me."

"I made things worse. You could have drowned trying to rescue me. Next time, I tell you to go—go."

She smiled. "Not a chance."

"Why?" he asked, the question slipping past his

lips. "Why would you risk your life for me? You should hate me, Brianna. I made mistakes in the investigation. Derek didn't steal the paintings, and he's dead now because I sent him to jail. I screwed up. I didn't ask the right questions. I didn't look beyond the obvious. I didn't imagine there were so many twists and turns, that—"

Brianna put her fingers against his mouth, cutting him off. "Don't, Jason. Don't blame yourself for not seeing what Derek took such pains to hide. He went to jail because he *tried* to steal the paintings, even if he didn't succeed, even if he was double-crossed. He was still involved and guilty, because he *did* knock out that security guard."

"You're letting me off the hook," he asked in amazement.

"It's past time I did. Maybe you didn't have all the answers when it came to Derek, but neither did I. We were both duped—me most of all. But Derek's death didn't have anything to do with either of us. That was a tragic accident. The rest was of Derek's own making. I've learned a lot about my husband in the past week. Like that damned Eve, Derek had more than one face. He had plenty of time to tell me the truth, to reveal himself to me, and he chose not to. Not even in his last letter did he come clean."

"Because he didn't want to disappoint you," Jason said, knowing that just this once he had to stick up for Derek. "You believed that he was better than he was, and he wanted to be that man for you. He loved you, Brianna. He told me so that day in my garage. He said he'd finally found the woman he'd been looking for. She'd been in the mirror all along."

"He saw something in the glass that wasn't there, and I guess I did, too." She drew in a breath and let it out. "Derek was as fake as his paintings; beautiful but not real." Her fingers slid down the side of his face. "You're the real thing, Jason."

His heart pounded at the look in her eyes. He'd wanted to see love there since the first moment he'd met her.

"You're honest," she continued. "You stand up for what you believe in, no matter the cost. You have a strong moral compass, and I like it." Her lips trembled, and her eyes glittered with emotion. "In case you didn't know, I'm falling in love with you."

"I'm already there," he confessed, "but you take all the time you need to be sure. I know the Kanes mean a lot to you, and I don't want to hurt them either."

"They do mean the world to me. They're the main reason I stuck it out with Derek. It actually would have been easier to divorce Derek than them. I hope eventually they'll come around to the idea of you and me, because I love them, and Lucas needs his grandparents. But I can't make my decisions based on them. I want you in my life. The rest we'll figure out along the way."

"Sounds like a good plan," he said with amazed relief.

She smiled back and then flung her arms wide.

"I feel *free!* Completely and totally free, for the first time in forever."

The shadows were gone from her eyes, and she was once again that girl in the bar with a lifetime of possibilities in front of her. Thank God she wanted him to be one of those possibilities.

"So are you going to kiss me, or what?" she demanded.

"I thought you'd never ask."

He pulled her head down, wanting to taste every sweet inch of her. He'd been waiting his entire life for her, the one woman who made him want to jump off a cliff—or at the very least, run into a flooding cave.

As the wind picked up, he felt her shiver in his arms, reminding him that they were soaking wet and night was falling. "We need to get dry."

"And we need to find Katherine," Brianna said, jumping to her feet. "She's the one who took me into the caves."

"I saw her driving away. Why did you follow her in there?"

"She told me she thought the paintings were here, based on the sketch Derek had drawn. She was acting so friendly, so helpful. In fact, she told me that Gloria and Derek had had an affair and that she was sure Gloria was the unseen partner. It made perfect sense. When we got here, she said she'd go in on her own. She didn't force me to go with her, so I wasn't at all suspicious.

"Once we got deep into the caves, she admitted

everything—that she was Derek's partner, that she set him up to take the fall, because she was pissed off that he'd gotten engaged to me. She let him rot in prison to pay him back for not choosing her. Derek couldn't rat Katherine out, because she knew about other things he'd done. We have to stop her before she gets the paintings and runs. I am *not* going to let her get away with this."

"Don't worry. She's not getting away."

"How do you know?"

"Because I already found the paintings, Brianna." He smiled. "A lot happened today. While you were with Katherine, I was with Wyatt and the Markhams. After they saw the forgeries, they realized that Katherine had to be responsible. Apparently, until this point, they all secretly blamed the other. Gloria thought Wyatt had double-crossed her because he was related to Victor, and Wyatt thought the Markhams had done it because of Gloria's ties to Ramón. She was descended from him, by the way."

Brianna's jaw dropped. "Are you serious?"

"Oh, yeah. I'll tell you the rest on the way."


When they pulled up in front of the Markham Gallery, night had fallen, but the building was ablaze with lights. A police car was parked outside. Brianna walked ahead of Jason into the building. She saw Gloria, Steve, and Wyatt standing with Joe Silveira and another officer. The first thing she noticed was that the wall of mirrors had been ripped apart, with large pieces of glass lying on the floor.

"What happened to you two?" Joe asked, taking in their sopping appearance.

"Katherine lured Brianna into the caves and left her there," Jason said shortly. "We barely made it out alive."

Brianna heard Gloria gasp and wasn't sure she believed the sincerity of that reaction. She didn't know if Gloria's affair with Derek was one of Katherine's lies, but she suspected it was not.

"I'm glad you got out," Joe said, concern in his eyes. "The Markhams shut down the gallery early according to plan. Katherine showed up as soon as everyone was gone. She turned off the security camera, or so she thought, took the mirrors off the wall, and pulled the paintings off the backs. We got it on our own cameras. She had quite a look of satisfaction on her face."

"You let Katherine steal the paintings?" Brianna asked in shock.

"Not exactly," Jason said, a pleased smile on his face. "We took the mirrors down, removed the originals, and replaced them with the copies. We needed to catch Katherine in the act, and we figured she'd try to snatch them as soon as she could, knowing the trail would lead to her."

"So Katherine has the fakes?"

Jason nodded. He tipped his head to Steve Markham, who moved around the reception area and pulled out the paintings. One by one the *Three Faces of Eve* were placed on the counter as the group gathered around.

For a while, there was nothing but reverent silence.

Brianna stared at each of Eve's faces and let out a sigh. "I really hate Eve, but I'm glad she's back."

"I'm sorry, Brianna," Wyatt said gruffly. "I knew Derek was guilty, but I should have realized he didn't have the smarts to do it all on his own."

She didn't know if that was a compliment or an insult, but it didn't matter anymore. She glanced at Jason. "How did you know they were behind the mirrors?"

"We were standing by the door, talking about where Katherine might have put the paintings," Jason replied. "Since she lives with her mother, home wasn't an option. It seemed likely that she'd want to keep the paintings close by, like here at the gallery. Wyatt mentioned how Katherine and Derek used to play with mirrors when they were painting, which reminded me of your sketches, and the first time you met Derek."

"When he saw me in the mirror," Brianna said. "And the gallery entrance—the mirrors were in one of his sketches that he did in prison."

"Exactly," Jason said, meeting her gaze. "I looked at the mirrors, saw my reflection, and thought maybe . . ."

"Very intuitive," she said.

He tipped his head. "It was time for us to get a break."

"So what happens now?"

"We pick up Katherine."

"Already done," Joe interjected as he hung up the phone. "Laughton picked her up on the outskirts of town. She's on her way to the station."

"It's over, Brianna," Jason said. "We've got her in possession of the stolen art. She's going to go to prison."

Brianna felt a wave of relief. "Thank God."

"Do you want to come to the station?" Jason asked.

She shook her head. "No, I'm done with Katherine. I'm done with all of this," she said waving her hand toward the paintings. "I'm going to tell the Kanes what happened, and then I'm taking my son home. We're going to carve pumpkins and have dinner and make plans for the future." Her eyes teared up as she realized she'd really come to the end. Her questions had been answered. Maybe not in the way she'd hoped, but at least she had the truth now. She could move on, and she was more than ready to do that.

Jason put his hands on her shoulders as the others moved away. "I know you wanted to clear Derek's name for Lucas, that you wanted him to have a father he could be proud of."

"I'll make sure Lucas knows that Derek was more than just the crime he committed. Maybe you can help."

"Whatever I can do," he said solemnly. "I'm not trying to take his place, you know. He was your husband. He was Lucas's father. I respect that."

"I know you do. We're going to make this work," she said, feeling more sure of herself than she had in a long time.

"I want that more than anything, Brianna."

"Me, too," she said, stealing a quick kiss. "When you get done at the station, come over. I'll be waiting."

"The sweetest words I've ever heard."

She smiled. "I'm just getting started."

He grinned back at her. "So am I."

# EPILOGUE

Ten days later

The streets of Angel's Bay were filled with ghosts and goblins, spooky cobwebs, and bright shining pumpkins.

"Are we almost at the last house?" Lucas asked wearily. He'd finally run out of steam from trick-or-treating, and his plastic pumpkin was overflowing with candy.

"This is it," Brianna said with a smile.

Lucas turned to Jason and raised his arms in a silent plea to be carried. Jason laughed and lifted him up. "You want a ride, buddy? That might cost you a Snickers bar. They're my favorite."

"Okay," Lucas said sleepily, resting his head on Jason's broad shoulder.

"Maybe we should go home," Brianna suggested. "It is getting late."

"No, I'm awake," Lucas said, perking up again. He hated to miss any action, and Jason had been telling him about the Lynches' Halloween party for days.

"We'll just stay a little while," Jason said, leading the way up to Kara's front door.

Kara and Colin had gone all out for Halloween. There were ghosts hanging from the trees, spider webs adorning the porch railings and a few grave stones erupting from the lawn. The house was filled to the brim with adults and children, most dressed in costume. Lucas saw one of his friends and immediately jumped out of Jason's arms. He handed Brianna his pumpkin and took off to play.

"That was fast," Jason said with a laugh. He leaned over and kissed her. "Maybe we should take this opportunity to wander around some dark streets for a while. I doubt he'd notice we were gone."

"The streets don't have to be dark. We're not hiding anymore." She slipped her hand into his.

"The Kanes were a little less chilly tonight," Jason said.

"They're making an effort, especially now that they know the truth about Derek. They have to try. I want all of you in my life."

"Hey, there you are," Kara interrupted, giving them both a kiss and a hug. "We're just about to go into the backyard and dunk for apples."

"I'll pass," Jason said, sliding his arms about Brianna's shoulders. "I'm more than comfortable right here."

"I can see that," Kara said, giving them a beaming smile. "You two look happy."

"We are," Brianna said, smiling back. "More than I ever could have imagined."

"You both deserve it. I've been waiting for Jason to find someone for a long time."

"She was worth waiting for," Jason said, love shining in his eyes. "And worth fighting for."

Brianna's heart swelled with emotion. She wouldn't regret loving Derek, because despite the secrets, they'd made a child together. But she and Derek had never really known each other. With Jason, it was different. The honesty between them took their love to a deeper level.

"I guess it's no more three musketeers," Kara said to Jason. "Now there's four."

"Yeah, I'm finally not outnumbered by you and Colin. By the way, I hear you're trying out for the Winter Workshop."

"Victoria and the Hartleys talked me into auditioning, but I'm sure I won't get it," Kara said. "They're just being nice, wanting to include some locals in with the L.A. company that's going to be arriving shortly."

"You're pretty good at drama," Jason teased.

"I'm going to take that as a compliment." She grinned.

"As you should."

A sudden crash of glass interrupted their conversation. Across the room a pregnant teenager was doubled over, grimacing in pain. Charlotte and Joe rushed to her side.

"Oh, my God," Kara said. "I think Annie is going into labor. Should I call nine-one-one?"

"Joe has it covered," Jason said, as the chief and Charlotte helped Annie toward the door.

"I better clean up the glass." Kara slipped away.

"The excitement never ends," Jason said.

"No, it doesn't. I wonder if the father of Annie's baby will finally show his face."

"What do you know about that?"

"Just what I hear at the quilt shop," Brianna said with a laugh. "It's quite the topic of conversation. There are a lot of suspects."

Lucas ran up to them. "Mommy, that lady is having a baby!"

"I know. It's wonderful."

"Are you going to have another baby?"

Her jaw droped. "Uh . . ."

Jason laughed at her expression. "Want to give us an answer, Brianna?"

"Not tonight," she said quickly. "Right now, I just want to celebrate being with my two favorite guys."

As Lucas ran off, Jason said, "I can live with that."

"I'm not ruling out more kids." The idea of having Jason's baby was rather appealing, but first things first.

"There's no rush," Jason said. "We've got plenty of time for everything. I love you, Brianna."

"I love you, too."

He might not have been the first man in her life—but he would be the last.

Can't get enough of Angel's Bay?

Turn the page to find out
what some of your favorite characters
have been up to . . .

**From *Suddenly One Summer*'s Jenna Davies**

Dear Readers:

When you first met me, I was on the run with my daughter Lexie. We thought we'd find peace and security in Angel's Bay, but we found a lot more. I fell in love with Reid Tanner, a cynical, sarcastic, gorgeous hunk of a man who thankfully fell in love with me, too. Neither Reid nor I believed in angels until we came to this beautiful seaside town and witnessed our own special miracle.

Finding Angel's Bay and each other changed both of us. Reid's stint as a tabloid reporter is over. He's back to covering hard news and just returned from the Middle East. He's taken a more permanent job in Los Angeles, so we're going to say good-bye to the bay for a while, but we'll be back. We purchased Rose Littleton's house and we'll keep it in the family as long as we can. Knowing that my roots extend to the original survivors of the shipwreck and the founders of this town makes this place home, no matter where we are.

I'm still teaching piano, but when we move to L.A., I'll play with an orchestra there. It's about the music now and not about the business, which gives me great joy. Lexie is seeing a therapist to deal with all the tragedy she's seen in her short life, but she's thriving. She adores Reid and can't wait to be the flower girl at our wedding next summer. Hope to see you there!

Jenna

## From *On Shadow Beach*'s Lauren Jamison

Dear Readers,

I came back to Angel's Bay to take care of my father. I thought I could get in and out of town without anyone noticing—without dragging up all the old history. I should have known better. I hadn't been in town more than a few minutes when my father took off in his boat, and I had to get someone to help me chase him down. That someone was Shane Murray, my high school boyfriend, my first love, and the man who'd been accused of murdering my sister, Abby. Shane and I had a lot to work through, but somehow we found our way back to each other. I like to think that Abby had a hand in that.

My father and I are building a new house, one without the painful memories. Dad and I are much closer now, and I cherish all the moments we have together. He doesn't always remember who I am or even who he is, but I'm happy to share this part of his life with him.

I finally fulfilled my dream of having my own bakery. I opened up Sugar and Spice this year and I'm up to my neck in flour and sugar. Shane says he gets high just smelling my hair. He's been my biggest supporter. And while he still has his boat on the bay, he's spending a lot more time on land. He still keeps his mother's secret, as do I. Sometimes love is more important than truth.

Speaking of love, Shane and I are planning a winter wedding. I know it's soon, but I want my dad to walk me down the aisle. Kara and Charlotte will be bridesmaids, along with Shane's sister, Dee. Shane's brothers, Michael and Patrick, as well as Kara's husband, Colin, will stand up for Shane. I'm hoping my mother and brother will be in the first row. I'd like to have my whole family together one more time.

Oh, and did I tell you where Shane proposed? You probably guessed—the tree house. It was where we fell in love as kids and came back together as adults. I can't wait to see our own kids playing there. Don't tell Shane I said that. He's just getting used to the idea of marriage. But I'm pretty sure I can talk him into the idea. Underneath that rough and tough exterior, he has the biggest heart of anyone I've ever known.

Lauren

Dear Readers,

I never thought I would fall in love with my worst enemy, but it turns out that the wrong man was actually the right one. Since we found the paintings and learned the truth, Jason and I have been able to let go of the past. Lucas adores Jason, and the feeling is mutual. The Kanes are slowly coming around. It's difficult for them to see Jason in Derek's place. They still miss their son, but they want Lucas and me to be happy, and for that I'm grateful.

Jason's dad is still dating Patty. No wedding plans yet, but the two of them are giddy with love. They've decided to move in together, and Jason is coming around to the idea of having another stepmother. I'm still working at the quilt shop and hoping to get a teaching job, but in the meantime I'm making a lot of friends and getting to hear all the gossip.

I didn't just find a new love in Angel's Bay, I found myself. Jason has been teaching me to surf, and yesterday I rode my first big wave all the way to the beach. It was a thrill. Jason is still doing carpentry in his spare time. He told me he's working on a secret project that I'm going to love. I can't wait to find out what it is. Can you?

Brianna

**From Kara Lynch**

Dear Readers,

Okay, you probably think you know my story. Colin got shot by a madman, then spent three months in a coma while I prayed for him to wake up. Stubbornly, I refused to leave his side when I went into labor, thinking that our baby would bring him back to life. Well, it didn't happen then, but he did eventually come back to me and Faith. I thought everything would be perfect when he opened his eyes, but we've had some rocky times since then. Things are better now. We have a second chance at happiness, and we're going to grab it.

Colin is almost ready to go back to work for the police department. I'm not sure how I'll feel seeing him in a uniform again, since I almost lost him to his job, but Colin loves being a cop and protecting this town. The angels watched out for him before. I hope they will again.

I'm thrilled to be planning Lauren's wedding. I'm so happy that my brother and his first love have reunited. Charlotte and I are going to be bridesmaids, although Charlotte is a little busy right now. Annie just had her baby, and, well, I'll let her tell you about what's going on there.

In other town news, the community theater is getting ready to open for the Winter Workshop, and I'm auditioning. More things have also been washing ashore from the shipwreck. My sister Dee tells me that a couple of treasure hunters have been down at the marina. The *Gabriella* hasn't been found in a hundred and fifty years, but it seems like she's getting ready to show herself. Wouldn't that be something?

Kara

## From Charlotte Adams

Dear Readers,

You must think I'm the luckiest woman in town to have two men interested in me. But let's take a reality check. I already dated Andrew in high school and he might be the golden boy now, but he had more than a few faults back then. He made some mistakes and so did I, mistakes I'm not sure I want to share with him. I don't know why he's pushing so hard to reconnect. Sometimes I think there's more going on behind his polite, compassionate minister's smile than meets the eye. Maybe Andrew has some secrets of his own.

And then there's Joe Silveira, gorgeous, hot . . . and married. Well, he's getting a divorce, but that takes time, and I don't want to be his rebound woman. He was in love with Rachel since he was fifteen. Is he really over her now? Maybe I can get some information out of Joe's sister, Isabella, who just arrived in town.

Men aside, I have other things to worry about. Annie just had her baby and she's under pressure to give up her child for adoption. Problem is, one of those adoptive fathers is the baby's biological dad, but he wants to keep it a secret. Can I stand by and let Annie perpetuate this lie? But it's not my choice. Or is it? Annie is late coming home. My mom and I are watching the baby, and neither one of us has a good feeling about it. For once, my mother and I might be on the same side—a shocking thought.

There's a lot going on here in Angel's Bay. Hope you'll come back for a visit.

Cheers,
Charlotte

And now,
a special look at
the next touching Angel's Bay romance
from bestselling author

Barbara Freethy,

featuring Isabella Silveira,
the sister of Angel's Bay Police Chief
Joe Silveira

Coming soon from Pocket Books

Dark clouds blotted out the sun setting over the ocean, and the threatening storm sent a chill down Isabella Silveira's spine. Her hands tightened on the steering wheel as the Pacific Coast Highway took another terrifying twist on the steep cliff that dropped abruptly into the wild, crashing waves below. She'd always been a spontaneous person, rarely looking back, always moving forward, but this trip was giving her plenty of second thoughts.

It had to be weariness—she hadn't slept more than a few hours in almost two weeks, haunted by tormenting dreams. They'd begun shortly after she'd received a birthday present from her brother Joe, an antique turquoise and gold butterfly pendant that he'd found in the house he'd inherited from their Uncle Carlos. He'd told her that the turquoise reminded him of her unusual eyes. All of her other siblings were dark, but in the Irish-Hispanic mix of her parents, she'd ended up with dark hair, olive skin, and bright blue eyes.

Her eyes were part of her gift, her grandmother Elena had told her—the gift of insight, shared by only a few women in her family. Af far as she was concerned, it was more of a distraction than a gift. Most of what she saw in her head was unimportant or could have been anticipated, like the Christmas tree being knocked over or the car running out of gas. But occasionally her visions were more complicated and disturbing, usually triggered by some emotional connection to another person.

To keep the troubling insights at bay, she tried to stay busy and ignore whatever odd, unexplainable images flashed through her head. For months, her brain had been quiet—until she'd put on the butterfly pendant. That night she'd dreamed of Angel's Bay.

She'd never been to the town where Joe had taken over as police chief almost a year ago. But the images haunting her had included this highway and the Angel's Bay sign she'd passed three miles back as well as other shadows and silhouettes swirling around landmarks and people that seemed familiar meaningful in some unfathomable way. Just when she came to the brink of discovery, she woke up sweating and shaking, with a certainty that she was supposed to do something, save someone . . . but she didn't know what to do or who to save.

She'd taken to exercise—running, spinning, kick boxing, anything that would leave her too exhausted to dream. She'd lost five pounds, but the dreams had continued. There was a voice in her head demand ing to be heard. Finally, she'd stopped fighting. The pendant had come from Joe; what if he was in some kind of trouble, and she did nothing? She'd never forgive herself.

Fortunately, she had some time off. She worked as a costume designer and the movie project she'd been hired to do had been pushed back until January, leaving her free for the next two months. While she normally worked at her sister's clothing boutique between film projects, she'd decided to go to Angel's Bay this time. Even if she couldn't figure out her dreams, at least she'd get to see Joe and the town that had stolen his heart. He'd even agreed to divorce Rachel rather than move back to L.A. Angel's Bay had certainly spun its web around him.

She turned on her headlights as dusk turned to night, then turned on the windshield wipers as raindrops splashed down. Thank God the road had widened, the hills on her right side falling back to wide-open meadows, fruit stands on the edge of farm land, and the occasional rural road heading inland towards another range of mountains. There weren't many cars and very few lights. She felt isolated and alone.

A crack of thunder jolted her already tense nerves and goose bumps ran along her arms. She hit the defrost button as her window began to fog, telling herself she was fine. She just had to hang on for a few more miles.

As she drove around another turn, high beams blinded her from an oncoming car that wove recklessly across the highway. She hit the brakes as the car suddenly turned in front of her, skidding onto a dirt road. Her brakes sent her car into a wild skid. She hung onto the wheel, fighting for control, but she was heading straight toward the cliff on the ocean side of the road.

She jammed the brake to the floor, but there was no way to stop her forward momentum. She screamed as her car ripped through the guard rail, plunging down the rocky hillside. Then the nose of the car hit something solid, and the windshield shattered. She threw up her hands as the air bag suddenly pinned her against the seat, stars exploding before her eyes. Was this the end? She'd seen other things—why hadn't she seen this?

Seconds or minutes or maybe hours later, she heard someone yelling, tugging at the car door until it sprang open. Rain hit her face and she blinked in bewilderment. The front window had splintered, and smoke was coming from the hood of her car.

"Are you all right?"

She stared at the man in front of her. He was soaking wet, his hair and eyes dark, fear and determination tightening his jaw.

"You've been in accident," he told her. "Are you hurt?"

She put a hand to her forehead and winced as she saw the blood on her fingers.

"The cut on your head doesn't look too bad," he told her. "Can you move? I want to get you out of here. There's no telling how long the rocks will hold."

He'd barely finished speaking when the car slid

forward a few inches. She grabbed his arm in panic. "Don't let me go."

His eyes burned with determination. "I won't." He reached across her to release her seat belt.

She tried to get out, but her left foot was pinned where the side of her car had smashed against the rocks. "My foot is stuck."

As he pulled at the metal she yanked her foot free, and the vigorous movement unsettled the car's precarious position. The wall of rocks holding them back from the sea began to break apart, and terror ran through her as the car began to slide.

The man grabbed her arm and pulled her out, then rolled on top of her, holding her tight as he dug his feet into the soil. As they clung to the hillside, her car plummeted over the edge of the bluff and into the sea.

Shock stole her breath as she realized how close she'd come to dying. If he hadn't come when he had . . .

"You saved my life," she said.

His breath came rough and ragged. "It was lucky that I saw your car go off the road. But don't thank me yet. We still have to get back up to the highway." He sat up, his hand tight on her arm, and pulled her toward an outcropping of rock where the ground was more stable.

There she finally let out a breath, feeling a little less vulnerable now. The steady rain had stopped and a slice of moonlight broke through the clouds. As Isabella's gaze met his, goose bumps ran down her arm. She recognized his face—it was the man she'd seen in her dreams. "It's you," she said in amazement.

He stared at her in confusion. "Have we met?"

Then sirens split the air, followed by strobe lights bouncing off the hillside. Help had arrived.

The man got to his feet, waving his arms in the air so the rescuers could see them.

She wrapped her arms around her body, chilled to the bone. Not just by the storm or the accident, but by the certainty that luck had had nothing to do with their meeting.

Love a good book? So do we!
# Pick up a bestselling Romance from Pocket Books.

≈≈

### FEEL THE HEAT
A BLACK OPS, INC. NOVEL
*Cindy Gerard*
A relentless enemy…
A merciless temptation.

### UNTRACEABLE
*Laura Griffin*
Be careful what you look for…
You just might find it.

### MAKE HER PAY
*Roxanne St.Claire*
A BULLET CATCHERS NOVEL
Sometimes it takes a thief to catch a thief…

### OUR LITTLE SECRET
*Starr Ambrose*
Keeping secrets can be deadly
…or delicious.

### A DIFFERENT LIGHT
*Mariah Stewart*
The beloved classic—now revised and
revisited by the bestselling author!

≈≈

Available wherever books are sold or at
www.simonandschuster.com

# Experience the **excitement**
## of bestselling romances from Pocket Books!

### Eileen Carr
# HOLD BACK THE DARK

When a clinical psychologist and a detective investigate an unspeakable crime, they learn that every passion has its dark side.....

### Laura Griffin
# WHISPER OF WARNING

Blamed for a murder she witnessed, Courtney chooses to trust the sexy detective pursuing her. Will he help prove her innocence...or lead a killer to her door?

### Susan Mallery
# Sunset Bay

What if you got another chance at the life that got away? Amid the turmoil of broken dreams lies the promise of a future Megan never expected....

*Available wherever books are sold or at*
www.simonandschuster.com

20471